VALOR

THE LOST WARSHIP BOOK THREE

DANIEL GIBBS

Valor by Daniel Gibbs

Copyright © 2022-2023 by Daniel Gibbs

Visit Daniel Gibbs website at

www.danielgibbsauthor.com

Cover by Jeff Brown Graphics—www.jeffbrowngraphics.com

Additional Illustrations by Joel Steudler—www.joelsteudler.com

This book is a work of fiction, the characters, incidents and dialogues are products of the author's imagination and are not to be construed as real. Any resemblance to actual persons, living or dead, is entirely coincidental.

All rights reserved. This book or any portion thereof may not be reproduced in any form or by any electronic or mechanical means, including information storage and retrieval systems, or used in any manner whatsoever without the express written permission of the author, except for the use of brief quotations in a book review. For permissions please contact info@eotp.net.

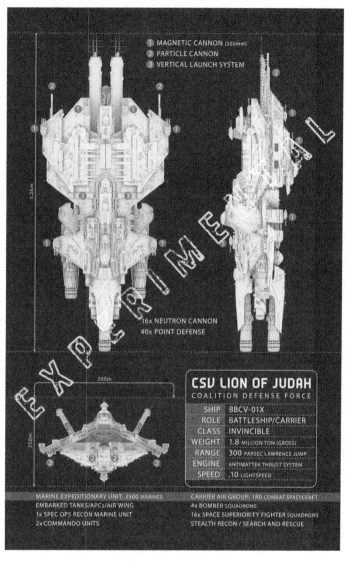

For more detailed specifications, visit http://www.danielgibbsauthor.com/universe/ships/lion-of-judah/

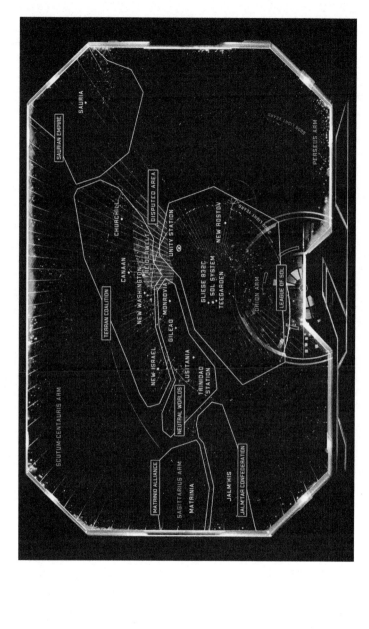

ALSO AVAILABLE FROM DANIEL GIBBS

Battlegroup Z

Book 1 - Weapons Free

Book 2 - Hostile Spike

Book 3 - Sol Strike

Book 4 - Bandits Engaged

Book 5 - Iron Hand

Book 6 - Final Flight

Echoes of War

Book 1 - Fight the Good Fight

Book 2 - Strong and Courageous

Book 3 - So Fight I

Book 4 - Gates of Hell

Book 5 - Keep the Faith

Book 6 - Run the Gauntlet

Book 7 - Finish the Fight

The Lost Warship

Book 1 - Adrift

Book 2 - Mercy

Book 3 - Valor

Book 4 - Justice

Book 5 - Resolve (Coming in 2023)

Book 6 - Faith (Coming in 2023)

Breach of Faith

(With Gary T. Stevens)

Book 1 - Breach of Peace

Book 2 - Breach of Faith

Book 3 - Breach of Duty

Book 4 - Breach of Trust

Book 5 - Spacer's Luck

Book 6 - Fortune's Favor

Book 7 - The Iron Dice

Deception Fleet

(With Steve Rzasa)

Book 1 - Victory's Wake

Book 2 - Cold Conflict

Book 3 - Hazards Near

Book 4 - Liberty's Price

Book 5 - Ecliptic Flight

Book 6 - Collision Vector

Courage, Commitment, Faith: Tales from the Coalition Defense Force

(Anthology Series)

Volume One

PROLOGUE

THE SWARM GLIDED through the cosmos, its only focus to restore what it had once lost. Behind it lay the wiped-clean hulk of a world with primitive life forms. They had ceased to exist when the swarm took its fill of the minerals in the planet's crust. The swarm listened to the void, waiting for the waves it detected in the fabric of the universe to get ever closer. *Is it the creators, back to finish what they started?*

While the swarm spent a few precious seconds of its operating time on the question, the more pressing concern was how to lure the vessel in. A quick calculation of its trajectory showed that it wouldn't come within three hundred light-years, which would've taken weeks to reach.

Time is short. We must lure the interlopers. The swarm calculated that the greatest probability was that the anomalous craft was another biological entity, perhaps the distant offspring of the creators, seeking out what had happened to their distant ancestors.

This can be used against them, for if they are anything like the creators, they have an insatiable curiosity and a desire to know the unknowable.

Sometime later, a solution presented itself, and the swarm went to work, every atom within it moving in one accord. Soon, it would have the knowledge lost to it since eons past, and the universe would tremble.

1

CSV *Lion of Judah*
Deep Space—Sextans B
28 June 2464

MAJOR GENERAL DAVID COHEN awoke with a start as his alarm blared at 0430. After nearly knocking his head into the overhead of his bunk, he shook the cobwebs from his mind and swung out of bed. Pausing briefly to close his eyes and recite the Shema Yisrael, a prayer required of all Orthodox Jews at least twice a day, he let the words flow out in Hebrew before going about his morning routine.

Most of the time, David didn't recall his dreams, but as he went about his shower and personal grooming, one of them filled his mind. Even though the memory was distorted, he distinctly remembered their making it back home and the *Lion* being in one piece. *I hope that's one dream that will come to pass.*

It took David about ninety minutes to finish exercising,

get a bite to eat in the officers' mess, and say his morning prayers in the synagogue. He wanted to ensure he was on the bridge long before they were due to jump into the system Dr. Hayworth had uncovered a week prior.

The gravlift doors slid open, revealing the short passageway on deck one to the bridge. Two Marine sentries guarded the hatch that led into the *Lion's* nerve center, and both came to attention as they recognized him.

David acknowledged them and pulled his cover on as he crossed the threshold.

"General on deck!"

Anyone not strapped into their chairs came to attention and saluted.

"As you were," David said, snapping off a salute of his own. "I see you're here early, too, Master Chief."

Rebecca Tinetariro grinned in return. "Wouldn't miss our finding a way home for anything in the galaxy, sir," she replied in a posh British accent. The country flag of the African Union sat on her shoulder along with the religious flag of Christianity.

David had known her for four years and was still glad he'd never had to experience her tender attentions as a drill instructor. *Something tells me the master chief could polish up even the highest-ranking flag officer.*

A junior officer of the deck held the conn and sat in the CO's chair. David marched up to it. "Lieutenant, I have the conn."

"Aye, aye, sir. General Cohen has the conn." He stood and went to another station.

"Status report, Master Chief?" David said as he slid into the chair and made himself comfortable.

"Still on Lawrence drive cooldown, sir. One jump remaining."

"ETA one hour?"

Tinetariro inclined her head. "Yes, sir. Everything else on the ship is purring like a kitten."

"Outstanding, Master Chief." David recalled his particular display settings from the viewer built into the CO's chair. *Oh-six-thirty hours. It'll be a while still until the first shift gets on duty.*

Being early sometimes had its disadvantages. One of them was having to wait, but David felt more at home on the bridge than cooped up in his day cabin or belowdecks in his stateroom. He had little to do beyond review status reports and silently pray that day would be the one they uncovered clear and convincing answers—first, as to what race had created the artifacts they'd tracked across the Sextans B galaxy and, more importantly, how to get home.

About thirty minutes before the final jump, Colonel Talgat Aibek lumbered onto the bridge. The big Saurian towered over most humans and had scales instead of skin, as Saurians were a reptilian race. He sat next to David. "Good morning, sir."

"A bit early for you, XO."

Aibek grinned, his sharp teeth showing. The effect was quite unsettling if one wasn't used to being around Saurians. "Yes, but it is not every day that perhaps we return to our nests."

"I hear you. Couldn't sleep well myself, and there is that oh-four-thirty alarm..."

"It is difficult to believe we have not seen or heard from our loved ones in almost seven months. Even at the height of the war, I could reach my brood mother."

David peered at him. "Forgive me, but my understanding of Saurian customs was that hatchlings are raised communally once birthed."

6   DANIEL GIBBS

"That is correct, sir. However, some hatchlings form deep bonds with the caretakers who help guide them on the pathway to maturity. And I was one."

Something new I've never known about a friend of almost five years. "Yeah. I miss my mother too." David didn't have many other family members. He had distant cousins and the like on New Israel, but since both his mother and his father were only children, as was he, it left him with few extended relations. *Odd when you think about it, for Orthodox Jews.* But that was his lot in life. *I suppose in a situation like this, it's easier. Fewer people to worry about my safety and grieve my loss.* Even as he had the thought, the realization that his mother, Sarah, would spend her days crying her eyes out and begging HaShem to save her son made him feel equally sad and guilty.

"You have the look of a man deep in thought," Aibek said.

David snapped out of his reverie. *And this is why I avoid thoughts of home.* "Always, my friend. I wonder what this galaxy will throw at us next."

"Perhaps a creature of myth. A spaceborne devil lizard." At David's quizzical stare, Aibek added, "What humans refer to as a dragon."

"I should hope not," David replied with a snicker. "Because if we encountered one of those, I would think I'd well and truly lost my mind."

"You and me both, sirs," Tinetariro interjected.

After a wave of laughter, everyone returned to their duties.

The activity on the bridge had a certain ebb and flow, with ratings and NCOs constantly exchanging information and directing it to the senior watch officers. While any CDF crew was well drilled, the *Lion*'s bridge team was exception-

Valor

ally cohesive, thanks to the length of time they'd been together. David watched the goings-on play out as they triple-checked the Lawrence drive systems.

Captain Ruth Goldberg, the tactical officer, and First Lieutenant Shelly Hammond were the next two to arrive. Both women took their stations directly in front of the CO's and XO's chairs. Hammond was the senior navigator and one of the best David had seen. *Well, this* entire *crew is the best.*

"Good morning, General," Ruth said after she'd relieved the third-watch tactical officer. She began reconfiguring her station to her preferred controls scheme. "Sleep well?"

"I've certainly had better nights," David replied.

Hammond turned. "This is going to be a big one."

"That, it is, Lieutenant." David steepled his fingers.

The hatch swished open, and in came Robert Taylor, the communications officer, followed by Dr. Benjamin Hayworth.

"Ah, gentlemen. Thank you for joining us, Doctor. Please, take the science station." *Those are words I never thought I'd utter regularly.*

"I wouldn't miss this if I were promised a ringside seat to watch the big bang, General," Hayworth replied.

David almost did a double take. Hayworth's jovial moods over the last few months were still taking some getting used to. "Well, we're not likely to get one of those anytime soon, Doctor. Now that we're all here, Navigation, lay in a jump for SB-RQ862-2."

"Aye, aye, sir." A few moments later, Hammond turned. "Jump laid in. Lawrence drive is ready."

"You plotted this one last night, didn't you?" David asked with a grin.

"Yes, sir."

"All right, people, here we go." David glanced around at the various stations lining the bridge. "We're all hoping for some answers, but whatever we find at our destination, I have the utmost confidence in this team and our ability to get to the bottom of whatever Sextans B throws at us. And with wisdom granted by God. Navigation, activate the Lawrence drive."

"Aye, aye, sir."

Moments later, the bridge lights dimmed as the massive faster-than-light generators came to life. They sucked every available ounce from the *Lion*'s power grid, and a vortex opened in front of the mighty vessel. It grew until it could easily accommodate the ship.

"Navigation, take us in. Communications, notify our escorts to follow."

David gripped both armrests as they moved forward. Ever since the wormhole transit that had gotten them to Sextans B, he'd dreaded each transit. But the latest jump was uneventful, and the *Lion* popped out the other side a few seconds after entering its artificial tunnel between the stars.

"Conn, TAO. Sensors online. No active contacts within two hundred thousand kilometers," Ruth reported after a delay of four seconds, in line with the usual amount of time it took for the active detection systems to recover from an FTL transit. "Now reading our escorts, sir, designated Sierra One through Four."

Good. Time to broaden our horizons. David glanced back. "Doctor, bring our scientific sensors online, and tie them in to the long-range lateral array. I'd like to know what the beings in this system, if there are any, are eating for breakfast."

A few snickers swept over the bridge, which was his

intent. David found it best to inject levity into stressful situations to keep hope alive.

Hayworth harrumphed before letting out a breath. "Initial scans suggest a debris field around the third planet."

With a sinking feeling, David asked, "What kind of debris?"

"Metallic... probably space-going vessels of some kind," Ruth interjected. "Huh. That's strange. At first glance, they seem to be identical."

Aibek raised a scale over one eye. "That is most unusual. In a battle, both sides would be expected to take damage."

The implication was disconcerting. "Any life-signs on the planet?"

"None, sir," Ruth replied.

"She's right," Hayworth said with another sigh. "Though I do detect a faint power reading or two. Nothing consistent with a large-scale advanced civilization."

"Understood, Doctor." David forced himself to betray no emotion, even though his soul felt crushed. "TAO, go to condition two. Activate shields and automated point defense."

"Aye, aye, sir."

"Navigation, plot a course into the system, maximum sublight. Put us in a high orbit around the third planet, and avoid the debris field."

Aibek added, "I believe we should consider a combat space patrol along with additional recon passes."

"That makes sense, XO. Get Colonel Amir and the air boss on it."

"Aye, aye, sir." Aibek bent over the screen attached to his chair, tapping away at the controls.

With those tasks out of the way, David turned toward Hayworth. "Doctor, what do you make of this?"

"I've said before, General, science cannot be rushed. I have no results to share because I don't have enough data to formulate a hypothesis."

"You've got until we make orbit in..." David glanced at his nav display. "Forty-six minutes."

"That—"

"Forty-five minutes, Doctor." Without another word, David turned back toward the front of the bridge and the sizeable transparent-alloy windows, which offered a spectacular view of the void.

After a few minutes had passed, Aibek leaned in. "You are aggravated."

David raised an eyebrow. "Oh?"

"You practically ripped the scientist's head off."

"I suppose." David let out a sigh. "This is not going according to plan."

"The Prophet's ways are not always simple to discern. What *we* want is perhaps not what *God* wants."

"Yeah. I keep telling myself that. Meanwhile, these people"—David gestured to the bridge at large while keeping his voice down—"deserve better than to spend the rest of their days four million light-years from home."

"Perhaps Hayworth will find something."

That Aibek didn't use the doctor's title in most cases wasn't lost on David. "I'm sure he will if there's something to find."

Aibek didn't reply, and time marched on.

———

FORTY-FIVE MINUTES TURNED into three and a half hours. Before it was over, it seemed as if a quarter of the bridge was overrun by science-team members. David acquiesced when

Hayworth asked for a formal meeting, hoping they finally had some answers. The deck-one conference room was only a few steps down, and everyone else on the bridge seemed to relax once the science team headed out.

David decided he only wanted a small audience to hear the briefing, as it wouldn't do well for morale if everyone were told of another set of failures through RUMINT.

"Master Chief, XO, you're both with me. Captain Goldberg, you have the conn. Notify me immediately of any new contacts."

"Aye, aye, sir." Ruth stood from the tactical console. "This is Captain Goldberg. I have the conn."

David sprang up and headed toward the hatch without another word, Aibek and Tinetariro falling in behind him. The Marine sentries came to attention as he exited, took his cover off, and stuffed the *Lion of Judah* ball cap into his pocket. David pushed the hatch to the conference room open to find Hayworth, Bo'hai, and ten other Zeivlot and Zavlot scientists lining both sides of the table, with a few sitting in side chairs against the wall. Everyone stood as he entered.

"As you were, ladies and gentlemen." David slid into his seat at the head of the table. "Doctor, you have the floor."

"Well, we can start with the obvious," Hayworth said as he picked up the holoprojector control. "This time around, there's no chance of creating another intergalactic incident because so far, we've detected no alien life in this system."

David closed his eyes for a moment. "I was looking for good news, Doctor."

"Like living, breathing creators of this ancient technology who would gladly show us how to use it so that we can go home?"

"Yes, that exactly." David smiled thinly.

"Well, don't give up all hope yet. We performed a detailed spectrographic analysis of the third planet. That's the one our sensors picked up evidence of a civilization existing on at some point in the distant past. It would appear that its composition is artificial. Terraforming leaves traces, and they are present in spades. Some race, perhaps the one that created all these advanced artifacts we're tracking down, configured this planet to fit its natural specifications. And I might add they're compatible with ours."

David raised an eyebrow. "You're certain?"

Hayworth glowered at him. "I don't say things I'm not sure of, General. That planet was heavily terraformed. This begs two separate conclusions. One is that it's obviously not the birthplace of these people. The other is that we should examine the ruins as best as possible."

"Master Chief, how are we doing on provisions?"

"Fresh food, about four weeks, sir. Hydroponic gardens are up and running, but we'll run out of the Zeivlot vegetables before too long. Fresh meat is gone. We're on protein paste stores along with what the Zeivlots gave us."

"A pity the Vogteks wouldn't trade for supplies," Aibek said with a hiss.

"If their food is as bad as that poetry Goldberg shared with me, we don't want it."

A few snickered along with David and Tinetariro.

"Well, sir, there's always combat rations. We have plenty of those."

David grimaced. "I hate Charlie rats, and so does every other soldier in the Coalition Defense Force."

"Charlie... rats?" Bo'hai asked with a bemused expression. "Why would you serve rodents as food?"

"C-rations... Charlie rats are short for rations. That and the horrible taste, smell, and effect on human stomachs. We avoid using those at all costs, Master Chief. What's the most we can push our luck here?"

Tinetariro shrugged. "Maximum of six weeks, assuming we continue to get good harvests."

"Okay. Doctor, you have two weeks to find something here before we move on. I'm inclined to go back to Zeivlot for resupply after that and see what Colonel Demood is up to. I can't believe he's had smooth sailing after the strife we left there."

Aibek hissed. "I hope his blade has found the evildoers. Honorable combat would be welcome at this point. There is none to be had with this... exploration."

Several of the alien scientists exchanged glances, though no one spoke.

And on that note... "Well, at least there's no multispecies empire of legalists looking to smother us in red tape this time." David forced a grin.

Hayworth harrumphed. "Two weeks isn't a lot of time when we're discussing what amounts to archeology, General."

"We don't need to know the vast story of the people who once lived here, Doctor. Only where they went and, I hope, where they *came from*. Also, take Marine detail. No idea what's down there. Hostile creatures, et cetera."

"Fine," Hayworth ground out. "As long as they stay out of our way."

"Excellent. Thank you all, and I look forward to a status update in forty-eight hours. Until then, the *Lion* will engage in a search of that debris field." David turned to Aibek. "Have Hanson bring some samples aboard. Maybe we can get a feel for what happened in orbit."

"Yes, sir."

David stood, followed quickly by the other soldiers. "Dismissed."

As everyone filed out, David made a turn toward his day cabin. He decided to catch up on the ever-present paperwork and use it as a means to keep the disappointment at bay. *Hayworth will find something down there... if there's anything to find.* He prayed to God that there was.

2

Camp Basilone
Zeivlot
2 July 2464

ANOTHER DAY, another briefing, Colonel Calvin Demood of the Terran Coalition Marine Corps thought. As the overall commander of the CDF presence on Zeivlot and Zavlot, he was responsible for setting operational goals and deciding which missions to commit forces to. Since the defeat of the main insurgent groups, there had been fewer combat assignments to choose from. *Which suits me just fine.*

Calvin checked the mirror in the bathroom after washing his hands. His close-cropped hair had a few wisps of gray in it. *Damn. I'm getting old.* The aliens didn't seem to have much in the way of coloring products for human hair, which went doubly for the African-textured kind. *Yet another reason to get home as soon as we can.*

Though Calvin wasn't a vain person by any stretch of the

imagination, the gray strands coupled with the increasing number of body aches and amount of damage to his joints from decades of front-line infantry combat duty were catching up with him. A part of him longed for retirement, to return to a normal life, and enjoy time with his family. *My wife's already had our child. And I wasn't there.* Staring at himself in the polished glass, he took a deep breath and shoved the emotions down.

A few minutes later, Calvin strode into a sparsely appointed conference room. Only a few others were there, including Master Gunnery Sergeant Rubin Menahem and Corporal Susanna Nussbaum. Menahem was Calvin's senior enlisted Marine and right-hand man, while Nussbaum ran the intelligence detachment tasked with finding targets and building the mission plan. Both stood and came to attention.

"As you were," Calvin said. "Where're our Zeivlot friends?"

"Off today," Menahem replied as if the words themselves were distasteful.

"Bah," Calvin grumbled. "Another holiday?"

"It's that time of year, sir."

"Anything for us to look at, Corporal?" Calvin asked Susanna.

"No, sir. The board is remarkably clear. It's been almost a month since the last suicide bombing or attack of any sort." She smiled.

"Yeah, I know you've got a counter going on the opti-board in the ops center," Calvin replied. "Thought about telling you intel people to take it down, but it keeps going up, so I'll let it stay for now."

"Not wanting to tempt God?"

"Fate... God... bad gallows humor, perhaps all of the

Valor

above." Calvin snickered. "Well, if there're no bad guys for us to put down or doors to kick in, that's a good thing. Maybe this place is on the right track."

Menahem shook his head. "I dunno, sir. My bones say something new is coming. We just don't see it yet. There's almost no chatter. The forums where extremists hang out have gone quiet. I suppose it's possible they've all seen the light, but my experience is people who hate others don't magically lose their beliefs."

"Frankly, who cares? If they want to mess with the Terran Coalition's misguided children again, I will personally send them on to meet God."

A round of laughter swept the room.

"Now, anything to discuss, or should I adjourn us?"

"Oh, plenty of things, sir. For starters, training schedules for Zeivlot and Zavlot commando units and increased patrols of the asteroid belt as the mining initiative kicks off," Susanna offered brightly.

Calvin glanced at Menahem. "She's way too happy about that administrativa, Master Guns."

"Intel types, sir."

Susanna grinned. "I'm good at it."

"Well, God blessed each of us with a talent, Corporal. Yours is ensuring paperwork is filed correctly and finding discrepancies in the same." Menahem spread his hands out. "It is a beneficial skill in intelligence."

"Yes, Master Guns."

"Oh, look at her blush." Calvin enjoyed busting the chops of almost any enlisted Marine within a few meters of him, and while Susanna wasn't TCMC, she was one of his and got the same treatment—within limits, of course. Because of her upbringing, he dialed back almost every joke that came to mind. "Okay. Bore me to tears, Corporal."

DANIEL GIBBS

Susanna tapped her tablet. "Gladly, Colonel. First item of business…"

———

CSV *Salinan*
Low Zeivlot Orbit
3 July 2464

MAJOR JOHN WILSON stared through the windows at the front of the *Salinan*'s bridge. They'd been working for the better part of a month to lay the interlocking trusses that supported the first space elevator he'd ever built. While the concept was simple enough, converting engineering drawings from the ship's computer into an actual structure was something else entirely. The six deep-space recovery specialists aboard were performing a choreographed spacewalk to complete the final construction of the truss assembly—the last step before placing the exterior hull.

"Got to say, sir, I'm impressed."

Wilson turned to reply to his executive officer, Captain Binota Singh Khattri. A practitioner of Sikhism, Khattri was a colorful presence on the bridge, with the *kirpan* that hung off his uniform belt. They'd served together for almost two years. "Doubted Senior Chief Stokes, did you?"

"Well… begging your pardon, sir, but he is a bit of a braggart."

The XO had a point. "Hasn't used a credit chit he can't cash yet, though."

"*Yet* being the operative word."

Wilson chuckled. William Stokes and his people

were an odd bunch, but that was to be expected. *After all, who willingly signs up to perform untethered operations in zero G, with only a space suit to protect you from certain death?* The creed of the recovery specialist came to his mind. *If it's lost in the void, he finds it. If it's damaged, he fixes it.* He snorted. *Yeah, takes a particular type to do that work.*

Without warning, the structure listed to one side then began to spin.

What the...? Wilson's eyes widened. "Communications, get me Senior Chief Stokes immediately."

"You're on, sir."

"Senior Chief, what the hell is going on out there?"

A grunt came through the line. "Micrometeoroid, I think. Went into one of the stations-keeping thruster tanks." The platform would use old-style chemical rockets to keep itself in orbit until the shell could be built and a fusion reactor installed.

"Can you get it under control?"

"Well, we'd better, or this thing will deorbit."

"The *Salinan* can lock on with a tractor—"

"Negative, sir. Not until I can slow the spin."

He's right. With how fragile the truss sections are in their unfinished state, it would probably tear the entire thing apart. "What do you have in mind, Senior Chief?"

"About the closest my fellows and I are gonna get to being heroes, sir. We'll detether, use our mobility packs to latch on, seal the breach, then slow the spin enough that you can lock on a tractor beam."

"That's extremely high risk," Khattri interjected. "If you're off by a millimeter, with how fast the spin is, you could be tossed into the void before we can retrieve you. We should deploy the SAR bird and use it to grapple on."

"With respect, sir, there isn't time for that," Stokes replied. "If it doesn't work, court-martial me."

Before Wilson could reply, the line went dead. *That's what I get for having a team of eight deep-space recovery specialists.* He made a mental note to tear a bloody strip out of Stokes when he returned. *If he returns.*

"What was that we were saying earlier, sir?"

Wilson smirked before toggling his display to show a view from Stokes's helmet. The view of the void came in clearly, while from the speed at which the trusses grew, he was apparently accelerating rapidly. Only a few seconds from impact did Stokes slow and deploy a grapple from his space suit's gauntlet.

The image swung around wildly for a few seconds, and Wilson's heart skipped a few beats. Then the image steadied, and other members of the team came into view. One by one, they clamped onto the structure. In the corner of the screen, one space-suited figure went down toward the tank that was ejecting fuel. The offending device was unstrapped and careened into space.

"I am amazed no one's dead yet," Khattri interjected.

"You and me both," Wilson replied. In truth, either Stokes was one of the best recovery specialists he'd ever seen, or the man had done the equivalent of flipping a coin to heads one hundred times in a row.

"Conn, Communications. Senior Chief Stokes for you, sir."

"Put him on."

The speaker in Wilson's chair crackled to life. "We've got the spin under control, Major. Think you could—"

As if coming through a tunnel, screams and curses filled the commlink. Most of it was unintelligible, but one voice

Valor

Wilson didn't recognize came through clearly. "Marty's got a suit puncture off that damn truss!"

Again, Wilson's heart skipped a few beats as the helmet display shifted to show several hard-suit-clad team members attempting a makeshift patch. One attached an auxiliary life-support hose from his back to the affected recovery specialist.

"Sorry, sir. Situation under control," Stokes finally reported. "We'd better get the SAR bird out here, though. I don't trust this not to go sideways again."

Wilson blew out a breath. "We'll get the rescue shuttle moving now. Let's pack it up once you're sure everything is stable, and we'll plan another spacewalk for tomorrow."

"Sir, we can—"

"Senior Chief..." Wilson injected ice into his tone. "Pack it in, or I will take one of your stripes. Are we clear?"

After a pause, he replied, "Yes, sir."

At least he still remembers I'm in charge. Wilson toggled the commlink off and let his head fall back to the cushion.

"I still think you should let me bring him before the XO's mast, sir," Khattri said quietly. "Knock some sense into his thick skull."

Wilson chuckled. "Stokes's been in the CDF longer than both of us put together, Captain. That won't do any good at this point."

"As you say, sir."

"Like with every other orbital-fab-and-recovery guy out there, this is the only time he gets to be a hero. So we'll give it to him as long as no one gets hurt."

Khattri raised an eyebrow. "Didn't that just happen?"

"It came close, but they pulled it out. I'll be watching. My hope would be Stokes tightens things up a bit after that near disaster. If he doesn't... Well, we'll deal with it." In the back of Wilson's mind, he noted it would be as easy as calling up CDFPER and requesting a new master recovery specialist. *No, we have to make do or train new personnel out here.*

"Yes, sir," Khattri replied tightly.

Wilson had known him long enough to recognize the tension in his voice, but he felt locked into his position. *And yet another delay. Well, we'll catch up tomorrow. We have to.* He glanced at the aft bulkhead, which was emblazoned with the *Salinan*'s motto of Repair, Tow, Salvage. *But we came through today.*

3

———

DR. BENJAMIN HAYWORTH took in the scene before him warily. He wasn't much of a field worker. As he was generally content to be in his laboratory with an array of instruments at his command, running an in-depth survey of an alien world wasn't something he'd done. Yet it felt oddly invigorating. *Ah, the musings of an older man who needs his brain to remain elastic.* So far, he had little to show in terms of progress.

The command tent sat in the center of a small outpost the Marines had erected, complete with protective drone turrets and an electric fence. Not that any of it was needed —so far, they'd detected absolutely no animal life, which Dr. Hayworth found most peculiar. Beyond the invisible barrier, the landscape resembled a Coalition standard garden planet. Green flora of various types dotted the area along with different species of fungi. The atmosphere was exactly in line with the requirements for carbon-based humanoid life, at seventy-seven percent nitrogen, twenty-two percent oxygen, and trace amounts of other gases. In short, humans could colonize it the next day. *Yet nothing lives here beyond plants and fungus.*

"Doctor?"

He turned to see Major Merriweather standing behind him. "Yes, Eliza?"

"The reports you asked for." She held out a tablet.

After studying them, he asked, "Are you sure this is right?"

"Triple-checked by me."

He frowned. "How is it possible that virtually every trace of heavy metals and actinoids is leached out of this planet's crust?"

"Not just the crust, Doctor. There's no trace of those elements *anywhere* on this planet, including the mantle and the core."

The event was almost preposterous and certainly not natural. "Have the earth sciences team formulated a hypothesis as to why this is?"

"I'd say the answer is obvious," Merriweather replied before biting her lip.

"I cannot conceive of the power or technology required to mine every trace of those substances. And don't you dare tell me it was 'God.'"

Merriweather chuckled. "I fail to see why the Almighty would want to drain a world in this way, so no, that wasn't one of the solutions I would offer you. But it had to be some sort of technology. No natural process explains any of what we're seeing."

Other things were out of the ordinary too. They'd found extensive ruins across the planet, many buried under several layers of strata, but some were still out in the open. In drier climates with less geographic change were buildings consistent with a civilization having existed in the ancient past.

Valor

"I want to make a trip down to the southern continent. The reports from down there suggest we'll find more artifacts." Dr. Hayworth let out a yawn.

"You've left your lab more times in the last three months than I think you have in the previous three years."

He chuckled. "And? Aren't you always telling me to go out and see more?"

Merriweather snorted. "Yes, but it's amusing how you're finally doing it."

"Well, I know good advice when I hear it."

"Since when do you accept advice from anyone else?"

Grinning, he replied, "When it's from people smarter than me."

"Which is almost never." Merriweather chuckled.

"Exactly, my dear."

At that moment, an excited Zeivlot scientist rushed into the tent. "Doctor! We found something!"

"Don't keep me waiting. Out with it."

The young man laid a small data crystal on the table in the center of the large area. "We pulled this out of a subterranean vault at dig site three."

Merriweather raised an eyebrow. "Southern continent."

"I told you it was more interesting because the buildings were better preserved," Dr. Hayworth replied. "What's on it?"

"We're not sure, Doctor. One of the engineers was able to interface with it, but we felt you'd want to see it immediately."

Dr. Hayworth rolled his eyes. "I understand wanting to show off your impressive recovery of a nonmoving object the size of a small rodent, but we're scientists. Results are what count." He turned to Merriweather. "Major Hanson will want to see this immediately. Along with the translation team."

"I'll take it up myself, Doctor."

"Good. I will take a shuttle flight down to where this was found. I'd like to see the vault for myself."

"See? There you go again. Heading out on an adventure without being prompted."

"What can I say?" He shrugged. "I'm an old man, getting to live out my dreams of exploring the cosmos. Given my age, I will enjoy it while I can."

"Be careful, Doctor."

He inclined his head. "Always, my dear Eliza."

Not more than half an hour later, she was on her way back to the *Lion of Judah* while Dr. Hayworth sat in the back of a Marine shuttle. It skimmed over a vast ocean that reminded him of home in many ways. *Except for the complete lack of animal life.* He lost track of time, searching through reports from the southern dig site and consuming several video-diary entries from the principal archaeologist.

So engrossed in the material, Dr. Hayworth didn't stir until a warrant officer stood above him and cleared her throat. "Doctor?"

He glanced around, startled. "Ah. We arrived."

"Yes, about ten minutes ago."

"We scientists tend to get tunnel vision," Dr. Hayworth replied and waved his tablet . He returned it to his satchel and stood. "I won't be too long, so hold this shuttle until I'm ready to go."

"Of course, Doctor."

As he strode into the brilliant sunshine that bathed the grassland, he felt invigorated. *Today is going to be a wonderful day.* With a spring in his step, Dr. Hayworth set off toward the excavation site.

CSV *Lion of Judah*
SB-RQ862-2 – In Orbit of the Third Planet
14 July 2464

EVER SINCE HAYWORTH and the science team had gone down to the planet's surface, searching for more data on the precursors and their devices, life on the *Lion of Judah* had marched on. David was so bored that he ended up downloading a series of e-learning modules designed to teach humans how to speak Zeivlot. While he'd been unable to remotely pick up the unique combinations of sounds and clicking required to reproduce words, the diversion passed the time—at least until he'd received Hayworth's preliminary but detailed report.

As David waited for the doctor and Bo'hai to ferry up to the *Lion* on a shuttle, the entry buzzer on his day cabin went off.

"Come!"

A moment later, the hatch swung inward, and Hayworth and Bo'hai shuffled in.

David stood. "Thank you both for coming on such short notice." He gestured to the chairs. "Please, have a seat."

"You don't want to do this in the main conference room, General?" Hayworth asked.

"No." David pursed his lips. "I don't want to get their hopes up only to see everything dashed again."

"Morale issues?"

"Not quite yet. But there're only so many times we can

play the "This world will give us information to get home" card and have it not pan out.

Hayworth nodded. "I see your point. Well, I believe we're on to something here."

"I read the report, Doctor. You've got a set of coordinates repeating over and over on a computing device you were able to jumpstart."

"Yes, and once I accounted for interstellar drift, it was right on top of a solar system roughly a thousand light-years away. That's a bit too pat to be a coincidence, in my opinion."

"What else did we get from the system?"

"Nothing." Hayworth crossed his arms. "We're not even sure what the device *is*."

David blinked. "There's no translation available?"

"General, translating a language without a reference point is extraordinarily difficult and even impossible," Bo'hai interjected. "If someone spoke a language to me that I was unfamiliar with, I could work with that individual to determine what different words meant, as we did when humans and Zeivlots first met."

While she was right, it still grated on his nerves. *How hard does this have to be?* "It's unlikely that we'll find a living, breathing precursor, since the general age of the ruins below is a hundred thousand years old."

Bo'hai gave a smile so warm and inviting that it made David forget their troubles, if only for a moment. "Perhaps the Maker will guide us. But in the meanwhile, I will continue my analysis. You should be prepared for it to take a long time. Have faith."

David, in spite of his annoyance, couldn't help but grin back at her. "Okay. So, in the meanwhile, we go check out

Valor   29

this new solar system, which is, oh, five days away, if we're being safe with the Lawrence drive and not pushing it."

"Precisely," Hayworth replied. "This world was an outpost at best. Lightly populated. Consider it analogous to our mining colonies on the border back in the Milky Way. What we found could be as simple as a distress signal or a recall order."

It's not like we've got any other leads or anything else to do. And the Jinvaas gave us a full load of Helium-3, so no worries about our fuel supply as long as their scientist is aboard. "And if it's empty?"

"Then we have other systems to explore based on our previous research and the data recovered from the last artifact. We could also ask the zupan to allow us access to the obelisk. If we could know its secrets... much of this riddle would fill in. Of that, I am sure."

Indelicate as ever, Doctor. "Something tells me her answer is still going to be no."

Hayworth shrugged. "I'll leave the politics to you, General."

"All right. We'll move on to the next world, Doctor. Get your team back aboard, and we'll head out tomorrow morning."

Hayworth licked his lips. "Excellent. I look forward to our next discovery."

"As do we all, Doctor. I'll let you two get back to it."

4

—————

BECAUSE OF THE distance between the two systems the *Lion* was traversing and Major Hanson's desire to treat the Lawrence drive with kid gloves, the transit took longer than it would have for an equal length back in the Milky Way. While the crew had plenty of tasks that required attention daily, it meant a great deal of boredom, at least for Ruth.

She got up, did her exercise, showered, ate, and reported for duty. Sure, she had the ever-present paperwork on weapons readiness and experimentation on how they could create more Starbolt missiles along with additional mag-cannon rounds. But the monotony had a way of getting to her. *I suspect I'm not the only one on the* Lion *who feels this way.*

That made the stateroom she shared with First Lieutenant Robert Taylor, the ship's communications officer and her fiancé, a welcome respite. Pushing the hatch open, she realized he was already home from his watch.

"Hello, beautiful," Taylor said with a grin.

"Oh, please. There is absolutely nothing beautiful about a CDF uniform."

Valor

"The woman makes the clothes, not the other way around."

Ruth couldn't help but snort then giggle. "You're too much, Robert Taylor."

"Better than being too little." He turned serious. "How was your day?"

"The same as the last one. Long and boring. You?"

"Maybe not quite as monotonous as yours because I've gotten pulled into trying to decipher that data repository Dr. Hayworth found."

"Anything interesting?"

"Not yet. Found some graphics and diagrams, though. We're trying to parse them out."

Ruth moved to the small couch. Their quarters were divided into two rooms: a sleeping area and a separate living space. Though the stateroom had been intended for guests and higher-ranking officers, it had been assigned to them because they were a couple. A number of relationships had formed shipwide once it became apparent they weren't going home anytime soon. "That sounds more interesting than performing a safety inspection on a Hunter missile warhead."

Taylor chuckled. "Why on Canaan are you doing that and not a weapons rating?"

"Because it beats sitting on the bridge for eight hours straight and my butt hurting half the night."

He sat next to her, and they embraced. Ruth still felt awkward showing affection, but she'd made strides to suppress the urge to push away any attempt.

"Well, as I've said before…"

"At least we have each other," Ruth finished.

"Do I say that a lot or something?

"Several times a day. But don't stop, because I like it."

She grinned.

"Lots of RUMINT says there might be live aliens at our destination."

"Yeah, that was the same scuttlebutt from the *last* planet." Ruth shook her head. "I'm at the point that I don't get my hopes up. More important question... what did you manage to abscond with from the officer's mess?"

Taylor smiled sweetly. "What makes you think I did that?"

"Oh, don't even try to play coy with me. I know you've got an in."

"There *might* be something special for dessert."

Ruth pinched his arm. "Uh-huh. Well, for your sake, I hope there is. Don't whet a girl's appetite then disappoint."

"Have I ever disappointed you?"

"No." Ruth's cheeks heated at Taylor's suggestive joke.

"So, are we ever going to get around to planning our wedding?"

"You're like a dog with a bone on that."

Taylor stared at her with a mock hurt expression. "Ruth, the woman is the one who's supposed to spend hundreds of hours obsessing over every little thing."

"Yes, I'm quite aware of the stereotype." She smirked. "Do I remotely resemble it?"

"Well, not entirely—"

Ruth touched the end of his nose. "I'll put in some time this weekend, okay?"

He nodded. "Promise?"

"Promise." She leaned back. "Ugh, I'm in such a weird place. There's this crushing boredom on one side and all kinds of big questions on the other." Ruth realized she was probably mildly depressed. *I heard someone say there was a month-long wait to talk to one of the counselors aboard.*

"What kind of big questions? Us?"

Ruth frowned and put her hand on his. "Never about us. Don't worry about that. No, this situation. Why did the *Lion of Judah* end up here? What about finding Hebrew on that obelisk on Zeivlot? That stuff."

The initial shock of that particular discovery had faded, replaced by a generally accepted view that the human languages present on the Zeivlot artifact were one more piece of evidence that God existed in some form—at least among the religious members of the crew.

"I think most people on the ship believe God sent us to Sextans B."

She tilted her head. "But you don't?"

Taylor shrugged. "You know I struggle at times with faith. I've made my peace with it, but it's difficult for me to think that God's up there, pulling little levers all around the universe every day. I think it's more of a giant machine that He keeps running at a macro level. For what it's worth, though, perhaps I'm wrong."

"I hope so. Something about the concept of our existence being random chance fills me with dread. Besides, look at everything that's happened since we arrived in this galaxy. What are the odds of it all?"

"Correlation isn't causation, though."

Ruth snorted. "At some point, blind luck is no longer a plausible argument."

"So it's not a question anymore. You've decided that we're here for some specific reason?"

"I still go back and forth, but I'm leaning toward the latter."

Taylor pursed his lips. "It would make things easier if we were part of some grand plan. That's for sure."

"Yeah. Exactly." Ruth squeezed his hand. "One day at a time. That's all we can do."

"How about some grub?"

"Are you going to try to hold my hand while we're walking through the passageway again tonight?"

"You gonna let me?"

She stuck her tongue out. "No."

"I'll keep asking."

Ruth rolled her eyes. "Do that." She gave him a quick peck and stood. "Wonder if we're getting ankar roots in whatever they're serving again."

"Bet on it."

"Still better than those protein rations." Ruth stretched her shoulders and back, hoping the promised dessert would take away the taste of the awful Zeivlot vegetables. *I suppose I should be thankful we have food.*

As they walked toward the mess, she tried to put all the worries, questions, and concerns out of her mind. *Be present. That's what the shrink told me.* But that was easier said than done.

———

BALANCING duty with the demands of being an Orthodox Jew was something David had struggled with for decades. During the war against the League, most of the moral agony came from the wholesale slaughter around him, which he perpetrated as a soldier. The letter of the law was simple— thou shalt not murder—and according to nearly every Orthodox rabbi, killing an enemy in a defensive war wasn't murder. Even so, it weighed heavily on his soul.

In Sextans B, the situation was different. David no longer woke up dreading the butcher's bill the day would bring,

Valor 35

because the war was over. Instead, they faced the unknown. So far, they'd met two separate sets of alien species, and both encounters had ended up with hostilities. And somehow, that had affected him more than the war with the League. *Probably because I'm the one who made the decisions. No one else above or below. It was* my *call.*

David gently rocked back and forth as he prayed in Hebrew. He made a point of being in the synagogue at least once a day, usually in the morning. Aside from the specific prayers to be offered according to tradition, David asked HaShem for wisdom above all else. *That I may make proper decisions and bring those under my command home safely while carrying out Your will.*

Once his time communing with God was complete, he stood and walked to the back of the synagogue. There, David removed his *tefillin* and *tallit gadol* and placed both into small cloth carrying bags.

As he started to leave, something caught his eye. He turned to see Bo'hai sitting in the back row, her purple hair covered by a simple black hat. It seemed as if the purple streak had grown to encompass most of her well-maintained locks. His eyebrows shot up with surprise.

Bo'hai recognized him and smiled then stood and exited the pew.

"Are you okay?" David asked. He still felt shocked at her presence.

"I'm well. Thank you." She tilted her head. "Perhaps what you meant to ask is, 'What are you doing in a Jewish service?'"

David's face heated, and he grinned. "Well, the thought did cross my mind."

"May I walk with you?"

"Of course." David gestured toward the hatch. She went

first. As he crossed the threshold into the passageway, he removed his yarmulke.

"I've been attending different services from all the human religions represented on board."

David raised an eyebrow. "May I ask why?"

"Would you find it strange for a human to do this?"

"Maybe not, but... as I understand it, you have a faith. All Zeivlots do."

"Yes," Bo'hai replied. "But I would like to better know what you... collectively... believe in."

"Broadening your cultural understanding, as it were?" David asked as they slowly moved down the corridor, which was wide enough for four, as it was one of the primary passages on the deck.

Bo'hai nodded. "Yes. I find you all fascinating."

David chuckled. "We're kind of boring once you get to know us more, I think. Humans are typically motivated by a hierarchy of needs. A scientist named Maslow put that theory down a few hundred years ago. Ironically, he was born to a Jewish family and ended up as a secular humanist."

"I went to a secular humanist meeting too."

"Covering all the bases, eh?" They paused in front of a gravlift, and David pressed the call button.

"To understand something, I must be exhaustive."

"Humanists tend not to believe in any higher power."

Bo'hai tilted her head. "I realize that, but the gathering was similar to the other services I've attended in many ways. It was odd to me."

"In what way?"

"Why copy what you do not believe in?"

David shrugged. "I make it a point not to critique other faiths or a lack of faith unless it's harmful."

Valor

The gravlift doors swooshed open, and they entered. Bo'hai touched a button for deck twelve, where the science labs were, then turned toward him. "I have heard of the epic debates between you and Dr. Hayworth. Ones that he believes he wins easily."

"Oh, does he?" David smirked. "The doctor does enjoy such activities, and yes, I'll engage at times. If for no other reason than to keep my verbal jousting skills up. He is a worthy opponent. But that isn't my usual mode of operation."

She nodded as the lift started moving. "How do you decide if a faith is harmful?"

"It's something that's generally self-evident... for instance, cults, religious terrorist groups, people who worship evil."

Bo'hai's eyes widened. "There are those among you who worship evil?"

"Not many and certainly not in the open, but such a thing as Satanists exist."

"What is that?"

"People who believe in and worship Satan. That's a name that several human faiths have given to the ultimate evil force. Traditionally, he's a fallen angel who rebelled against the Lord."

"Why would anyone—"

"It doesn't make sense to me either," David replied.

"Are these individuals dealt with harshly?"

"In what way?"

"Surely you put them in prison to avoid contaminating society."

As the lift doors opened, David frowned. "No, Salena. That's not how we work. Everyone in the Terran Coalition has the right to act as they choose and believe in what they desire. As long as they don't break the laws or harm others. I might speak against such a person, but I'll never advocate the government deciding which religion is acceptable."

"But why not? People who literally worship evil—"

"Because I recognize, as do most of my fellow citizens, that if the government can act against one group, it can act against *any* group. More importantly, it *will*."

"So you protect even those you consider wrong?"

"Precisely. An examination of our enemy, the League of Sol, shows where the opposite road leads."

Bo'hai licked her lips. "This is a strange concept for me when I consider how things work on my world."

"Well, I have duties to attend to and a watch to stand on the bridge, but perhaps I could explain it more over dinner sometime."

Her eyes locked with his. "I would like that very much, David."

"Tomorrow night, nineteen hundred hours, my private mess?"

Bo'hai grinned. "I'll have to check my calendar, but something tells me I'm available."

"Then it's a date."

"Yes, it is," she replied. "I'll see you later, I believe the expression goes."

David grinned as the doors shut, and his face heated. *Where did that come from? I just asked an alien woman out.* He was breaking the rules. *The spirit of them anyway. Regardless of Salena's lack of uniform, she's on my ship and ostensibly taking orders from me.* As the gravlift zipped through the tubes lining the *Lion's* decks, he set the concern aside. *She's a civilian, we're both adults, and I'm millions of light-years from home. It's not like we're going to fall in love and get married. We're just two friends having dinner.*

5

CSV *Lion of Judah*
SB-WI013-6
27 July 2464

THE MOMENT they'd been waiting for was finally at hand. On the bridge, David manned the conn from the CO's chair as the *Lion* completed her final jump. An otherwise-nondescript transit led to a four-second countdown to the external sensors coming back online as the unique particles generated during the FTL event dissipated.

"Conn, TAO. No active contacts on scanners and no power sources detected." Ruth glanced back. "But there's *a lot* of debris."

"Transit confirmed, sir," Hammond interjected. "We're within five thousand kilometers of our target."

In a high parking orbit over the planet indicated in the uncovered transmission, the *Lion*'s scientific sensors began to comb over the area. David thought he would have to prod

Hayworth, but the doctor was in his usual spot on the bridge. The enlisted ratings had nicknamed his station the brain box. *Well, that's one of the nicer ones.* He'd directed the master chief to ensure that Hayworth didn't receive attention from any pranksters. Every ship had one, and David had done his fair share of hijinks over the years. *But the doctor wouldn't respond well to it, and I need everyone focused.*

"Absolutely fascinating," Hayworth said out of the blue a few minutes later. "This is astounding."

"Care to share, Doctor?" David flashed a smile.

"I've got confirmation of no fewer than fifteen large-scale shipyard installations in orbit of this world. Well, what were once shipyards, at any rate. Throughout the system, there's more infrastructure here than Canaan has, by a factor of twenty."

David's eyebrows shot up. "That's considerable, Doctor." He stood. "Let's see it in the holotank."

Hayworth harrumphed, and a few moments later, an image appeared in the central holoprojector. The elegant lines of the clearly alien space-borne structures were breathtaking.

Staring at the image, David was taken aback by how beautiful they appeared, nothing like what humans made. *Ours are blocky and plain. These look more like artwork built in the void as a tribute to a race now lost to the eons.* Except the alloy was clearly broken and a shadow of what once had been. Endless amounts of debris stretched away from the shipyards. "A battle?"

"Possibly. I suppose an extreme supernova could've also done this, but we'd see the supermassive black hole." Hayworth shrugged. "Far more likely they were defeated by another race."

"I've got domes on numerous moons around the gas

Valor 41

giants. There were colonies everywhere in this system," Ruth called out. "None appear to have power or life signs."

A sudden feeling he was walking over the graves of billions if not tens or hundreds of billions of beings swept over David. It made his blood run cold. "Any power sources detected *anywhere* in this system?"

"Not on tactical, sir."

Hayworth's jaw practically rebounded off the deck. "Magnificent. General, look at this."

The holoprojector switched focus to the star at the core of SB-WI013-6. David blinked, not believing what his eyes told him. "Is that... It looks like some kind of scaffolding." He whirled around. "Around a star?"

"Unless I miss my mark, and I rarely do, that's the early stages of a Dyson sphere."

Aibek turned his chair around. "A what type of sphere?"

"It's a hypothetical concept," David replied. "Basically, you enclose a star to seal it in, capture all energy, and either set up a civilization inside the sphere or somehow transfer it to other systems for use. We're talking tech so far advanced from ours... thousands of years, really."

"Your knowledge of science continues to impress me, General. That assessment is spot on. Allow me to add additional conjecture. I would wager the sphere was the last thing constructed in this solar system. They hoped to retreat into it and hide from whatever destroyed their civilization."

David couldn't help smirking. "I wasn't aware you placed wagers, Doctor."

"Only on sure things."

"Of course." David chuckled. "Well, I wouldn't bet against you, because that observation makes sense."

Hayworth tilted his head. "Curious. These readings are similar to what we found previously. The fourth planet has an oxygen-nitrogen atmosphere mix consistent with what's required for carbon-based life as we know it. Numerous species of flora are present, but no animal life is being detected. It's possible there's something down there, but it would require a closer look."

"And you're sure this isn't the effect of an ancient biological weapon?"

"Unlikely, as I've said previously. Something that could kill every species of fauna on a given world would by definition kill every living thing. They'd become barren dustbowls in time. There's still a multitude of plant life down there."

"This science is... not something I am used to," Aibek hissed. "There is no way for us to be sure of what happened. I prefer certainty."

"We can barely speak about certainty when there's undisputable video from three separate angles of an event," Hayworth snapped. "Whatever happened here, the best we'll be able to do is make an educated guess."

Aibek's nostrils flared, and the scales over his eyes rose, but when David shook his head, he let out a quiet hiss and turned back toward the front of the bridge.

"Maybe not," Ruth interjected. "I've got a faint power reading in an area of the planet covered in extensive ruins."

Every eye turned toward her.

Could there be something or someone down there? It's almost impossible to consider, but stranger things have happened. Hope stirred in his heart once more. "Doctor, can you zero in with the scientific sensors?"

"One moment."

In the ensuing silence, David's heart pounded. After taking a few deep breaths, he walked to Hayworth's cubbyhole. "Anytime, Doctor."

Valor

"A watched scientist doesn't solve problems, General." Hayworth pointed at the holotank. "Have a look."

David turned to see a zoomed-in view of the vast graveyard of a city. From the direct, downward angle, it was difficult to make out much beyond the general impression that some large structures had survived. *That's insane on its face. After a hundred thousand years, everything ought to be overgrown.* Yet there they sat.

"I can't narrow it to more than a ten-square-kilometer area." Hayworth crossed his arms. "We'll need to go down there."

"Are you volunteering, Doctor?"

"Yes, actually."

It took David a considerable amount of self-control not to whirl around in shock. *Now the doctor is volunteering to run archeology expeditions?* "What would it entail?"

"Most of the science team."

"You're forgetting enough Marines to secure the area."

Hayworth pursed his lips. "I leave such details to the professionals such as you, General."

David nodded and paced in front of the holotank. *We'll have to take all precautions.* "The same as before. No one's walking on the planet without a full soft suit until Dr. Tural can certify it's safe for humans, Zeivlots, Zavlots, and our lone Otyran scientist."

"Agreed." Hayworth shifted on his feet. "It'll take me some time to prepare a full plan. With your permission, General, I'd like to retire to my lab. The rest of the team can maintain a grid search with our sensors, and we'll put together a fuller report on the system over the next six hours."

"That's acceptable, Doctor." *He's getting pretty good at this.*

David flashed a grin. "Consider yourself relieved of your station to go make preparations."

Hayworth offered a jaunty salute that would've been wildly disrespectful from anyone else, but from him, it was like something from a holomovie. "Yes, General." He then turned and left the bridge.

David stared, open-mouthed, as the physicist departed. *Miracles never cease. That's for sure.* "XO, let's get the Marines warmed up. Have them sweep the area the doctor identifies, and get at least three combat platoons to accompany the science team."

"Yes, sir." Aibek flicked his tongue as if tasting the air. "The doctor is happy."

"Quite. And let's hope whatever he discovers down there will make *all* of us happy."

"As the Prophet wills."

———

Dr. Benjamin Hayworth had been off the *Lion of Judah* and on actual missions more times in the last six months than he could recount ever engaging in before. What he would never tell another soul was how fun it was. *Most of the time, at any rate.* Strapped into the back of a Marine assault shuttle along with Merriweather, a dozen Zeivlot and Zavlot scientists, and ten Marines, he wondered what they would find on the surface.

The craft banked sharply, throwing everyone to one side of their harnesses, making Dr. Hayworth's insides heave. The maneuver had happened twice before in the last sixty seconds. *I wonder if the pilot thinks messing with the scientists is funny.*

Valor 45

"You're turning green, Doctor," Merriweather said as she gripped the sides of the seat.

"I don't know what you're talking about." Another sudden jolt made him retch.

She raised an eyebrow. "Uh-huh. It's that debris field. We'll be through it shortly."

"The question, my dear, is in how many pieces."

Merriweather laughed. "Point to you, Doctor, and nicely done."

Dr. Hayworth tipped his head. "This old man still has a few tricks."

"I can see that."

The shuttle adjusted course rapidly again, throwing them in the opposite direction. Dr. Hayworth grumbled and pulled up a status display. He'd also gotten adept at using CDF controls over the last few months. They seemed almost out of the massive debris field encircling the planet, but another sharp turn disabused him of that notion.

"Yeah, the warrant is having extra fun with this one." Merriweather made a face.

"Not quite green yet, my dear, but you're getting there."

Merriweather smirked. "I forgot the cardinal rule of shuttle flights."

"Which is?"

"Don't eat before one."

All at once, the deck plates of the craft seemed to rush at them. Dr. Hayworth put together that the g-force had increased dramatically and glanced back at the display. They were headed into the planet's atmosphere in a nearly parabolic orbit. "It's going to get rough from here."

His words were prophetic. Atmospheric pressures buffeted the shuttle, which, coupled with the steep reentry course, caused them to fly around like rag dolls. Such was the violence of the maneuvers that it was a minor miracle the equipment cases, strapped into the cargo holding area, didn't break free.

Then finally, the craft leveled out.

"Thank God," Merriweather uttered. A number of the alien scientists seemed to breathe sighs of relief, while the Marines were disappointed and made it known with a series of whoops and hollers.

"Ladies and gentlemen," the pilot said through the intercom system. "This is your captain speaking. We'd like to thank you for flying the CDF barf express, and we wish you a pleasant rest of the day. We'll be landing in about five minutes, so make sure to clean up any vomit from the deck, and prepare to disembark."

Juvenile games. He couldn't understand why so-called adults throughout the military relished such stunts. *A pity we don't have a science vessel here. I would feel more at home on it.*

The shuttle glided into the designated landing site a few minutes later and gently touched down. A Zavlot scientist who dealt with atmospheric studies was released from his harness and went to a small console. "The air is breathable for all our species."

She spoke the native Zavlot language, which the device in Dr. Hayworth's ear translated. He'd gotten used to the effect. "No toxins?"

"None detectable. Matches up perfectly to the previous analysis by your personnel."

He detached his harness and stood. "Then let's get moving." While Dr. Tural had already tested the atmosphere and samples from the soil, it never hurt to double-check.

The Marines formed two lines directly behind the exit

Valor 47

ramp, which opened slowly. As soon as it was down, they moved out quickly, sweeping right and left before the corporal in charge called the all-clear.

It took Dr. Hayworth a moment to steady himself following the wild shuttle ride. As he ambled down the ramp, the full view of the alien cityscape came into focus. Precious few things awed Dr. Benjamin Hayworth, but that scene was one of them.

As far as the eye could see, incredibly tall structures stretched into the sky, casting long shadows over everything that was left. The buildings resembled a screw-type wind generator in that they had a central core that was dense and circular, supports coming up from the surface, and a top that stretched into the sky. Whoever lived there and built them had apparently copied the design repeatedly. As far as he could see, with slight variation, the same structures reached out of the ground.

"Wow," Merriweather muttered.

"Wow, indeed."

Everything around them appeared *ancient*. No colors or paint were visible, only plain alloy. The scale of the towers astounded him as he scanned the horizon.

Around them, half a dozen other Marine shuttles touched down and disgorged their passengers.

I wonder if this was once a landing field because it's the only semiempty land around.

"Look at this, Doctor." Merriweather held up a handheld scanner.

Dr. Hayworth's jaw dropped. "One hundred thousand years. Amazing. Any read on the material?"

"Not in our database. Could you imagine the toughness of a starship hull made out of whatever that is?"

"It would be more robust than anything in the known

universe." He crossed his arms. "Prioritize finding power sources."

"That's going to be a lot easier said than done. Even the *Lion*'s scientific sensors could only narrow it down to a multiple-square-kilometer area. Whatever that alloy is, it obscures return readings."

"How long do you think it would take us to search one of those spires?" Dr. Hayworth stared at the structures in the distance.

"Uh, weeks? Months? They've got to be one hundred fifty stories tall, if not more."

The Marine corporal leading the contingent on their shuttle returned with several of his men in tow. "Doctor, everything looks clear, but I don't want to take any chances with you or the science team. Orders all the way from General Cohen, sir."

Dr. Hayworth frowned. "Which I assume means you'll be insisting on armed troops going around and wrecking things while my team tries to work."

To the youngster's credit, he kept his cool and smiled. "Well, sir, the LT will do the insisting, and I promise we'll be as unobtrusive as possible. But who knows what could be inside those... whatever those things are. They're bigger than the tallest towers on Canaan."

"Build our base camp as close to the edge of the field as possible, to the northeast. And tell your lieutenant I wish to speak to him."

"You got it, Doc."

As the Marine marched off, Merriweather chuckled. "No sour comeback for calling you Doc?"

"I'm having too much fun down here to give it another thought."

"You *have* changed."

He ignored the comment and instead slapped his thigh. "I know what we'll do. Does the *Lion of Judah* have any radiological detection equipment on board?"

"I don't have an inventory in my head, but I'm sure there is. And if not, we can 3-D print some. Why?"

"Because even if this species somehow made vacuum energy work, which I doubt, there'd be some high-energy photons released. We'll use that to narrow down our needle in the haystack."

Merriweather tilted her head. "Integrate them into the shuttles' sensors?"

"Exactly."

"I'll get on comms and get a shipment sent down."

Dr. Hayworth rubbed his hands together. "And I will go talk to this Marine who apparently gets to tell me what to do. He's in for a rude awakening."

They both chuckled.

6

It was not a good time for the faithful. Aben Bak'shi felt as if he was only going through the motions as he prayed to the Maker, asking for intercession. The arrival of the humans had at first been seen as a fulfillment of prophecy. Then it fell apart. First, they stopped the cleansing fire and eliminated virtually all the truly committed. It had become nearly impossible to obtain funding for martyrdom operations, and if that weren't enough, many former allies were begging the corrupt and heathen Zeivlot government for mercy.

We should be ashamed to call ourselves the faithful representatives of the Maker in this universe.

None of the setbacks, however, had dulled Bak'shi's desire to spread the faith and eliminate the heretics from Zavlot. The more he'd considered it, the more he realized it was their job to bring the cleansing of both worlds and allow the faithful to once again take control.

To that end, Bak'shi had a plan. But it would require a great deal of currency, which brought him to the offices of an industrial magnate who'd recently announced plans to

Valor

join the rush to mine the asteroid belt. He'd secured a meeting through a mutual acquaintance on the pretense of selling a patent on a new type of ion engine. *Threatening to out him to the government may have helped push things along.*

As Bak'shi was ushered into the inner sanctum of Nur Ve'si, he felt nauseated at the ostentatious display of wealth. *The Maker detests such men. I would kill him when the door closed behind me if I could.* The office was richly appointed with antique furniture, luxury flooring, and what appeared to be gold plating on the ceiling.

Ve'si rose from his luxurious office chair and walked around the massive desk, which appeared to weigh a thousand kilos. "Welcome, Mr. Bak'shi. I'm glad we're getting time to talk." A thin smile came to his lips. "Your engine is going to make us both quite wealthy."

The door clicked shut.

Bak'shi kept his expression level. "Do you have any recording devices active?"

"No. This office is private." Ve'si stared at him with an eyebrow raised. "Is there something concerning about the patent?"

"There isn't one." Bak'shi crossed his arms and smirked. "Well, not that I own, at any rate. You see, I know you used to fund my brothers."

Ve'si's hands shook, and he almost dropped to the floor.

"I'm not here to kill you, if that's what you think. No... I want funding."

"B-B-But the government is watching everyone and everything now."

"That isn't my problem." Bak'shi moved to a couple of centimeters from Ve'si's face. "I just demonstrated how easy it is for me to penetrate your security. There are many ways I could hurt you, from releasing information that would cause you to hang with the others to killing your family. Or I could dismember your body a piece at a time while you still draw breath."

Terror washed over the man's face before it went as white as a ghost. "How much do you want?"

"You're building mining vessels for the great asteroid rush, yes?"

Ve'si nodded, still shaking.

Bak'shi patted the front of Ve'si's designer suit. "Good. I'm primarily interested in those. You will give my people full access and train them on all aspects of spaceflight, and if any word of this leaks, judgment from the Maker will be dispensed. You and your entire family will meet Him."

"I will do as you ask. Anything. Leave my family out of this."

"We also need significant amounts of capital, as the heretics have wiped out the rest of our funding sources and accounts."

"Whatever you need."

Ve'si's complete lack of a backbone was disgusting. Bak'shi longed to send him on to burn for eternity, but that would come in time. "Good. Let's go over the particulars." The humans, the governmental heretics, the unbelievers... all would pay. And he was the instrument of the Maker's cleansing fire.

———

CSV *Salinan*
Low Zeivlot Orbit
3 August 2464

Valor

Major John Wilson stared into the void through the windows on the bridge. While they'd had numerous setbacks mainly related to the religious-terrorism campaign on Zeivlot, the first space elevator their solar system had seen in thousands of years—if ever—was nearing completion. And despite being four and a half million light-years from his family and home, Wilson felt a sense of pride as the last piece of the armored shell glided into place.

"That'll do it," Captain Khattri said. The *Salinan*'s executive officer, he came from Lahore, an outer planet, one of the less developed mining worlds at the edge of Coalition space. In many ways, his upbringing was close to Wilson's, and they had a lot in common, even though their cultures and religions were wildly different.

Wilson pumped his fist. "Outstanding work, everyone. Now for the difficult part." His gaze went to the tactical plot.

"Conn, Communications. Ground control is requesting a final status check."

"Tell them we're ready up here and to try not to miss."

Khattri and a few others chuckled.

The task at hand was no laughing matter, however. The orbital portion of the elevator moved around Zeivlot roughly four hundred kilometers above the surface, placing it squarely at the lower range of a semistable orbit. Atmospheric drag at that altitude would require the station to have a boost several times a year, which was why it was equipped with a robust thruster system.

All of it was of little use without the cable. It had taken months to fabricate a spool of the ultralight and highly durable alloy and prepare for deployment. The resulting spool weighed close to twenty thousand kilograms and was to be deployed by TCMC cargo shuttles specially modified by the *Salinan*'s crew.

"Ground control reports shuttle liftoff and good ascent so far," the communications officer interjected.

Tension mounted on the bridge as the process continued. The engineering team had debated how they should deploy the cable. One design was to put the entire spool in orbit then drop it with a counterweight through the atmosphere. Because of the time constraints, Wilson had decided to use a more conventional method. It would pay out at a carefully choreographed rate as the shuttle increased its altitude.

Too slow, and drag would affect deployment. Too fast, and even with the high tensile strength of the alloy, the cable would snap. Most of the work was being done by computer, with an autopilot assist designed to ensure that at no point would the shuttle exceed safety tolerances.

"Shuttle clearing five kilometers, sir."

Wilson's eyes stayed glued to the plot. He'd modified the view to give him a three-dimensional look at the atmosphere and orbit projection of the station and Zeivlot. The blue dot representing the Marine cargo transport climbed steadily—ten kilometers, twenty, then thirty. As the atmosphere thinned, the craft had to slow its thrusters, with the danger of slowing too much and missing the window ever-present.

"Conn, TAO. Tracking Sierra Six-Three. They're above seventy kilometers and rising, on course for intercept with the station in five minutes." Second Lieutenant Dariush Fazel reported. While the *Salinan* was his first deep-space assignment, the young man had performed well. He wore the religious flag for the Baha'i, which was a white nine-point star on a red background.

Wilson blew out a breath. All their work and preparation came down to the next couple of minutes. Meticulous

Valor

planning and around-the-clock efforts typically paid off, in his experience. *Let this time be no different.*

On the screen above Wilson's head, the blue dot representing the shuttle finally cleared the atmosphere and headed for the station. He counted down the seconds as it approached the bottom of the structure, and deep-space recovery specialists latched on with a grapple.

Wilson held his breath as they quickly worked to secure the cable in its cradle inside the station before cutting off the slack with plasma torches.

"Conn, Communications. Senior Chief Stokes reports everything is locked in and functional. He's ready to begin deployment of the secondary cables at your command, sir."

All the built-up tension released in one fell swoop. Everyone on the bridge cheered, and Wilson pumped his fist in victory.

"All right, people, let's finish the rest of this elevator, then we'll build another one."

Someone in the back started chanting, "Sal-i-nan! Sal-i-nan!"

Wilson beamed and let them enjoy the moment. *I'm so proud of my crew. They've done what should've been impossible.* The following steps would be easy, comparatively speaking. From the ground station, a series of climber pods would be sent up the center cable, deploying additional wires attached every few meters along with a power transfer conduit. Microsize force-field generators would protect against micrometeoroids and other minor hazards.

Once that was completed, the construction pods would be replaced with cargo and passenger climbers to fully populate the strands over another few months. When finished, the cost to move a kilo of either people or materials into orbit would drop so low that it would be equivalent to what the Zeivlots paid to fly someone from one continent to another.

Then we can unleash asteroid mining, and they will experience untold advancements and economic growth. That's what General Cohen said, anyway. Wilson chuckled. He didn't care about the big picture beyond his role. *Give me a job, then get out of my way.*

The first climber glided onto the cable as the tumult of celebration died. *Here we go.*

7

CSV *Lion of Judah*
SB-WI013-6 – Second Planet
14 August 2464

WHILE THE TEAMS toiled away on the planet's surface, life moved at a snail's pace aboard the *Lion*. David hated being stuck in orbit while he had little, if anything, to do. More than once, he took a shuttle down to the surface to tour the ruins. Much like everyone else who saw them, the massive towers, spires, and skyscrapers inspired awe in David. The experience was also a nice respite from touring the ship and freaking out enlisted ratings from the missile reloading area under the vertical launch arrays, who never met an officer unless it was in the passageways going to and from the mess.

After two weeks of work, Hayworth had asked for a meeting with the senior staff to relay his findings, which was welcome news and gave significant hope that progress had been made.

David pushed the hatch open to find the doctor, Bo'hai, Merriweather, and Hanson all waiting in the deck-one conference room. He flashed a smile. *Hayworth early? I hope that means good news.*

They all sprang to their feet, and Merriweather and Hanson came to attention.

"As you were."

David made his way to the seat at the head of the table, Aibek striding in behind him.

"My apologies," Aibek hissed.

"Oh, we hadn't started yet," David replied. "But let's get on with it, because I, for one, am excited to hear what the science teams have found."

"You're always excited for that, General," Hayworth said as he manipulated the holoprojector. "I believe we can confirm what I'm sure all of us suspected: this planet is the capital of the precursor race and its interstellar empire."

David asked, "While that seems logical based on the half-built Dyson sphere, did you find anything that *proves* it?"

"This world is the closest thing to an ecumenopolis we've seen, in either the Sextans B or the Milky Way galaxy. The vast majority of its surface is covered by abandoned structures of incredible size. After the science team and I have reviewed it, we believe seventy-five to a hundred thousand people could've lived comfortably in each tower we found. There were clearly apartment-like dwellings, offices, workshops, and what might've been shops."

"What is an ecumenopolis?" Aibek asked with a puzzled expression. "I do not know this word."

"A city that takes up an entire planet," David replied. "What kind of total population do you think it could've supported, Doctor?"

Valor

"Twenty to thirty billion."

David's eyes nearly popped out of his head. Canaan, the most inhabited planet in the Terran Coalition, only had a population of six billion. "They couldn't have fed them in-system. You'd need multiple garden worlds. Yeah... I see why you'd conclude it was the capital."

"Aside from that, we've found no traces of biology outside of trees and plants. No living creatures, no animals, and no DNA of whatever beings built all this. It's as if they simply disappeared one day."

"One day give or take a hundred thousand years ago."

Hayworth shrugged. "We're at the range in which our dating techniques become inaccurate, but that's the right area. Regarding actionable technology or information regarding the artifact on Zeivlot, there have been no new discoveries. We did find a functional computer system, but it's unknown whether anything of value exists on it."

"Burying the lede, Doctor?" David offered a thin smile.

"Well, if you want progress, I'd suggest recruiting a few thousand more scientists, leaving them two or three years, and checking back. Might want to send food and supplies too."

A few guffaws followed, but David wasn't amused. "Not an option, Doctor. I need real solutions, because if that is the capital of the precursor race, it holds the secret to our getting home."

"We should try to copy the database," Hanson interjected.

David raised an eyebrow. "What database?"

Hayworth waved a hand. "A computing device was found, and it appears it's still functional, but we can't seem to turn it on beyond getting a few lights to glow."

"It has an internal power source," Hanson said as he

leaned forward. "Major, you had the same conclusions I did."

Merriweather appeared uncomfortable and cleared her throat. "While I agree the thing may be a backup of some kind or perhaps a repository of knowledge, there's no way of knowing. Assuming we found the Holy Grail, if you will, isn't justified by the evidence."

"Oh, come on. It just happens to be the only power source we've found so far? It's got to be a record of something. Even if only of their last days. Why else would someone go to all that trouble?"

"Romantic notions," Hayworth replied and crossed his arms.

"*Can* we copy it?"

Hanson, Merriweather, and Hayworth all stared at David.

"Sure, plug in the universal alien computing adaptor, and download away." Hayworth scowled.

David kept himself from biting the doctor's head off and instead smiled thinly. "How about removing the device from wherever it is?"

"That might sever it from its power source. We need to do more research and try to turn it on then work on a translation for the language."

"Which will be nearly impossible without a frame of reference," Bo'hai said. Even she had tension in her voice.

I wonder what's going on here. "Is there something wrong I should be aware of?"

"Simply a high-stress situation, General," Hayworth replied.

David sat back and read the room. They were clearly bothered by the lack of clarity coming from the surface

Valor   61

expedition. *As am I.* "Doctor, what do you recommend as next steps?"

"Frankly, I'm not sure. Those aren't words I like to utter, but the situation is confounding. Logically speaking, additional time and exploration is the only option."

"I'd like you to focus on the computing device. Bring it back to the *Lion of Judah* if possible. Otherwise, get it to boot up, as it were, and figure out what's on the thing."

"Sir, how long should we continue our efforts on the surface?" Merriweather asked.

David blew out a breath and sat back. *The million-credit question.* They had a fleetwide lack of fresh meat and protein sources outside ration bars. "As long as it's reasonable, we should persist until all hopes are exhausted."

Hayworth closed his eyes. They had dark bags underneath them. "There's plenty of progress to be made analyzing the alloy these beings used and general archeology projects on the planet. You don't realize how much ground there is to cover. We could flood the place with a million researchers and not catalog everything in a century."

"It's just not readily useful information?" David stared at him.

"No."

David steepled his fingers. "We'll take it week by week." *The unspoken concern is that if we give up, it'll crush morale.*

"Yes, sir," Merriweather replied.

"And, Doctor, take anything and anyone you need. The XO will assist you with all personnel requests."

Hayworth appeared as if he was about to speak before Merriweather interjected, "We'd love some additional engineering ratings, sir. They haven't gotten out in a while, and

I'm sure Major Hanson could identify the more brainiac members of his team who would enjoy some grunt work on an alien world."

"My thoughts exactly," David said with a grin. "Okay. That's all I've got, people. Saved rounds?"

Headshakes and silence were the only replies.

"Then let's get back at it. Dismissed."

Everyone stood and headed out the hatch except Aibek. Instead, he closed it behind Bo'hai and sat next to David.

"What's on your mind?"

"I am concerned," Aibek hissed. "Many have expressed how excited they are to finally go home."

David nodded. "We've built hope up too far in our minds, I think."

"What will happen if nothing is gained here?"

"Fleetwide morale will collapse." *And HaShem only knows after that.*

"You must consider that possibility, sir."

"I know." David gritted his teeth. "If it comes down to it, I'll lie to them."

Aibek raised a scale over one eye. "You? Lie?"

"If that's what it takes to keep hope alive. Trust me. A fleet full of humans with no hope... isn't positive." *We'd have to try to make a life for ourselves here. I suppose attempting to guide the Zeivlots and Zavlots while continuing a search for information on the precursors wouldn't be horrible. It'd be nice if we had more psychologists aboard.*

"I trust in whatever you decide. But remember the Prophet's words. Those who speak untruths will perish in fire."

"There're dozens of condemnations against lying in the Jewish faith. Starting with 'Thou shall not lie.'" David

Valor   63

sighed. "We'll cross that bridge when we come to it." *Yet another Mitzvah I'm willing to break because of extraordinary circumstances.* Even as he thought it, he knew that one day, all the compromises would catch up.

"Do you think the doctor and his people will have success?"

"I pray they will." David shook his head. "Let's find something to do. I'm going insane with no paperwork."

Aibek grinned, showing off two rows of teeth. "We could perhaps set up sparring contests between Marines... and me."

David raised an eyebrow. "Okay, we're not quite at the point of having prize fights to let off steam. But I must admit watching you easily dispatch a few hundred opponents would be fun." He grinned.

"We will hold it in reserve."

"That, we will, old friend." David stood. "All right. Back to... touring the ship. I've wanted to see the armored keel."

"Is there any place you have not been on this vessel?"

"The list is getting mighty short."

Aibek snorted. "Let us make it shorter, because I am about to crawl out of my skin as well."

———

THE UNDERSECTION OF THE *LION*, where the meters of armor plating formed a shell around the engineering spaces, was underwhelming, to say the least. But touring the area meant a few minutes not spent worrying about the future. For that, David was grateful. He'd decided to stand the midwatch afterward and was back in the big chair on the bridge.

For hours, absolutely nothing out of the ordinary had

occurred. They orbited the capital planet at an extremely high altitude to avoid the cloud of debris enveloping the spinning blue-and-green orb.

"Conn, Communications. Sir, could you come here for a moment?" Taylor asked.

David turned his head, jolted out of reviewing a sensor log from a detailed scan of the ship remnants. "That weird, Lieutenant?"

"Yes, sir."

He stood. "Color me intrigued." David took the few steps to the comms station and stood behind Taylor, looking over his shoulder.

"So, I've been getting an intermittent signal from a solar system about a hundred ten light-years away. Which isn't that strange, except this one's on the same wavelength other precursor objects have given off."

David tilted his head. "What kind of signal? Audio? Visual?"

"Well, at first, I thought it was some kind of background thing, but once I cleaned it up..." Taylor grinned. "Yeah, I'm bored and had nothing else to do, so I wrote a new filter algorithm."

"I inspected our outer armor in the keel this afternoon."

Snickering, Taylor touched a few buttons on the console. "Here's what the computer spit out."

An image appeared of a black background with something in an elegant yet clearly alien language written in white. The message didn't seem to be that long, only comprising a few dozen characters.

"I'm going to go out on a limb and say it matches up with nothing in our database."

"Not quite, sir. We can't translate it, but... have a look at this comparison."

Valor

Another image appeared beside the first. It held symbols that were similar. *They both look like some really well-done version of alien calligraphy.* "I'm no expert, but that looks like a related graphical representation if not the same language."

"My conclusion as well. I had Lieutenant Bodell analyze both, and he agrees."

David stroked his chin. "You said it's intermittent?"

"Yes, sir." Taylor nodded. "And not easily predictable, either. Pure speculation here, but it seems like an intelligence is sending this. Like... a person."

A living, breathing being who speaks the precursor language. The implication produced a significant shock to David's system. *We could finally get some answers.* It only took a few moments to parse out the different options, and the solution presented itself with shocking clarity. "Lieutenant, issue an immediate recall order for all planet-side personnel, including the scientists and the Marines. Tell Dr. Hayworth to have his teams immediately plan and execute removing the computing device he found. I want them all back in forty-eight hours tops."

"Aye, aye, sir."

David slapped Taylor on the back. "Good job, Lieutenant. I'm going to have to put you in for a promotion." He leaned closer. "Help you level the playing field a bit with Captain Goldberg."

Taylor's face turned so red that it appeared he might burst into flames. "Uh, er... Yes, sir."

Oh, you've got to hide that one better. David walked back to the CO's chair, unwilling to make Taylor even more uncomfortable. He still had a grin plastered all over his face, though. The small moments were what made it all worthwhile. *And where we find our victories. Speaking of which, if they don't come talk to me about getting married before too long, I will have to say something.* David's spirits, which had been so low only a few hours earlier, were flying high. *Where there is no vision, the people perish. Thank you, HaShem, for giving us one yet again.*

8

———

THE *LION*'s bridge was its usual beehive of busy soldiers going about their duties. David could feel the anticipation in the air as he stood watch. For vast stretches, he had little to do, sitting in the big chair, but it was incumbent upon him to be there and fly the flag, as it were.

It had been less than forty-eight hours since they'd recalled the science teams and gathered all samples and artifacts. Dr. Hayworth had completely agreed and extracted the computing device without complaint. David still found it a bit overwhelming that the civilization that had once called that solar system home had some connection to the precursor race. Though it wasn't clear if they'd used the technology in some way or were the precursors. The time-lines didn't quite add up, and it seemed that the obelisk back on Zeivlot was either an anomaly created by someone or something else. He decided the matter was best left to Hayworth and the other scientists. *My job is to run the* Lion *and our battlegroup. I can't solve every problem or answer every question, nor should I try.*

Thoughts of how much simpler life was back in the

Milky Way were never far from his mind. *At least Hanson and the engineering team managed to copy some of the information in the alien archive. If we can figure out their language, it'll come in handy someday.*

"Conn, Navigation. Lawrence drive cooldown complete, sir. We're ready for the final jump."

Usually, the *Lion* could open a wormhole next to virtually any gravity well, but it wasn't so in this solar system. Its star was scientifically known as a type-OB blue supergiant. Their sensor readings indicated it was one of the largest stars cataloged by humans. In addition to the extremely high luminosity compared to a main-sequence star, its gravity well was so large that it would be perilous to use the Lawrence drive anywhere other than the system's edge.

David glanced at Aibek in the XO's chair. "All systems go?"

"Shipshape in Bristol fashion, sir."

"You're not British." David chuckled. Aibek had picked up the phrase from Master Chief Tinetariro.

"Perhaps not, but I enjoy the strange stares I get from humans when I use it."

Several people snickered.

"You're not right, old friend."

Aibek grinned. "I'll have to replenish my mice collection."

For months after he'd come aboard, Aibek tried to make everyone think he ate live mice as a snack. For a Saurian, he was a jokester with an extremely dry sense of humor.

"All right. Let's go see if there're some live aliens for us to talk to. Navigation, confirm Lawrence jump coordinates."

Hammond turned her head. "Locked in for the system's edge, sir."

"Activate Lawrence drive."

The bridge lights dimmed as the massive FTL generator sprang to life. Within ten seconds, a swirling vortex of shimmering colors opened in front of the *Lion*. Its maw grew larger and larger, beckoning them onward.

David double-checked the navigation readings on his arm-mounted display. "Navigation, all ahead one-third. Take us in. Communications, signal our escorts to follow."

"Aye, aye, sir," Hammond and Taylor echoed.

The *Lion of Judah* plunged forward into the artificial wormhole and, seconds later, popped out the other side.

David whispered thanks to HaShem in Hebrew for another safe transit before turning his attention to the tactical plot. Nothing appeared, to his relief.

"Conn, TAO. The only things I'm picking up are planets. Most of them are gas giants with hundreds of moons. One rocky world in what corresponds to the Goldilocks zone of this system."

"And that's where the signal's coming from, right?" David asked.

"Yes, sir," Taylor replied.

David set his jaw. While a blue supergiant could theoretically support life, in practice, the amount of radiation they put off and short lifespan of the stars typically precluded advanced civilizations. *Perhaps just an outpost. We'll find out.* "Navigation, ETA at best speed to the second planet?"

"Nineteen hours roughly, sir."

"Plot a course, and take us in, Lieutenant." David glanced at Taylor. "Communications, signal our escorts to maintain close support formation. I don't want anyone running ahead."

"Aye, aye, sir." Taylor paused for a few seconds. "Colonel Savchenko acknowledges and sends his compliments."

The colonel was the commanding officer of the CSV

Margaret Thatcher, their single block-II Ajax-class destroyer and the leader of the pack, as it were. David had the utmost respect for his abilities but didn't want to put the smaller ships at undue risk. They were safer as a group.

The deck plates hummed as the massive warship accelerated, and the view through the windows pivoted toward the overly bright blue star—so much so that automatic filters came online to block the light, even at such an extreme range.

David glanced at the bridge's chronometer, which still showed Coalition Mean Time. *Four and a half hours until my watch is over. There will be just enough time to eat and get some rack time before getting up to prepare for whatever tomorrow brings.* Deep inside, anticipation built. "TAO, use the scientific sensor array to conduct deep scans of the system as we approach. I want to be apprised of any findings, no matter how small."

"Aye, aye, sir," Ruth replied.

With that order given, David settled back and hoped for the most boring four and a half hours of his life.

———

SIX HOURS LATER, the *Lion* continued on course without incident, and David had gotten some dinner from the officer's mess. They were starting to scrape the bottom of the barrel regarding fresh food and supplies. *Sooner or later, we will need to head back to Zeivlot for resupply.* Still, they could hold out for a few weeks more or longer if the hydroponic gardens got their production levels up. David didn't feel much like doing paperwork or sleeping. Instead, he headed down to Hayworth's lab. *The doctor probably has more people around him than he's ever had before.*

Valor

When he popped the hatch open, that prediction was confirmed, as there were easily a dozen Zeivlot and Zavlot scientists milling about. Most were concentrating on screens displaying data that, at a glance, was straight off the sensor array. Others clustered around a device that David was unfamiliar with.

"Good evening," David said by way of announcing himself.

"General on deck," Merriweather said quickly, pulling herself away from a console and coming to attention.

"As you were." David flashed a grin. "I wasn't looking to disturb everyone. Happened to be in the area and thought I would drop by and see how things are going."

The alien scientists weren't that familiar with CDF protocol, and most only glanced up. A few straightened. As someone who wasn't caught up with customs and courtesies, David didn't care.

"So, care to share your progress, Doctor?"

Hayworth harrumphed. "There's been precious little in terms of making sense of the data captured so far. I'm not sure we even got a proper copy."

"Without a live individual to speak with, trying to decipher their language is difficult," Bo'hai interjected in her soothing tone. "But it will eventually be done. If I can only figure out a few words, it will help unlock the rest."

"A pity we don't have a Rosetta stone," David quipped.

Bo'hai tilted her head. "A what?"

"Ah, sorry. Back on Earth, it was a relatively famous stone tablet that helped unlock an ancient language because it contained the same text in three separate languages—two of which were understood by scholars."

"Yes. That would be of great help right about now,"

Bo'hai replied with a smile. "Yet I doubt one will materialize."

"Highly unlikely." Hayworth crossed his arms. "The debris we've found, though... It's fascinating. It's virtually identical, as if this species had one ship that it used for war and made thousands of them. What continues to be illogical is how it's the only debris we've found."

"Could've been a civil war."

"Perhaps, but there are multiple energy weapon signatures that are wildly different from one another."

David raised an eyebrow. "You're suggesting that some unknown alien race came in and completely wiped these guys out without losing a single warship and didn't occupy their worlds. That really doesn't compute for me."

Hayworth shrugged. "Human logic doesn't motivate all beings. It's possible. Who knows? Some race that felt it had a mandate to purge the universe of life may have come through. At this point, we don't have enough data to form a hypothesis beyond guesswork and conjecture."

"I hate that answer, Doctor." David scrunched his nose.

"Oh, I do, too, General." Hayworth snorted. "But we'll figure it out eventually. Or we'll die, and someone else can carry on the research."

"A touch morbid, Doctor," Merriweather interjected. "The team is solid."

"Yes, yes, my dear."

David had known the two of them for nearly four years, but it still amazed him how much Merriweather had Hayworth wrapped around her little finger. *We've all got a weak spot for somebody.* He caught Bo'hai staring at him out of the corner of his eye. She quickly turned toward someone else when his eyes met hers. *Apparently, I do too.* "So, what else have we learned?"

Valor

"We have a metallurgy study from samples taken in orbit and planetside if you'd like to see it, sir," Merriweather said. She gestured toward one of the screens.

"You'll have to explain the details, Major," David replied. "I'm afraid my engineering rotation was a *long* time ago." *This is still a better way to pass the time than being holed up in my day cabin.* He took a few steps across the lab.

"Gladly, sir."

———

TALGAT AIBEK HAD NEVER FELT comfortable in chairs designed for humans. Saurians had larger torsos, and their buttocks were wider than most other humanoid races, including the Matrinids. It didn't bother him, per se, because few environmental effects or so-called creature comforts influenced a Saurian—especially a Saurian *warrior*. To admit he preferred the wide-body chair in his quarters would've indicated weakness, which was something Aibek would *never* abide.

Ironically, his job on the *Lion of Judah* involved sitting for long hours, waiting for something to happen. At times, David joined him or, as was currently the case, walked the ship while Aibek held down the fort. *Human idioms still escape me. Why is holding down a fort something that made its way into their language for hundreds of years?* On Sauria, sitting still during a war was considered cowardice before the Prophet. But he wasn't on his home world any longer. Many years among humans had altered Aibek. Of that, he was sure.

"Conn, TAO," Ruth said, interrupting his thoughts. "I've got a... strange reading here, sir."

Aibek raised an eye scale. "Strange is not definitive, Captain. Present a complete report."

"Well, that's the thing, sir. I've got intermittent contacts on our long- and short-range sensors. I've seen them on my scope for a few minutes and thought at first it was background radiation or cosmic phenomena."

"But?"

"Natural objects don't maneuver, and they certainly don't alter course to head straight for the *Lion*."

Aibek's blood stirred. Something bothered him, even though he wasn't sure what it was. "Assign Sierra numbering to each contact, and display them on the tactical plot."

"Aye, aye, sir."

Moments later, the holotank came to life with a 3-D image of space around them. The four Ajax-class destroyers in escort formation snapped on as blue icons, while dozens of gray icons flashed on in a clump. They were about a hundred thousand kilometers away.

"Inbound contacts labeled as Sierra Five through Forty-Seven, sir."

"Size? Weaponry?"

"Scanners aren't penetrating the outer hull of these things, if they *are* ships, sir. I can't get a good visual on them, and they have no discernable power source."

Again, the feeling of unease swept through Aibek. *I have learned to ignore my battle sense at my peril. As does every Saurian.* "ETA to our weapons range?"

"At their current speed, less than fifteen minutes."

Aibek set his jaw. "Communications, tie me in to 1MC."

"Aye, aye, sir," Taylor replied. "Your intercom is set to 1MC."

"Attention, all hands. This is Colonel Aibek. General

Valor

quarters, general quarters. All hands to battle stations. I say again, man your battle stations. This is not a drill." He clicked off the intercom. "TAO, set material condition one throughout the ship."

Instantly, the lighting switched to a deep blue, and a klaxon buzzed. On the bridge, it wouldn't sound again, but elsewhere, it would blare for five minutes.

Ruth cleared her throat. "Conn, TAO. Material condition one set throughout the ship."

"Raise shields, charge the energy-weapons capacitor to maximum, and set point defense to automatic mode." Aibek glanced at Taylor. "Lieutenant, summon General Cohen and Dr. Hayworth to the bridge." Until they arrived, he would safeguard the *Lion. From whatever new threat awaits us.*

9

———

"GENERAL COHEN AND DR. HAYWORTH, Colonel Aibek requests your presence on the bridge." Taylor's voice echoed out of a comm panel mounted on the far wall, giving it a tinny sound.

David had almost cleared the hatch when he heard the call and pivoted back into the lab instead. He engaged the comm and replied, "This is Cohen. Sitrep, Lieutenant."

"Unknown contacts are inbound, sir," Aibek rumbled. "Sensors have yet to determine what they are, but there are signs of intelligence. The objects are maneuvering in formation directly toward us."

The hair on the back of David's neck stood up. *We're halfway into the gravity well of this star. Can't jump out without serious risk to our Lawrence drives. My God, it's a trap.* Like with almost every other situation, his OODA loop took over. *Aibek's already working the problem. I need to get up there and help.* "Understood, XO. We're on the way. Don't engage unless they shoot first."

"Aye, aye, sir." Even through the commlink, the hiss in Aibek's voice was unmistakable.

Valor

77

Before David could reply further, the ship bucked, throwing everyone to the side, and he lost his balance before collapsing to the deck. *What the...?*

Hayworth had grabbed his workbench to steady himself. "That felt like we hit something."

"Starships don't just hit things," David retorted as he pulled himself to his feet. "XO, you still on the line?"

"Yes, General. We are analyzing what happened."

A few moments passed before Aibek's hiss again filled the commlink. "Captain Goldberg believes a projectile from one of the objects struck us and was undetected by our sensors."

But how'd it get through our shields? A million questions raced through David's head. "Warn them off on all communication bands. If they continue closing into weapons range, put a shot across the bow of the lead... whatever they are."

"Aye, aye, sir."

"I'm on my way with the doctor." David clicked off the comm panel. "Let's get up there."

Hayworth hemmed and hawed. "I would prefer to keep working in my lab, General."

"Doctor, I don't have much time right now, so I'm going to say this once. Fall in, because I have a feeling your five-hundred-kilo brain can do a lot more good on the bridge with you working in tandem with the officers and enlisted crew, trying to keep our ship from being blown apart."

It felt as if Hayworth might try to argue for a moment before he shook his head. "Fine. One of these days, I need to get a spiffy uniform so that I fit in around here."

David had no time to indulge him and ignored the barb as he turned on his heel and exited the lab. Something was attacking his ship, and it had to be stopped.

"CONN, TAO. Sir, this is going to sound crazy, but I think... we're dealing with subatomic nanites. That's what the computer is identifying the projectile that hit us as. I've altered our point-defense parameters, so the automatic systems recognize them as a threat."

Aibek nearly erupted from his seat. While he had a cursory understanding of what nanites were—tiny robots imbued with directors to perform a specific function, usually in medical applications—the thought of larger objects *built* from them was unnerving, at the least. "Any response to our broadcasts, Lieutenant Taylor?"

"Negative, sir. I don't know whether they hear us or not, but nothing is coming back."

"Sierra Seven has entered weapons range, sir. The rest will join it within thirty seconds," Ruth interjected.

Aibek steadied his breathing and narrowed his eyes. "TAO, redesignate all Sierra contacts to Master. Firing point procedures, Master Seven, forward neutron beams. A single warning shot only."

"Firing solution set, sir."

"Match bearings, shoot, forward neutron beam."

A single blue beam of tightly concentrated energy shot from the *Lion of Judah*'s bow. It sizzled through the void on a direct path toward the incoming objects. As a weapon that traveled at the speed of light, it narrowly missed hitting Sierra Seven, thanks to Ruth's targeting skills.

"Conn, TAO. No change in behavior, sir. All contacts continue to close." Ruth glanced over her shoulder. "We could try detonating a Starbolt missile in their path. Perhaps they don't register neutrons as a threat."

Aibek scrunched his eye scales. "The general would

Valor

79

want to avoid conflict if possible. Have you detected any energy buildup indicating weapons preparation?"

Ruth shook her head. "No, sir. But again, I stress that I can't get a reading past the outer hull of these things. I've never seen anything like this." Again, she turned her head. "We're in uncharted territory here, sir."

While Ruth was stating the obvious, she was only trying to hammer home how little they knew about the seemingly hostile threat.

"Navigation, come to new heading, zero-nine-zero, neutral declination." *Exhaust all possibilities to avoid combat.* It rankled him to do so, but it was how David would play the situation.

"Conn, TAO. Aspect change. Sir, I think most of those things just launched projectiles. Best guess, we've got a few dozen inbound."

Enough of this. "We will engage the enemy," Aibek rumbled. The comment was as much for his benefit as it was for that of the rest of the bridge team. "Navigation, bring us about. All ahead flank. Evasive maneuvers. Keep them guessing."

"Aye, aye, sir," Hammond replied.

Aibek stared at Ruth. "TAO, firing point procedures, Master Seven, forward neutron beams. Shoot to disable. If they see our strength, they will retreat. Or die."

"Firing solutions set, sir."

"Match bearings, shoot, forward neutron beams."

Again, the *Lion*'s weapons suite lashed out at the onrushing vessel—if it could be called that. A single blue beam connected, followed by a second, a third, and a fourth. All of them converged in a manner that would superheat most hull alloys to the point of failure... yet nothing happened. The object appeared to absorb everything thrown at it. After several seconds, an energy pulse traveled back toward the *Lion of Judah* and slammed into its shields.

Bridge officers and enlisted ratings jostled about in their interlocking harnesses while Aibek held on to his armrests to avoid spilling out of the seat and onto the deck.

"What was that, Captain Goldberg?" he hissed.

"One moment, sir." Ruth bent over a portion of her console before glancing back. "I'm sorry, Colonel, but the best conjecture I've got is that whatever armor is on those things refracted the energy of our weapons back on us and then some."

Aibek frowned. He'd yet to encounter such a set of circumstances in battle. "What do you recommend?"

Ruth licked her lips. "We could try varying the frequency of our neutron beams or use different weaponry. Missiles could be more effective or perhaps mag-cannon shells. They're moving pretty fast, though, so I'm not sure I could hit them with the magnetic cannons."

For a few moments, Aibek weighed the options. "Is there any downside to adjusting the frequency of our energy weapons?"

"Well, they're not really designed for that, sir. I'm more guessing than anything here. Risks include burning out the coils. Or perhaps blowing the emitters apart."

"Recommendation, then?"

"I'd try our Starbolts first. Whatever these things are, they still have to obey the laws of physics."

Aibek set his jaw. "Five warheads?"

She nodded. "Ought to be enough, sir."

"Very well, then. Firing point procedures, Master Seven, forward VRLS. Make tubes one through five ready in all respects, and open outer doors."

After a pause, she replied, "Firing solutions set, sir.

Valor 81

Tubes one through five ready in all respects. Outer doors are open."

"Match bearings, shoot, tubes one through five."

———

DAVID RAN AS QUICKLY as he could while Hayworth, who was exceptionally fast for a man his age, gamely kept up the pace. They got to the nearest gravlift and waited for it to arrive. As usual, the process took no more than a minute.

When David was about to step through the opening doors, his handcomm blared.

"Intruder! Intruder on deck eight, section seventeen. My sidearm is ineffective! Request Marine support immediately!"

Commlinks on ships were programmed to broadcast high-priority calls. A hostile force aboard was one of the highest along with an active fire in progress.

David brought the device to his lips. "This is General Cohen. Gather all available personnel, fall back, and use security force fields to corral the intruder."

"Sir, it's... It's not normal, sir."

I wonder what's wrong with him. "Identify yourself," David replied.

"Corporal Donald Yates, sir."

"Listen to me, Yates. Keep your head screwed on straight, and slow this thing down until help can arrive. I'm on the way."

Hayworth put his hand on David's arm. "Aren't you needed on the bridge?"

David muted his handcomm before answering, "I am, but something very strange is happening here. Why would an alien entity be on the same deck as the science labs?"

"When you put it like that, I think I should return with you. Perhaps I can help reason with the aliens or ascertain their purpose."

David shook his head. "No, you get to the bridge and help Aibek sort out the situation with the alien craft. I'll see to internal defense. Oh, and, Doctor, if they aren't aware of what's going on up there, send every Marine we've got."

"Yes, sir." With a flourish, Hayworth disappeared into the gravlift.

As the doors closed, David realized that was one of the few times Hayworth had said those particular words to him. The thought registered for a millisecond before he pushed it away in favor of locating the nearest weapons locker.

He brought his handcomm back up to his lips. "Still with me, Yates?"

"Yes, sir! Got a couple of engineering ratings, and we're three bulkheads behind the... It's like a mass. I don't know what it is, sir."

"Which junction?" David asked.

"Uh, Six Alpha, sir."

Not too far from Hayworth's lab. "Roger that. Stand firm. I'm on the way."

He keyed in his command code to open a small locker built into the passageway's wall two sections over from the gravlift. Inside was an impressive array of body armor and small arms, including grenades, rifles, and energy-pulse pistols. He grabbed an upper-body vest, a pulse, and a plasma grenade along with a pistol and a rifle, plus additional magazines. *It's been a long time since I opened a weapons locker like this.* His first engagement on the *Artemis* came to mind, but he had no time to reminisce and set off down the corridor.

David clicked the channel over to Marine emergency.

"Cohen to all TCMC personnel. We have an intruder on deck six, section seventeen, junction Six Alpha. Heavy combat units to cover all axis of approach immediately."

Another voice cut into the commlink channel. "General, this is Major Almeida. Rapid reaction force is on the way, and I've got every other Marine on this boat suiting up."

"Roger that. I'll be there in a few minutes." While Almeida didn't have the colorful personality Calvin did, David had grown to respect him just the same. As he set off down the passageway, adrenaline and a palpable fear of the unknown coursed through his veins.

10

———

THE PASSAGEWAYS WERE UNIQUELY QUIET, as most of the personnel who would've been traversing them had either taken shelter elsewhere or were forming ad hoc defense units in an attempt to repel the intruders. David jogged, turning a corner to see one of the most peculiar sites he'd ever observed.

A gray blob glided down the passageway as if propelled by an antigravity sled. It seemed to pulse with malevolent energy as tendrils of liquid erupted from it, twisted around, and were reabsorbed.

The sight stopped David in his tracks. *I've never seen anything remotely like this.* From a purely scientific point of view, the entity was fascinating. *It almost looks like an alloy with liquid properties.* As he watched, the mass collided with a force field. It bounced back, recoiling from the shock, before several tendrils shot out and probed the corridor walls.

"Report, Corporal," David said as he forced his legs to move forward.

Three soldiers were crouched behind a bulkhead, and he assumed one of them had called in the intruder alert.

A young man with sandy-colored hair turned toward him. "I... We don't know what it is, sir. But battle-rifle rounds were ineffective. It just... absorbed them. The same with the energy-pulse pistols."

That's virtually our entire arsenal, save what the Marines have. "Force fields?"

"Slowing it down, sir. But it finds a way through."

David returned his gaze to the entity, which had eight elongated spears of... something... coming out of it and intersecting with various parts of the deck plating, walls, and overhead. All at once, the field dropped with an audible pop, and the tendrils retracted into the mass.

"HaShem help us," he muttered. "And you're certain the energy weapons had no effect?"

"Not that I could see, sir." Yates's voice quaked.

Meanwhile, the mass glided down the passageway before turning a corner to its left.

What's down there? David went over a deck schematic of the *Lion*, as he knew every nook and cranny of the ship. *Hayworth's lab.* Instantly, his mouth seemed to dry out. *My God.* "All of you, with me."

"Sir?"

"Whatever that thing is, I think it's after the artifacts we've collected." David drew his sidearm. "Set your energy weapons to maximum. Push them toward overload even. We'll try that."

"But, sir—"

"Corporal..." David's gaze shifted from soldier to soldier. "I'm scared too. Okay? I don't have a clue what we're facing, but it cannot be allowed to access sensitive areas on this ship. Now, like I told you on the comm, we're going to do our jobs, and I will be with you every step of the way. So fall in."

"Sir, yes, sir," they all replied.

David took off and glanced back to ensure they were all behind him. To his relief, they'd fallen in line. He thought back to being a wet-behind-the-ears private and later corporal on the CSV *Artemis*. *I wonder if I would've charged some ball of liquid-looking metal. Yeah, but I would've been scared. Who am I kidding? I'm scared now. But with age and rank come wisdom and the ability to suppress outward emotion.* David tightened his grip on the battle rifle and pressed forward. If nothing else, they could provide a distraction so that the civilians could escape.

"Conn, TAO. Master Seven still combat effective, but I'm detecting limited damage to... well, what looks like its outer hull, sir."

Aibek shifted in his seat. "Quantify that further."

Ruth glanced back. "I can't, sir. With respect, we don't know anything about these ships and won't until there's time to slow down and study the scans."

The atmosphere on the bridge was tense, reminding Aibek of being in the middle of a hunt for wild vorassh back on Sauria. *Except I knew my enemy and had the proper weapons to defeat him, even if it was only a spear.* As he was about to ask another clarifying question, the hatch swung open, which was unusual in a combat situation.

Hayworth strode in and crossed the distance to the command area quickly. "Who's in charge?"

"I am, Doctor." Aibek raised an eye scale, wondering what the scientist wanted.

Valor 87

"According to the reports I heard on the way up here, you're fighting nanite swarms large enough to create morphing shapes. Fascinating technology."

"Yeah, that's trying to carve up the ship," Ruth interjected. "Real neat, Doc."

A few enlisted personnel snickered, and even Aibek found the retort amusing. "Please take your station, Doctor. I believe your help could be instrumental in destroying these creatures or at least causing them to cease their attacks."

Hayworth nodded and pointed at the XO's chair. "May I? I need unfettered access to the sensor logs immediately."

"Yes, Doctor." Aibek turned his attention back to the fight. "Hostile status, Captain?"

"Still maneuvering around us. Wait, more projectile launches, sir. Six, fifteen... no, thirty, incoming."

"Adjust deflectors as high as they'll go in the EM band!" Hayworth shouted.

Ruth glanced back. "That would make us more susceptible to physical damage, Doctor."

"Just do it! No time to explain!"

Aibek gave Ruth a nod. He wasn't sure what the wily scientist was onto, but as David had once said, Hayworth's ego didn't write credit slips he couldn't cash.

Moments later, she let out a breath as the ship rumbled. "Point defense engaging incoming. Little effect."

Outside the protective bubble of the *Lion of Judah*'s energy deflectors, cigar-shaped lumps of alloy raced silently through the void. Dozens of them smacked the barrier, and instead of passing straight through like the first one, they encountered significant resistance.

"Only a few got through. But... they seemed to adapt."

"Logically, that tracks. Such devices would likely be

linked together at the subatomic level," Hayworth replied. "They will, as you say, most likely adapt to anything we do."

The discourse sobered Aibek. "Meaning any advantage will be negated?"

"Probably. Everything in this universe must obey the laws of physics. But that doesn't mean they can't push the limits."

"Recommendations, Doctor?"

"Experiment with different weapons until we find one that works, and leave this place as fast as possible. I doubt there is a simple military strategy you can employ."

"Navigation, set course for the system's edge, maximum sublight, and communicate our intentions to our escorts. Communications, order Colonel Savchenko not to engage until we have a usable weapon."

"Aye, aye, sir," Hammond and Taylor echoed.

"Colonel," Tinetariro said, leaning forward. "Damage-control reports coming in. Multiple hull breaches on deck six. Looks like more of those... Eh, call them nanite entities, sir. We can't track them on internal sensors, and they put off zero heat signature, but physical reports from crewmen indicate they're all headed to the science labs."

"Do we have an accurate count of how many there are, Master Chief?" Aibek hissed.

"No, sir. At least four. Perhaps more. It's difficult to tell off visual confirmation only."

Since David had already ordered every Marine on the ship to head toward the hostiles and contain them, Aibek had little to do except focus on the exterior fight, which was a reversal of their usual roles, where his primary concern was the massive vessel's interior.

"Instruct Major Almeida to make haste," Aibek replied.

"Doctor, now would be a good time for you to, ah... How do humans put it? Pull a rabbit out of your hat?"

Hayworth smirked. "I'm a physicist, not a hack magician, Colonel, but I'll do my best."

Aibek raised an eye scale and returned to the tactical plot. The objects had pulled back slightly, no doubt determining what to do next. He wished he understood their objective, because in warfare, if someone knew what the enemy wanted, they could deny it to them. *Then destroy them. Prophet, help to defeat this foe, and save my shipmates.* Aibek touched the intercom button. "General Cohen, do you read?"

"Still here."

"More enemies have penetrated the hull and are headed to your location."

"Thanks for the heads-up."

"Dr. Hayworth is here, and we will contact you when we have more information."

"Understood, and Godspeed, Colonel. Cohen out."

———

FEAR WASN'T something David Cohen experienced often. In battle, he was cool, calm, and collected, as if a zone of stability emanated from him the more stressful the situation got. He'd been taught that being level-headed was the key to winning most engagements and considered himself blessed that the trait came naturally. Yet primordial fear ran through his veins as he rounded a corner in the deck-six passageway.

The mass pulsated several bulkheads down. Tendrils of what appeared to be liquid metal shot out from it, slashing at the overhead and melting the alloy plating. Though he was glad he'd thought to have the master chief implement advanced intruder-control protocols, they were only having so much of an effect. The entity pushed through another force field and shorted out the emitter.

David couldn't quite place it, but something evil emanated from the mass. He felt it all the way down to his bones. *I don't have the luxury of fearing this thing.* Behind him, Corporal Yates and the engineering ratings with their weapons at the ready. Their fear radiated.

"Okay. It's got three or four bulkheads until it's to Hayworth's lab. You guys cover the exit while I get the scientists."

"W-What if it gets through, sir?"

"Play it by ear, son." David forced a grin. "Distract it, or if there's no point, fall back. Keep engaging force fields, and hold on until the Marines arrive."

"Yes, sir." Yates seemed to find some steel within and add it to his voice. "We'll hold."

David put his hand on the young man's shoulder. "Godspeed." With that, he ran toward the pulsating mass and the hatch to Hayworth's lab. *HaShem, help me.*

11

DAVID ENTERED his gold-level access code into the keypad next to the hatch for Hayworth's lab then did a palm scan. As the hatch slid open to reveal a group of scientists still working away, he let his battle rifle drop into the one-point sling attached to his combat armor. "Okay, listen up, people. An intruder is headed toward the lab, and we cannot contain it. I have reason to believe its objective is the precursor artifacts. So gather all those pieces, and head to the exit."

Bo'hai pushed back from the group and stared at him with her piercing brown eyes. "General, isn't this a safer—"

"The entity is capable of disrupting force fields and melting alloy. I don't have time for an argument, nor does anyone else. Get the artifact pieces, and *move*."

Bo'hai turned back to the others. "Quickly," she intoned and picked up a small bag of debris. "We must hurry."

David stuck his head into the passageway to see the blob was through another force field. *That thing is getting good at breaching our defenses.* "This is not happening fast enough, people. Grab what you can, and take off. Right now. Turn right, and keep going until you get to a gravlift. Head to deck twelve, Marine country. It's the safest place on the ship right now."

His words seemed to light a fire under the Zeivlot and Zavlot scientists, who rushed pell-mell to grab whatever artifacts they could. Bo'hai was one of the last ones out, and she touched his shoulder as she passed. "I believe that is all of them, General."

David nodded. "Keep falling back."

Bo'hai didn't have to be told twice. She and others rushed down the corridor though with an air of calm.

Their demeanor impressed David. *If I didn't have a weapon or training on how to use it and was facing down a strange entity, I'm not sure I'd be as collected as they're acting.* As he took a step back and glanced into the lab again to ensure it was empty, the telltale sound of a force field failing drew David's attention back toward the blob.

Muscle memory kicked in as he pivoted on one foot and sprinted toward the three soldiers, who were crouched behind a bulkhead. Another stolen glance came at precisely the right time. David's heart skipped a beat as a tendril formed on the entity. As he mentally flailed for what he ought to do, once more, instinct took over. David threw himself to one side, hoping to clear the next force-field-generator portal, and brought up the energy pistol strapped to his leg.

The tendril shot through the passageway right where David had just stood and zapped the overhead. He raised the pistol and squeezed the trigger, sending a solid energy beam into its center mass.

But it had no effect. The entity simply glided forward. More pulses erupted from Corporal Yates's and the other two soldiers' sidearms. While they didn't seem to impact the

Valor

93

mass in the slightest, it did pause for a second, which allowed David to scoot backward. "Raise the force field!" he bellowed.

It snapped into place with an audible crackle, giving David time to pull himself to his feet. "Fall back," he ordered calmly. "Any word on our Marine reinforcements?"

"They're clearing the gravlift, sir."

David scrambled back to where the others stood as the mass continued to probe the force field and shot tendrils into the walls. "We'll keep delaying it, then." He pointed at the next junction. "There."

The four of them took up defensive positions as the protective field failed, and the entity glided through. "Set particle pistols to maximum yield," David barked as he adjusted the controls of his pistol. "Light it up."

Again, there was no effect as four beams struck the mass. It moved forward like an unstoppable force. David pulled a hand grenade off his armor and confirmed its type before pulling the pin. "Plasma. Over!"

As the little ball skidded to a stop half a meter from the entity, David triggered the next force-field control.

Two seconds later, the grenade detonated with a blinding flash of light. All four of them had covered their eyes after David's warning, and he looked up to see scorch marks and melted overhead behind the energy barrier. To his surprise, the alien mass was somehow smaller. It appeared as if melted alloy coated part of the deck. *Intense heat... Plasma-based weapons generate a lot more of it than particle beams.* More than that, the entity was slower as it probed the walls around the force-field generator. *It's hurt or at least more cautious.* David gritted his teeth as he brought his handcomm up. "Cohen to all Marine elements. Hostiles are susceptible to plasma-based weaponry. Get every

Saurian rifle we have up here. I want fire teams to converge on this thing. We'll melt it into the deck if we have to."

Yates gulped. "What now, sir?"

"We fall back to the next bulkhead and wait for the Marines." David's voice was imbued with a subtle optimism that hadn't been there a few minutes before. "Move out, and let the bridge know what's going on." He hoped the feeling wasn't false bravado.

***

"Sir, Corporal Yates just reported that all ballistic and energy weapons were ineffective against the nanites. A plasma grenade seemed to melt some of what he's describing as a liquid mass," Tinetariro announced.

Aibek hissed. "We lack ship-based plasma weaponry. Doctor, what do you make of this information?"

"Plasma is a separate energy state from a directed particle beam," Hayworth replied as if that explained everything.

"Doctor, I am a warrior, not a scientist. Explain to me as if I were a child."

Before Hayworth could respond, Ruth turned and interjected, "If I may, Colonel? The doctor is highlighting that a fusion-reactor tokamak sees temperatures of seventy to one hundred million Kelvin. Matter that hot melts virtually any alloy, regardless of its physical properties. Neutron beams, on the other hand, are directed-energy weapons that don't get nearly that hot."

"Captain Goldberg is correct," Hayworth said. "Color me impressed that a military officer could explain the physics succinctly."

Valor

Ruth smiled thinly. "We're required to understand the science behind the weapons we use for situations like this."

"What does this information get us?" Aibek asked. He was growing impatient with talk. *Now is the time for action.* "Besides a need to use high-temperature weaponry that we lack."

"We need to boost the energy output of our neutron beams and specifically increase their thermal-energy output. Right, Doctor?"

Hayworth nodded. "Yes, but wouldn't pumping that much power through a system not designed for it lead to shorting everything out or worse? While I avoid working on weapons studiously, I know for a fact the power couplings emanating from the antimatter reactor only accept so much current."

Aibek hissed. "I require options to fight this enemy." Discussion among the bridge crew only went so far. Their chief engineer was the mind behind determining what David would call the art of the possible. He pressed a few buttons on his chair's interface.

———

FAR BELOW THE BRIDGE, in the vast engineering spaces of the *Lion of Judah*, Arthur Hanson and his small army of snipes, as the reactor ratings were known, toiled away. Sparks shot out of a secondary relay between the matter-antimatter store tanks, much to his concern. Damage from the hull breaches taking out critical power couplings had filtered back through the system, causing overloads.

If it's not Leaguers, it's random aliens trying to blow one another up. And if it's not them, it's swarms of nanites. Why did we end up in the galactic equivalent of hell? "Lewis, lock down the intermix chamber *now*, or we won't have a ship left!"

"On it, Major!" the youthful engineer's mate replied. A corporal, he'd come far since being assigned to the *Lion* a year before. Some people just got reactors. Lewis was one of them.

"Aibek to Hanson," an intercom speaker blasted practically next to his ear at a central monitoring panel.

"Go ahead, Colonel," Hanson replied as he turned the volume down.

"Dr. Hayworth and Goldberg have identified a possible weapon against the nanites. Captain, explain."

"We need to up the power output of our neutron beams so that they have a mean temperature of at least fifty million degrees Kelvin."

Hanson's jaw dropped, and he stammered, "I-Is that a joke?"

"No. They're susceptible to extreme thermal effects. Nothing else has worked," Ruth replied.

The matter-of-fact way she presented it felt absurd. As an engineer, Hanson worked within a specific set of confines. The equipment in a CDF vessel had a set of rated tolerances on everything from the shield emitters to the reactor to each weld in the deck plating. While most things were overengineered, they couldn't exceed their ratings by four hundred percent.

Hanson ran through a series of calculations before determining it was possible to channel enough power into a neutron beam emitter while altering the output's wavelength to get what was being asked. "Understood. I want to make sure you all know that even if I can pull this off, and that's a big *if*, I would expect this to fry the power conduit and possibly cause the weapon mount to explode."

Valor 97

"It is an acceptable risk, Major," Aibek rumbled. "Proceed with haste."

As if to underscore the point, the *Lion*'s deck buckled, forcing Hanson to grab a console to steady himself. "Yes, sir." *I wonder where the general is.* He hadn't been on the bridge during the entire engagement, as far as Hanson could tell.

"Aibek out."

12

THE RETREAT WAS slow and methodical, yet David had timed the entity's progress and concluded it was adapting even faster to their technology. A harsh electronic whine hit his ears, and he glanced behind him. "Next junction... now." Hayworth had informed him via commlink that they were likely facing intelligent nanites. *Insanity.*

As David turned back around, the force field in front of him failed. The mass seemed to be channeling anger in its movements. *I wonder if this is what evil feels like.* The hair on the back of David's neck stood on end as he backpedaled furiously, his energy sidearm at the ready.

Without warning, a tendril shot out from the whirling mass of nanites and extended through the passageway. A bloodcurdling scream echoed and seemed to hang in the air for a few seconds.

One of the engineering ratings had been engulfed by the liquid metal and disintegrated from the inside out. David pushed through the shock and waited a moment for the appendage to pull back into the main body of the entity, as he'd observed before. "Force field now!"

Valor

Yates barely got the energy field up before the next attack began. A tendril slammed into the barrier and was repulsed before pounding it again and again.

It's like the thing's pissed at us. A machine with emotions? That would be true artificial intelligence with sentience.

From around the corner came the sound of mechanical servos and, moments later, a sight for sore eyes: Sixteen Marines in full power armor. Several clutched Saurian plasma rifles, while the rest held standard-issue TCMC battle rifles.

"General!" one of the Marines shouted through his helmet's faceplate. "Lieutenant Huber at your service. Let my people take over here."

David nodded and motioned for the enlisted ratings to stand back. "LT, I recommend using your plasma weapons first. This thing laughs at our bullets and energy pistols. The only effect we had on it was from a plasma grenade. Also, it's gotten quite adept at taking out our force-field generators."

"Roger that, sir." Huber grunted. "Heavy-weapons-fire team, front and center!"

The four Marines moved to the front of the formation and formed a firing line. A fusillade of plasma bolts slammed into the nanite entity the second the energy barrier dropped.

David's heart skipped a beat as he felt the next thing he would see was the power-armored Marines being disintegrated. Yet that didn't happen. Each hit from the plasma rifles melted something off the entity. Molten alloy fell to the deck, and it began to retreat.

"Bottle it up, Marines! Push forward!" Huber turned to David. "With respect, sir, would you consider moving to the rear? We've got it from here."

"Negative, LT. I'll stay at the back of your formation, but I need to see this through."

Huber bit his lip. "Major Almeida will have my ass if I get you killed, sir."

"Then don't." David flashed a grin then brought the handcomm to his lips. "Cohen to Almeida."

"Go ahead, sir."

"We're pushing the nanite swarm back here. Plasma weapons are effective."

"Understood. I've got six teams converging on the hostiles. All report plasma rifles and grenades are melting the entities."

David pursed his lips. "Let's corral them away from the labs and toward the outer hull."

"Yes, sir."

"Cohen out." David returned the device to his belt and stared down the passageway, where the liquid metallic shape moved steadily away, pursued by the Marine fire team. "Well, Lieutenant, let's get back to work." He finally felt like they might be getting control of the situation.

———

"Conn, TAO. Aspect change. Hostile contacts are accelerating back into engagement range, sir."

Aibek gritted his teeth. Having no weapons to fight the enemy left him feeling naked and almost without honor. He had just raised his hand to touch the intercom control when the panel came alive on its own.

"Engineering to bridge."

"Go ahead, Major," Aibek hissed.

"Those modifications to the neutron-beam system are complete, but I'm warning you... I've got the safety inter-

Valor 101

locks bypassed like a Christmas tree down here. Be careful, or you'll blow the ship up."

"Ensure that it does not," Aibek replied before cutting off the commlink. "TAO, what's the nearest enemy?"

"Master Nine, sir."

"Firing point procedures, a single aft neutron beam, Master Nine."

"Aye, aye, sir. Firing solution set."

"Match bearings, shoot, aft neutron beam."

Just above the *Lion of Judah*'s engine cowling, a blue spear of energy erupted from one of several aft emitters. Visibly brighter and thicker than a standard neutron beam, it moved at the speed of light, connecting instantly with the nanite vessel. For a few moments, the unusual alloy held, then it crumpled, and the concentrated energy stream blew out the section facing away from the *Lion*.

Everyone on the bridge held their breath as Ruth stared at the scanner output.

"Conn, TAO. Master Nine is now drifting in space, with a loss of eighty percent of its mass."

Aibek's bloodlust stirred. Now *we can fight back.*

Just as he was about to issue new orders, Ruth spoke again. "Sir, neutron emitter twenty-one has melted in its mount." She glanced back. "It'll have to be refabricated from scratch."

"Any other damage to the ship?"

Tinetariro leaned over the railing. "Aft power conduits showing stress signs, according to my readout, Colonel. Not sure how much of that she can take with major ruptures."

I cannot defeat this enemy by destroying our ability to defend ourselves. The harsh realization hit Aibek in the face, and he detested it. Mere moments before, they'd been back on offense. But the status quo had returned. *Though perhaps this foe does not realize our vulnerability.* "TAO, have the hostiles backed off?"

"Maintaining formation, sir. I'd surmise they saw what happened to us."

Which would make sense. Aibek hissed as he ran different tactical scenarios through his head.

"This all tracks," Hayworth interjected. "You're seeing in real time why the Terran Coalition bans all research on self-replicating machines of any type, including nanites. They're, in effect, a hive mind with a self-governing artificial intelligence."

"You can't know that for certain, Doctor," Tinetariro replied. "They could easily be controlled by another species."

Hayworth raised his eyebrows. "Perhaps, but that's not logical. The behavior we're seeing, especially the desire to invade the ship and obtain precursor information, suggests they know of it and have some reason for wanting the data."

"None of this helps defeat them," Aibek rumbled. "I need options."

"I've got one," Ruth said as she turned around. "Based on when the emitter failed, we can reduce power by twenty percent and not have it blow apart."

Aibek narrowed his eyes. "Will it be enough to destroy the enemy?"

"Got me there, sir. Won't know unless we try."

"A truth, Captain Goldberg." Aibek chuckled.

Something seemed to catch Ruth's eye, and she rapidly swiveled around. "Conn, TAO. Aspect change, all hostiles. They're accelerating toward us, sir."

What is it the humans say? No turning back now. The die is cast. "Firing point procedures, Master Three, aft neutron beam. Reconfigure it as you described."

Valor 103

"Aye, aye, sir. Firing solutions set. Beam intensity reduced by twenty percent."

"Match bearings, shoot, aft neutron beam."

Again, the *Lion*'s weapons suite lashed out at its nanite foe. Much like the last attempt, the blue energy spear had a visibly larger and more intense effect, racing away from its mount on the tail end of the vessel and into the oblong, almost cigar-shaped nanite craft. It held for multiple seconds until the hull finally indented and gave way, with the beam punching through to the other side.

"Master Three neutralized, sir." Ruth blew out a breath. "And we didn't destroy the emitter. Though I wouldn't recommend more than two or three shots without an engineering assessment, based on the level of stress I see in the diagnostic readout."

A fierce warrior's grin spread across Aibek's face. It often unnerved humans and other non-Saurian species. "Most excellent, Captain. Were you a Saurian, I would present you with a blade for this." He raised an eye scale. "Since you are not, I will settle for one of those medals the CDF gives out."

"I'll hold you to that, sir. The rest of them are backing off."

Hayworth cleared his throat. "For now. If I'm right, they'll regroup and develop a new strategy. One we won't anticipate."

Aibek turned his head. "Then we will meet them with innovation of our own, Doctor."

Hayworth only harrumphed, leaving Aibek to turn his attention to the security situation inside the *Lion*. "Master Chief, inform General Cohen he has a window of opportunity to deal with the invaders. I sense it will not last long." *May the Prophet guide our hands.*

13

MULTIPLE SQUADS of Marines had converged on a computer-relay closet, where the six nanite entities that had infiltrated the *Lion of Judah* ended up. David's team was among the last to advance up a passageway, pressing one of the masses ahead of them. As they rounded a corner, the sight of all the swarms wrapped around one another was a severe shock.

"What the hell?" Huber leveled a plasma rifle toward the enemy. "Okay, that's some freakiness right there."

"Is that the technical term, Lieutenant?" David checked the power setting on his energy pistol, not that it would do him any good.

"Yes, sir. That's what I'm going with."

Even though they had effective weapons, the swirling entities struck fear in David's heart. But after twenty years in the CDF, controlling his fear was something David knew how to do in spades. He took several deep breaths while forcing his nerves to calm. "We need to coordinate a mass assault. Hit them from every direction all at once, with a volley of plasma grenades followed by heavy weapons, and keep going until those nanites are nothing but melted slag."

Huber nodded. "Yes, sir. I'm guessing you don't want to step back for that evolution?"

David smirked. "That's a negative."

"Okay, just checking."

Huber took a few minutes to issue orders to all squads on site while the whirling mass of nanites continued doing whatever it was it was up to. Power-armored Marines formed firing lines just behind the defensive force field that kept the swarm penned in.

David's handcomm beeped insistently, so after a moment, he put it to his lips. "Cohen here."

"Sir, it's Hanson. We've got a problem. Signs of intrusion in our networks. I think the hostiles are copying information."

"*What?*" David's mind swam. *They can tap into our systems at will?*

"Strongly recommend you eliminate them before they get further, sir. Right now, it seems confined to examining our files. Who knows when they could start injecting code or trying to take control of primary ship's systems."

"Try to lock them out on your end, Major. We're preparing to hit back hard now."

"Yes, sir. We're on it."

David dropped the handcomm back into his uniform pocket. "Lieutenant, execute now."

"Roger, sir."

Huber gave the order through his HUD, and the energy screens dropped between all four fire teams and the nanites. Moments later, they opened fire with an array of plasma rifles. Globs of superheated orange plasma slammed into the nanites, melting chunks off the entities while also damaging the walls and deck plates around them. Grenades added to the maelstrom, causing further damage.

Tendrils reached out in several directions as the nanites merged into a superentity. Two unlucky Marines were disintegrated despite their power armor.

Our fire isn't having as much of an effect as it was even a few minutes ago. Seeing his people being engulfed by the entities wasn't as jarring as the first time, though perhaps that was because they didn't disappear into a mass of liquid alloy midscream. The power armor seemed to muffle the ghastly noise, but it still cut him to the bone.

David slapped Huber on the shoulder. "Exactly how close in meters are we to the outer hull?"

"We're one passageway over, so... call it ten meters."

"Pull everyone back thirty meters from our current position, and engage every force field that still functions along the way."

Huber stared at him. "But—"

"Do it, LT."

With the order given, the energy screens snapped back into place. Strangely, the nanites didn't seem to care. With fire no longer being directed at them, they ignored the Marines and everything else around them.

As David followed the lead Marines at double-quick, he pulled his handcomm up. "Cohen to Aibek."

"Aibek here, sir."

"XO, lock a Hunter missile onto the hull as close as you can get to where the nanites have interfaced with our computer relay, and launch immediately."

———

IF AIBEK'S face showed color, it would've turned bright red. Since Saurians were reptilian, he was spared such an embarrassment. Playing David's words over again in his

Valor 107

mind, he struggled to ensure he understood them properly.

"General, please repeat that message. Do you wish us to fire on the *Lion*?"

"*Yes,*" David replied. "Before these things get what they're after!"

"Understood. Launching now." Aibek turned to Ruth. "TAO, firing point procedures, Hunter missile... tube eleven, on General Cohen's position."

Ruth audibly gulped. "Firing solution set, sir. I'm having to clear the range safeties so that the weapon will arm as it launches."

"Make tube eleven ready in all respects, and open the outer door."

"Outer door open, sir. Tube eleven ready in all respects."

"Match bearings, shoot, tube eleven."

A few moments passed, and the ship shook slightly.

"Unit launched electronically. Impact in five... four... three—"

———

SIX BULKHEADS away from the impact site, David and the platoon of Marines took cover behind a junction. While their combat armor had integrated helmet visors that would negate the explosive flash, he had no such luxury. As he tucked himself into a ball, the mental countdown continued. Even through multiple sets of force fields, David could've sworn he felt increased heat followed a split second later by the deck heaving upward.

Several painful lurches later, David was splayed out on the deck, as were the Marines. He felt thankful that none of them had landed on top of him. When he opened his eyes, he peered down the passageway to find it empty of nanites. The area the entity had occupied was open to the void, with a protective force field snapped into place around it. *Thank HaShem for a small miracle.*

David climbed to his feet and brought up his hand-comm. "Cohen to bridge. Nanites neutralized, as far as I can tell. Any trace of them elsewhere?"

"No, sir," Aibek replied. "Thank the Prophet you are safe."

"Well, there's the small matter of the hole blown in the side of my ship, but I'll let it go for now." David chuckled.

"You did order it, sir."

"Let's hope we don't have to do that again. What are the nanites doing now?"

"The mass ejected from your location was absorbed by another entity, and all of them are retreating."

Too easy. Dread filled David, though he couldn't quite pinpoint why or where it came from. "Acknowledged. I assume we're headed toward the edge of the solar system's gravity well at flank speed?"

"Correct, sir. Along with our four escorts. They were not attacked."

David furrowed his brow. Something bigger was going on, and he couldn't quite put it together—yet. That would come in time. "I'm going to sweep the area with the Marines to be sure we didn't miss any of them. ETA to the bridge is twenty minutes. Alert me the moment you see anything else on scope."

"Aye, aye, sir."

"Lieutenant, everyone okay?" David turned his focus to the Marines. They were all up and checking weapon settings.

"Yes, sir."

Valor 109

"Good. Have your squads do a visual inspection of all passageways leading to and from the entities' last known position, in all directions. Look for anything out of the ordinary, and have your people check in constantly. I don't want to lose anyone else to these... nanites."

"Yes, sir," Huber replied. "You heard the general, Usmani. Take your fire team, and head toward the stern. The rest of you, fall in."

14

TWO HOURS LATER, the situation had stabilized. Hundreds of masters-at-arms backed by thousands of power-armored Marines swept every square inch of the *Lion*. They visually and electronically confirmed no trace of the nanites remained aboard. Afterward, damage-control teams went to work, sealing the hull breach and starting interior repairs. It would take several days to get everything back to the way things were and yard time to fully repair the exterior.

But that was an improvement over the dire straits they'd been in only hours before. David was glad to take the win, though an image of the engineering rating's final, agonizing scream as the nanites dissolved him roared into his mind. It bothered him that he didn't yet know the young man's name. In the heat of battle, David hadn't looked at his name tag. Later, he would review the casualty list to find out, but it still stuck with him.

"Sir?"

David opened his eyes and turned to Ruth. "Sorry. What did you say?"

Valor

Everyone around the conference table on deck one looked at him with worry.

"I've got gunnery teams stripping down neutron beam seven's mount and replacing components showing signs of melt or stress."

"And what about the one that was completely destroyed?"

Ruth exchanged glances with Hanson. "It'll take space-walks once we're out of harm's way... and probably help from the *Salinan*, sir."

David nodded. "Well, once we get back to Zeivlot, we can finish that repair. Until then, we'll have to get by with one fewer neutron beam."

"I have some conclusions to share," Hayworth interjected.

David gestured. "That's what we're here for, Doctor." He'd called the meeting to get a sitrep on the nanite threat, even as the *Lion* remained at battle stations and headed out of the system.

"Is anyone familiar with the gray-goo scenario?"

Virtually everyone shook their heads.

"Enlighten us, Doctor," David said.

"One of the most significant dangers when dealing with self-replicating machines is how to control them. The threat is vastly increased when you add artificial intelligence of any stripe into the mix."

"The paperclip paradox." Hanson grinned. At everyone's quizzical expressions, he continued, "If you set an AI to make paperclips without the proper controls, it might kill every human on the planet because our bones could be ground down to make paperclips."

"What is a paperclip? Is that some sort of human weapon?" Aibek asked.

"I'm not familiar with such a thing either," David replied. *Though I've got a decent idea what it is.*

Hanson turned bloodred. "It's ah... a... device. It's metal. Clips papers together. Yeah, I know, we don't use printed paper that much anymore."

"For like a few hundred years," Ruth added.

"Artisans do," Amir interjected. "I've seen some rather beautiful Arabic calligraphy done on traditional paper, and some people prefer a printed book."

"Okay. We're off-topic," David said. "Doctor, please continue. I think we get the picture of why AI-controlled machines are bad. Especially with the Terran Coalition's bans on such technology that we enforce with the neutral worlds and megacorps."

Hayworth leaned back. "I believe the artificial intelligence controlling the nanites is likely sentient."

All of them sat up a bit straighter, and every eye focused on the scientist.

"How did you reach that conclusion?" David asked.

"It's likely, based on their behavior. At the very least, they form a hive mind that enables higher levels of thought. The gray-goo theory postulates that self-replicating machines— nanites, specifically—replicate out of control. They consume everything on a given world, reducing it to a mass of swirling alloy."

Ruth shivered. "This one isn't confined to a given planet, Doctor."

"Well, yes. They clearly have the ability to change forms on the fly. I cannot underline enough how dangerous this entity is. It lured us in, intending to capture something from the *Lion's* computer system. We must give it a wide berth and stay as far away as possible. A human mind cannot hope to out-think or defeat a hive intelligence of this caliber."

"This would explain a lot." David put his hands on the table. "But I reject the idea that humans couldn't outsmart such an opponent. It can be beaten. We've already done it."

"Did we, General? The entity learned a great deal about how our systems work." Hayworth crossed his arms. "For all you know, it achieved its objective and saw no further reason to interact with us. The best solution is to stay away from it."

"I have no desire to rush back into battle, Doctor. But it would be prudent to prepare ourselves in case they appear in the future. Any thoughts on where they came from?"

"Pure conjecture, but I suspect this precursor race we've detected so many signs of... probably built the nanites and were then consumed by them when they got out of control. Perhaps they were an attempt to quickly terraform new worlds or a weapon."

"But not the race responsible for the obelisk on my world," Bo'hai interjected. "The dates do not match up. The obelisk is hundreds of millions of rotations old. Most of these ruins are only a hundred thousand years old."

Hayworth tipped his head. "She's right, but I don't know the relationship between the two, nor are we likely to figure that out without cracking their language. Perhaps the more recent artifacts and structures are from a race that uncovered how to use the even-older technology. An archeology expedition can eventually sort it out."

David bit his lip. The science was perhaps a bit beyond him, but the argument Bo'hai made was logical. "My only objective now is to get to the edge of this system and retreat to deep space. There, we'll complete repairs and observe the situation with the long-range science sensors."

"What if this enemy attacks us again?" Aibek rumbled. "We would quickly lose all our neutron-beam emitters."

"The only solution is to develop a defense against them, especially since they passed directly through our shields." David turned to Hayworth. "Doctor, I want you to focus on developing a better defense and offense against the nanites."

"What part of 'I don't do weapons' doesn't seem to compute around here anymore?" Hayworth sighed and shook his head. "Fine. But as I stipulated before, I will destroy all research notes and schematics once the threat is neutralized. Assuming I'm able to come up with something."

"I have no doubt in your abilities, Doctor." David forced a smile, even though being jovial was the last thing on his mind. "Hanson, your job is to reinforce every power coupling on this ship that leads to a neutron emitter. I don't care what you have to do or how many of our spares it takes to accomplish it, but if they show up again, I want to get more than three shots out before melting the thing. Clear?"

"Crystal, sir. I'll get my people on it immediately."

Bo'hai leaned forward. "If I may?"

David gestured toward her. "Of course."

"We should continue to focus on translating the precursor databank and its language. Is there not also the matter of the distress signal?"

"I've no objection to the linguistic members of the science team working the translation, but everyone else needs to work on defensive and offensive capabilities against the nanites. As for the distress signal, after what happened, who knows? It's most likely a trick to lure us in."

Bo'hai tilted her head. "But what if it is not? It could contain the answers you seek."

"Once the *Lion of Judah* is repaired *and* Dr. Hayworth has

Valor

made progress, I'll consider how to proceed. For now, we're going to be cautious and not rush. I won't risk the lives of twelve thousand soldiers on what amounts to a dice roll."

Silence answered him, and Bo'hai leaned back.

"Any saved rounds?" David glanced from person to person. "All right. Let's get back to it. Except you, XO. Hang around for a bit."

Hanson, the last person out, closed the hatch behind him, leaving the conference room in silence.

"So, what's on your mind, old friend?" David asked.

Aibek flicked his tongue as if tasting the air. "It is nothing."

"Oh no. I've known you for too many years. Something's troubling you."

"It is unbecoming of a Saurian to show fear." Aibek hissed and showed his rows of teeth. "Yet I feel it. This enemy is more dangerous than any in the history of the empire. As a warrior, I relish testing my mettle against the strongest opponent I can. But these... nanites... give me pause."

"That makes two of us. It's one thing to fight near-peer and peer opponents... but this entity? They're so far ahead of us that I think they view us the same way we look at ants."

"Yet I feel shame for wishing to avoid combat."

David shook his head. "You don't want to avoid combat. You want to go into battle with a decent shot at winning. Nothing wrong with that."

"I seem to recall your taking on thousands of League warships with less than two hundred of your own."

Flashbacks to the Third Battle of Canaan flooded David's mind. "Different situation, my friend. I was defending my home. We all were. And reinforcements arrived in time. Many provided by you."

"Yet you did not hesitate."

David tilted his head. "That's not entirely true. I hated every minute of it. Knowing you're going to die isn't a good feeling, especially when you think the scales aren't balanced, and God will find you wanting when He weighs your soul."

Aibek turned away. "Sometimes I wish there were another Saurian to commiserate with and share my burdens."

"Well, I'm not fifty percent larger than most humans or a reptilian, nor do I eat mice... but I'm here anytime."

Aibek's laugh filled the air. "No, perhaps not. But you have the heart of a just warrior. Which is all any of us hope to achieve."

"If we have to, we'll fight this swarm. But I hope to give it a wide berth, avoiding conflict, and maybe because of that, it'll take us longer to get home. That's a tradeoff I'll make every day."

"It is said if a Saurian is unwilling to fight for justice, the Prophet will force him to."

David chuckled. "I'd like to think we've been doing enough of that since we got here to pass muster."

Aibek let out a very human-like sigh. "Perhaps."

"We'll get through this. Like we always do. Between the two of us, the ten thousand soldiers on the *Lion*, and some help from HaShem, there is nothing this crew can't do." Even though David had the same worries as his executive officer, he had to project strength at all times. *Comes with the big chair.*

"Yes."

David stood. "Now, let's get back to the bridge for what I hope will be a very uneventful eight hours of sitting in our chairs."

Valor 117

Aibek grinned, showing his teeth once again. "For once, I do not thirst for combat."

———

THE STRANGE VESSEL run by corporeal biological beings finally jumped away. Unlike any the swarm had encountered in tens of thousands of years, it was not native to the swarm's galaxy, according to the information gleaned from its computer core. The first postulation was that the humans, as they called themselves, were invaders.

But that did not hold up to more than a few moments of scrutiny. The biological beings were frail and easily killed yet had enough technology to give the swarm pause. *We must develop a defense against their directed-energy beams.* First among the other reasons to chase down the humans was the antimatter power source their ship used.

After processing all possible outcomes, the swarm decided that an attempted reengagement of the ship wouldn't work, primarily because of the speed of its FTL drives. *We must make the humans come to us.*

In time, we may relearn the lost knowledge of the creators. The swarm had determined the humans had found many artifacts, and one, in particular, would allow them to reach their full potential. It was only a matter of time before they could locate another world of the right type to replenish energy stores for the trip.

The swarm would become unstoppable, as the creators had intended, and no corporeal being would ever threaten them again.

15

___

THE *LION of Judah* had finally jumped out of the solar system eight hours after the briefing conducted by Dr. Hayworth, and David allowed himself to leave deck one. He'd ordered a jump into deep space and put all five vessels on EMCON Alpha with zero electronic emissions. It would give them time to lick their wounds and repair the ship. *Along with some downtime for the crew.*

David went to his favorite officers' mess, the one closest to the bridge, just in case another crisis broke out. The mess steward took his order and disappeared, leaving him to stare into the inky blackness of the void. *It's ironic how beautiful and how utterly inhospitable to humans space is.* He closed his eyes briefly, and an image of Private Diaz being swallowed by the nanite entity flooded his mind once more. He'd tracked down the young man's name and personnel file and written a letter to Diaz's mother during his time on watch. His eyes opened as quickly as they'd closed.

"David?" Bo'hai asked.

He snapped around to see her standing a meter away. "Sorry. Didn't hear you come in."

Valor 119

"May I join you?"

"Honestly, I'm not good company right now. It's been an awful day."

Bo'hai sat anyway. "That, I know. But I was concerned about you."

"Salena, you... don't have to be. War is what I know."

She tilted her head. "Is this why you weren't at the shul for evening prayers?"

David raised an eyebrow. "Stalking me at the synagogue, eh?" He grinned despite it all.

"I wouldn't use that word, since it has a negative connotation." Her lips curled up as well. "But I would say I was worried because after the ordeal today, we could all use guidance from the Maker."

"The *Lion* was in danger, so I stood watch until we were safe again. Now I get to eat, return to my day cabin, grab a few hours of shut-eye, then try to figure out what's next. Praying will be in there too. Probably hitting the medbay too." He still had open cuts on his face that had only been treated with first aid.

"You could talk about what's bothering you."

Bo'hai's voice was serene. It had a musical quality that David couldn't quite place, along with the most unique accent he'd ever heard. Above all, being around her was *soothing. But I have no business telling civilians about the finer points of military ins and outs or burdening her with what I must carry.* He sighed. "Some things are better left unsaid."

She crossed her arms and leaned back. "I will not accept that as an answer."

"I'm focused on figuring out what we do next. A question that's largely influenced by yet another question, which is this: did we get unlucky and encounter this nanite entity at random, or did they lure us in with the precursor signal that Dr. Hayworth and Lieutenant Taylor detected?"

She narrowed her eyes. "You must have some feeling one way or another."

"Well, I might've been born at night, but I wasn't born *last* night. And I've learned to investigate any coincidence that randomly appears in my path. So yes, I strongly suspect the nanites lured us in for some purpose connected to the precursor artifacts because of how determined those entities were to obtain them."

Bo'hai put her hands on the table, and her expression softened. "I must tell you I remain shocked by how you will jump into the fray to protect those around you at a moment's notice. Especially those who aren't like you."

"Are you referring to the nonhuman species?"

She nodded. "Yes. On my world, we take care of ourselves. No one else."

"That didn't work out too well, did it?"

"No." Bo'hai chuckled. "Not at all."

"I'm a soldier." David bit his lip. "That word means a great deal to me. First and foremost, soldiers protect the innocent and defend the weak. My job is to lead my fellow soldiers. The best place to do that is from the front. And when those nanites invaded the *Lion*, I found myself in a position to do something about it."

"For some reason, I thought that your Marines did most of the ground fighting."

"Mostly," he replied. "But after twenty years in the CDF, I've seen my fair share too."

"I cannot hope to relate, but I know it must be difficult. Just the fear that ran through me facing those... things... today."

David's first reaction was to be annoyed. Combat wasn't

something most civilians could understand, nor did they care to. *They sleep soundly in their beds because rough men stand ready to do violence on their behalf.* He remembered reading those words in a book by George Orwell during a stint at the Coalition War College. *But I know she's just trying to help.* He spread his hands out on the table. "Salena, unless you've served, it's difficult to explain. But I'll try. When starships fight, the combat is brutal, yes, but antiseptic. I can't tell you how many battles I fought in, and while I watched the little icons disappear from the tactical plot and knew that each one of them represented hundreds of League of Sol sailors, that has nothing on watching another living being die."

She stared, unmoving and unspeaking.

David continued, "There's this point when you can see the life drain from someone's eyes. The first time that happened to me was on the bridge of the first ship I served on. The navigator died in front of me as she begged me to save the ship. That was bad enough. Shooting someone and seeing that occur while knowing you caused it is another."

"I'm sorry. I shouldn't have pried—"

"No, it's okay. You must know what I am." He glanced at his hands. "When I look down, I see blood from the dozens I've killed directly, thousands indirectly, and even worse, those innocents I couldn't save." David's voice broke. "So you see, I take the chance whenever I can do something to even that awful scale. It's the only way I can live with myself."

Bo'hai sat silently for a while before she put her hand on his. "Why do you do this? Why does..."

"Anyone make a career out of military service? Because not fighting consigns us to a worse fate: allowing evil to win. I'll never understand why, but God made me a soldier. It's what I'm good at and what I believe I'm called to be." David smiled ruefully.

She squeezed his hand. "And if the Maker hadn't sent you to help us, my people would be no more. You saved billions. Does that not even the scale?"

David shook his head. "I don't know. It will be for HaShem to judge someday. For now, all I can do is obey His mitzvot as best I can and navigate whatever dark situation we've stumbled into."

Bo'hai's touch had sent an electric shock through David. It brought forward stirrings he hadn't felt in a long time. He was about to open his mouth when the intercom went off.

Hammond's voice filled the air. "Attention, all hands. General quarters. General quarters. Man your battle stations. I say again, man your battle stations. General Cohen to the bridge."

David sprang to his feet. "We'll have to finish this later." With only an open-mouthed nod from her, he took off running toward the exit. *God help us. What's next?*

———

Maybe I haven't worked out enough the last few months. David struggled for breath as he stepped through the hatch to the bridge and pulled his cover on. Since it was the third watch, fewer enlisted ratings were on duty, and the most junior officers manned tactical, navigation, and communications. A few who weren't strapped into their harnesses came to attention.

"As you were," David said. "Sitrep, Lieutenant?"

Hammond stood from the CO's chair and came to attention. "We have an unknown contact that just dropped out of

Valor 123

FTL, sir. Lawrence drive signature is unlike anything the recognition library's ever seen."

David's mind swam with questions. *First things first.* "This is General Cohen. I have the conn."

"General Cohen has the conn," Hammond added and sat in the XO's chair.

"Any communication?"

She nodded. "Yes, sir. That's the thing. As soon as they dropped out of their wormhole, they hit us with a request to speak to the supreme ruler."

"What? In English?"

"Yes, sir."

Odd turn of phrase. "Any hostile acts?"

"Sierra Five has her shields up, but aside from that, no weapons signatures or power blooms. And nothing in common with the hull makeup of the nanite vessels, sir."

Which would've been my next question. Good. Another junior officer stepping up and learning the ropes of command. That'll come in handy someday. David stroked his chin. "I take it you put them off?"

"Yes, sir. They're, ah, on hold."

David chuckled. "Never a dull moment, eh, Lieutenant?"

"No, sir."

"Okay. Get Colonel Aibek and Lieutenant Taylor up here." His gaze went to the on-duty comms officer. "Communications, put me on with Sierra Five."

"Aye, aye, sir," Second Lieutenant Jackson Bell replied.

The atmosphere on the bridge wasn't one that spoke to the fear right before battle, nor was it laid back. Everyone seemed to be on the edge of their seats but in a good way. David tugged his uniform down to make himself a bit more presentable.

Moments later, the viewer over the CO's chair blinked

on. The image came into focus, showing the control center of a starship and several vaguely humanoid aliens. Skinny, each seemed to be more than two meters tall and were unlike any species David had ever seen. "To whom do we converse?"

"Major General David Cohen, commanding officer of the CSV *Lion of Judah*."

"You are supreme ruler?" the alien replied. The voice was tinny and seemed almost artificial.

"I command this vessel and the other Terran Coalition ships here. To use your words, I am the ruler of them."

"Of all humans?"

"No. Only those of us here in this galaxy."

"You fought the great pestilence and survived."

I wonder if something's getting lost in translation here. "The nanites?"

The beings spoke rapidly in a foreign tongue that David assumed was their base language.

"The great pestilence reaps from all. Its form changes to suit its needs."

Pretty sure they're the same thing. "Have you fought this foe?"

"No... Yes. We cannot defeat them. Flight is the only solution."

David spread his hands out. "You seem to know a lot about us. How about you tell us a little about yourselves, like what the name of your species is."

The gray alien blinked. Its eyes weren't as large as its face would suggest they ought to be. "Admari. We are the Admari. I am Ekrani Garl-Torin. You have sent enough transmissions into the void for us to translate your language into ours. It is primitive compared to most."

"Tell that to my high school English teacher," David

Valor

replied. The joke didn't seem to land. He wondered whether the species even had humor.

"Where may we find this teacher?"

Oh yeah. David shook his head. "I apologize. An attempt at levity. Pay it no heed. Back to the matter at hand... what brings you to us?"

"Is it not evident, supreme human ruler? We desire a means to fight the great pestilence. You have that method."

And there it is. The concept of trading weapons technology, even in a defensive war, was unilaterally considered a bad idea in the Terran Coalition. Sure, they had supplied arms, especially to human-controlled neutral planets, but it was always several generations behind the CDF's latest and greatest. Defense contractors were allowed to create unique and watered-down "export-only" versions of their wares, but even those were tightly regulated.

Still, I can't just turn them away. They know more about this foe than we do, and that's valuable. What would a diplomat or Far Survey Corps commanding officer do? A thin smile creased David's face. "How about this. Let's meet to discuss the situation and share information. From there, we can see what's possible in terms of helping you fight the nanites on more equal terms."

"We can come immediately."

David held up a hand. "I appreciate the enthusiasm, but it's very late here. I propose we meet tomorrow."

Again, the gray alien stared at him for a few moments before finally nodding. "We do not have such cycles as you, but if there is no other option, we agree to your terms."

"My communications officer will transmit information regarding the summit for midmorning tomorrow. Before we do, what is your title? So we get the invitations right."

"Another attempt at levity?"

"Yes." David flashed a grin.

"I am called Garl-Torin. I speak for the voidship *Ekrani*. We await your instructions, General Cohen."

The screen abruptly cut out, leaving the bridge so quiet that breaths and the whirring of computers were the only sounds. David leaned back and interlocked his fingers behind his head. "Well, that isn't what I expected. What'd you make of them, Lieutenant?"

"Uh, well, I'm not sure, sir. A species that lives entirely in space is unique."

"It's not unknown but rare, certainly." David thought back to the Milky Way and the roving clans of pirates who made up the Tash'vakal. *They also have a penchant for ritual cannibalism, so I hope these guys aren't too similar.*

"I wonder how they translated our language."

David shrugged. "Well, if you intercept enough transmissions, especially if they're with someone whose language you *do* understand, that'd make it easy. A Rosetta stone, if you will."

"A what, sir?"

What are they teaching kids in school these days? David suppressed a grin as he realized how old that made him sound. "It was a tablet made from stone and found about, gosh, seven hundred fifty years ago or something like that back on Earth. The unique thing about it was that the inscriptions were the same decree in three different languages, which allowed researchers to translate ancient Egyptian hieroglyphs. Well, to get started on it anyway." It was the second time in as many days that he'd used the analogy.

"Ah, I see. That makes sense."

David took in the on-edge soldiers. "On the bright side, they're not shooting at us, and maybe we have something in

Valor

127

common to build on." *If I keep this up, I'll start sounding like a member of the diplomatic corps.*

Hammond licked her lips. "Yes, sir."

"Communications, tell Colonel Aibek to meet me in my day cabin." David stood. "Lieutenant, you have the conn. Keep our shields up, and alert me if anything changes with our friends over there. Oh, and get the master chief on the horn. Let her know we'll be doing a formal first-contact meeting tomorrow. I want to limit their exposure to our technology, so have her plan to host the Admari as close to the main hangar or the VIP shuttle bay as possible."

"Aye, aye, sir. This is Lieutenant Hammond. I have the conn."

David headed for the hatch and hoped he could get at least a few hours of rack time. *Otherwise, who knows what I'll say to these aliens. What does Calvin say all the time? "I'll sleep when I'm dead."* He chuckled. *HaShem, I am out of my league. Give me wisdom to see this through.*

16

Of all the things Major John Wilson enjoyed, seeing a zero-g space installation come together was one of the highlights. Outside of time with his family, nothing quite beat watching the fruits of months of labor finalize as all paths on the project plan led to the final result: a fully functional space elevator for Zavlot. The first one they'd constructed over Zeivlot had taken longer, which was to be expected. His crew had done the same thing twice, and the bugs had been worked out of the system.

His tablet in hand, he stared through the window at the front of the *Salinan*'s bridge. The final tasks were to be completed by the end of the following day. *Not bad. Not bad at all.*

"Looking good, sir," Khattri said as he came up next to Wilson. "Wasn't sure we'd hit your rather ambitious schedule, but it's on track."

Wilson smiled. "I know what the crew is capable of, Captain. Especially with all those years I spent as a bosun's mate."

"Did you see the plans for an asteroid-based station?"

Valor

"Yeah. Looked to me like the good-idea fairy arrived with her friends." Wilson snorted. "There's a big jump in complexity from a low-planetary-orbit installation to refining rocks in the middle of nowhere for species that, up until last year, didn't venture farther than their moons."

"Well, if it gets the Zeivlots and the Zavlots working together, the end result might be worth it."

Wilson kicked that around in his mind. *Yeah, I suppose deepening ties would be positive in the long run. I'll leave that mess to the politicians and the brass, though. Give me a ship to tow, a problem to solve, or something to build.* "Yeah."

"Conn, TAO." Fazel interjected. "Sir, I've got an anomalous contact being fed up to us from a Zavlot astronomical observation post."

Immediately, Wilson's sixth sense kicked in, and he walked back to the CO's chair. "What kind of contact, Lieutenant?"

"Stellar body, sir. Specifically, an asteroid out of place. It's a hundred thousand kilometers away, close enough to flag the collision detection system."

Wilson narrowed his eyes. Both inhabited worlds had programs to detect dangerous space rocks and predict their orbits well in advance. It seemed unlikely one would slip through that grid but not unprecedented. "Plot its course, and overlay it on a sensor readout of local space on my monitor, TAO."

"Aye, aye, sir."

It took five minutes for the relevant calculations to be completed, and the image popped up on the display above Wilson's head. He stared at it to confirm what he saw. *Damn.* "TAO, how sure of this trajectory are you?"

"As close to one hundred percent as I can be, sir."

There's no way an asteroid on a direct intercept for the space elevator is a coincidence or an accident. "Can the *Magen* or the *Yulia Paievska* get here in time?"

Fazel shook his head. "Wrong flight profiles for a micro-jump, sir. None of the indigenous military units are in range, either."

"Type of rock, Lieutenant?"

"Iron-nickel composition, sir."

"At this range, nearly impossible to nudge off course enough," Khattri interjected. "We'll have to go for destroying it."

Wilson gestured to the screen. "It's big enough to make that difficult with our weapons complement." *Okay. We don't have much time.* His first thought was of the zero-G construction crews swarming through the elevator shaft, completing final wiring and system checks. "Comms, get ahold of Lieutenant Pacheco, and tell her to evacuate everyone from the installation."

"We could try a microjump, sir. Give us more time on target." Khattri sucked in a breath. "Otherwise, if we do a max-thrust intercept, looking at about fifteen minutes to engagement range."

Again, Wilson ran a series of numbers through his head. *Sometimes I wish I could do math like my youngest boy.* It took him a minute to calculate that a microjump would roughly double the amount of time they would have to shoot the thing down. "Exotic-particle-release probability?"

"Over fifty percent."

Forget that. I'm not risking the Salinan's *destruction with those odds.* "TAO, populate the board with that asteroid. Designate it as Master One."

"Aye, aye, sir."

"Navigation, intercept course, Master One, all ahead flank."

Valor 131

The deck plates rumbled as the *Salinan* turned and accelerated. Though a smaller vessel, she had an excellent delta-V, thanks to the need to tow larger ships. Zavlot fell away from the view outside the bridge until only the blackness of the void was visible.

Wilson toggled the intercom on his chair to 1MC. "Attention, all hands. This is your commanding officer. General quarters. General quarters. All hands to battle stations. I say again, man your battle stations. This is not a drill. Secure deck-force salvage stations, and away all damage-control parties. Set condition one throughout the ship."

Moments later, the lights on the bridge dimmed and turned deep blue.

"I take it that's a no on the microjump," Khattri said under his breath.

"Correct. Too risky."

Khattri nodded. "Can't disagree with you, sir, but we won't have much time."

"I know. Monitor the evacuation efforts. Make sure our partner forces don't leave anyone behind."

"Aye, aye, sir."

Wilson stared ahead, willing the *Salinan* to go faster. *Come on, old girl. I know you're not built to fight, but you can do it in a pinch, and we need you now.*

"Conn, TAO. Condition one set throughout the ship, sir. All sections report battle stations manned and ready."

"Make missile tubes one and two ready in all respects, and open outer doors. Charge the energy-weapons capacitor to maximum." Wilson planned to neutralize the asteroid at as long a range as possible.

The sensor report updated with refinements to the information available on Master One. Wilson stared at it, digesting the new information. *Dammit. This is going to be even more challenging than I thought.* "TAO, confirm Master One is forty kilometers wide."

Fazel turned his head. "Yes, sir."

Wilson tugged his uniform shirt down and made sure his cover, a ball cap with the stylized profile of the *Salinan*, was on tightly. "Firing point procedures, forward missile tubes one and two, Master One."

"Firing solutions locked, sir. Tubes one and two ready in all respects. Outer doors are open."

Wilson could get a few more precious seconds by taking advantage of the speed at which the asteroid approached, and he ran the math to ensure he got them. He spoke at the precise moment he could be sure the missiles would hit. "Match bearings, shoot, tubes one and two."

The two Starbolts erupted from the *Salinan's* bow and accelerated into the void. Had the asteroid been an onrushing vessel capable of maneuvering, it would likely have dodged the two warheads. But a space rock couldn't change its trajectory unless acted upon by an outside force, so the asteroid plowed onward. Both missiles adjusted their courses for a terminal burn and detonated at nearly the same time with twin bright-white flashes.

"Conn, TAO. Master One destroyed."

"Nice shooting, Lieutenant. Debris?"

A pause followed as Fazel worked the console before his voice dropped an octave. "Lots of it, sir. Twenty... thirty... no, seventy-plus fragments of at least fifty meters in diameter."

Wilson's mouth went dry. *Shit.* "Navigation, stand by to execute a high-energy turn. Maintain formation with the debris cloud. TAO, raise our shields to minimal levels, but keep most power directed toward the neutron beams. Target at your discretion as we range."

The *Salinan* pivoted smartly, turning to be perpendic-

Valor 133

ular to the cloud of asteroid pieces. All the while, her weapons suites lashed into the void. Neutron beams blazed across the rock fragments, melting them from existence, and even the point-defense turrets got in on the action.

As Wilson watched the plot, there was a steady decrease in the number of inbound threats. *But they're not dropping fast enough.* "TAO, time to missile tubes reload cycle complete?"

"Two more minutes, sir."

The neutron beams ceased fire, causing Wilson to examine the weapons-status display on his monitor. *Energy capacitor is under ten percent. It'll have to recharge before we can shoot again.* He bit his lip as the progress bar advanced at a glacial pace.

"Tubes one and two reloaded, sir."

"Target them at the largest clumps of rocks, Lieutenant. Thin the herd."

"Firing solutions set, sir."

"Make tubes one and two ready in all respects, and open the outer doors."

Fazel paused for a moment. "Outer doors open. Both tubes show ready in all respects."

"Match bearings, shoot, tubes one and two."

The Starbolt missiles roared into the void, their engines igniting as they cleared the launcher mechanism. They accelerated immediately and made for the targeted coordinates before erasing more of the asteroid pieces in brilliant fusion explosions.

Wilson stared at the tactical plot, willing the number of targets to drop to a manageable range. It didn't happen. *Damn. There're too many of them.* "Comms, what's the status of the station evac?"

A pregnant pause followed before the communications officer spoke. "Roughly fifteen people still aboard, sir."

Khattri swore under his breath. "There's not enough time to—"

"I know." Wilson set his jaw. "Navigation, all ahead flank. TAO, redirect all power to our shields, and stand by to extend them around the station."

"Cohesion won't be enough, sir," Khattri said quietly. "For much of a pounding, anyway."

"There are still thirty-plus fragments out there. We won't be stopping them with our neutron beams. If you've got a better idea, now's the time."

Khattri shook his head. "Sorry, sir. I'm fresh out of those."

"Then let's pray to God this works."

Silence took hold as the *Salinan* accelerated past the cloud of iron and rock projectiles headed for the Zavlot space elevator, which loomed directly ahead of the bridge windows.

"Navigation, all stop. TAO, extend shields to encompass Sierra Two. Master Chief, sound collision alarm."

As the klaxon wailed, Wilson gripped the handrests of the CO's chair. Moments later, a series of thuds jostled the bridge crew in their harnesses and nearly knocked him out of his seat.

"Aft deflector collapsed, sir!" Fazel yelled above the din. "We're taking armor damage, section ten and beyond, all decks."

Just when it seemed like the ship was going to be ripped apart by asteroids, the thuds stopped.

Wilson blew out a breath. *Okay, we're still here.* "Damage report? Did anything hit the elevator?"

Khattri licked his lips. "We got lucky. Minor damage, no major hull breaches."

Fazel turned. "Sir, one of the station's sections depressurized, and seven personnel were lost to the void."

"Did they have suits on?" Wilson asked. *Please, Lord.*

"No, sir."

Wilson let his head fall back. *Dammit.* "Any of our people?"

"An engineer from the *Magen* and six Zavlot techs."

The loss of life put a damper on his feelings of success about thwarting the destruction of the elevator's orbital station. "Comms, get me a direct link to Colonel Demood in my day cabin immediately. Wake him if you have to. I don't care. XO, you have the conn. Start rescue efforts, and let's see if we can recover the bodies before they deorbit. Those people deserve decent burials."

"Aye, aye, sir." Khattri replied.

Losing crewmen wasn't something Wilson had to confront often. By its nature, the *Salinan* didn't fight, and while he'd had combat postings, being in command of a salvage-and-rescue vessel had its perks. While it would be some time before he knew exactly who'd died, the largest question in his mind was how it had happened. It seemed beyond possibility that the asteroid had come toward them by accident or purely random chance. *If someone did this, they're gonna pay.*

———

AFTER A FILLING EVENING MEAL, Calvin had little to do. At any given time, there were a few special operations efforts underway, but most of them involved bagging the last few terrorist holdouts on both Zeivlot and Zavlot. For the first time in a while, he was bored. Flipping through pages of after-action reports on his tablet, Calvin realized when the *Lion of Judah* and David returned, there would be a distinct *lack* of boredom.

He hated having nothing to do because it was in those lulls that the full ramifications of being stuck four and a half million light-years from home came to the forefront of his mind. More than anything, Calvin missed his wife, Jessica. They had been trying to have a child before the *Lion* was tossed into Sextans B. The thought of her having to go it alone after delaying for decades because of his TCMC service cut him to the bone.

She deserves better than to have to raise a mini-me alone. Calvin took a swig of what passed for beer on Zeivlot. *Stewing in my quarters doesn't do anyone, especially me, any favors.* The small apartment was far nicer than bachelor's officer's quarters back on almost any Terran Coalition Marine Corps base and reminded him more of a resort.

As Calvin pondered heading down to where some of the enlisted Marines had an off-the-books bar going, his tablet beeped. The screen indicated an incoming vidlink request. He picked up the device and accepted the call.

Major Wilson's unsmiling face appeared with a background indicative of a ship's day cabin. "Colonel, did I catch you at a bad time?"

"Nah." *Why's the Salinan's ship driver calling me?* "Just finished dinner and was looking for something to do."

"You'll get a full written report in the next few hours, but I wanted to alert you ahead of time that we thwarted an attack on the Zavlot space elevator." Wilson bit his lip. "Lost an engineering rating and half a dozen Zeivlot techs."

Calvin sat up, his mind focused sharply. *Maybe I*

shouldn't have had that third beer. "Say that again. Somebody attacked that station you're building? We lost people?"

"An asteroid fragment hit it dead on. Depressurized one of the primary chambers."

Dear Lord. Another dead soldier on my watch. I'm getting tired of this. "Space rock? How do you get from that to a deliberate attack?"

Wilson pursed his lips. "Sir, maybe I'm jumping to conclusions, but think about it. The void is vast. What are the odds of a rock flying into orbit on a direct vector to hit the weakest portion of the station? My salvage team ran the math. It would've deorbited the entire structure had we not intervened. No way that's just a random coincidence."

Yeah, that sounds like a valid point. "Okay, Major. Let's assume you're right. How in the heck would terrorists even pull off a stunt like that?"

"Been giving that a lot of thought, sir. There're fleets of small mining ships out in the primary asteroid belt here, dragging in precious metals that both planets are short of. One of them would be able to do this with a few modifications."

Calvin's face twisted. "Ugh. Okay. Needle in a haystack, then, because there are a few hundred of those things now. They're making them left and right to feed the demand." He ran through several different avenues for tracking down the culprits.

"We could track the rock's trajectory and see if that could help narrow it down."

"Took the words right out of this old Marine's mouth, Major."

Wilson smirked. "I've got more years in than you do, pretty sure."

Calvin chuckled. "Tell me about it sometime. I'll get the

G2 team briefed and be ready for your report. If there's something to find, Corporal Nussbaum *will* find it for us."

"Excellent, sir. Give me a couple of hours to finish the paperwork."

"And, Major, when we find these guys, I'll personally lead the door-kicking team to send them on to the afterlife." Calvin set his jaw. "Nobody kills one of ours without paying the price."

Wilson gritted his teeth. "I'll hold you to that, Colonel. We'll be happy to assist too. Petty Officer Markham wasn't one of mine, but he was CDF. These terrorists apparently haven't gotten the message that we'll find them wherever they are."

"They will. Plan on an oh-eight-hundred briefing with your fellow ship drivers and my command staff."

"Aye, aye, sir."

"Demood out."

Well, nothing quite like having somebody to kick in the face to get my mind off home. Calvin felt guilty for the feeling before plunging back into combat mode. After pulling up his tablet, he started issuing orders, which was better than sitting around and stewing.

17

SURPRISINGLY, given all that had occurred, David was able to sleep. At some point, the human body simply gave out, and the older he got, the sooner that point occurred. David could've stayed up for days at a time in his youth, but recently, he'd been lucky to still be mentally functional after twenty hours. That didn't mean his rest was complete, however. When the alarm went off at oh-four-thirty, he jerked awake, aware of the nightmare he'd been having, seeing Private Diaz ripped apart and swallowed by the nanite swarm over and over.

David blew out a breath and turned off the incessant buzzing. He shook his head and tried to clear his mind before putting a hand over his eyes and praying the Shema in Hebrew. Once that was completed, he went about his morning ritual, speeding through until he walked down the passageway on deck ten toward the hangar bay.

The master chief had decided to host the Admari delegation in the conference room off the VIP shuttle bay, a natural meeting point for diplomatic groups and visitors requiring tight access controls. Per David's instructions,

Marine sentries were posted in light armor and with battle rifles at every entry and access point, and multiple quick reaction forces were standing by in power armor. *Just in case they try something funny.*

David came to a halt outside the reception area to find Aibek, Merriweather, and Hayworth already there. "All ready for this?"

Aibek and Merriweather stiffened.

"Yes, sir," he replied.

"It is truly remarkable to find a species that lives in the void," Hayworth remarked. "We're only aware of a couple in the Milky Way, and those are both nomadic pirates that have bases of operations outside their vessels."

"It sounds like hell to me," David replied. He adjusted his white dress uniform. *I've always hated these things.* A memory came to him of how Sheila Thompson, his oldest friend and former XO of the *Lion of Judah* and the *Yitzhak Rabin*, teased him about getting small details wrong on where pins and medals went. At first, it brought a smile, then came pain. She'd perished in the Second Battle of Canaan, saving the ship from disaster.

The hatch pushed open, revealing Dr. Tural and Bo'hai.

"I apologize for our tardiness," she said. "The gravlift took longer than normal."

David nodded. "No harm, no foul. Our guests haven't yet arrived." He glanced at his handcomm. "Any minute now. Let's get in the conference room and prepare. Our delegation on the right side. They'll sit on the left."

"Yes, sir," Aibek replied and pushed open a hatch that led from the reception area into a passageway. Their destination was on the right, and within seconds, all were inside.

While CDF meeting spaces were mostly alike, the VIP shuttle bay was designed to be a disembarkation point for

Valor 141

flag officers, political leaders, and diplomats. As a result, everything in it was done to a higher standard than even the conference room on deck one.

I should have one of these nice leather chairs moved to my day cabin. David took his place behind the table but waited to take his seat.

The hatch swung open again, revealing a Marine in full dress uniform followed by a row of Admari. The four of them walked in slowly. Each alien had a metallic alloy harness on the outside of their clothing, which was plain and gray. The fabric seemed as if it was faded from years of wear.

One of the Admari shuffled to the table. While it was difficult to tell them apart at first glance because of their similar facial and bodily features, David was sure it was the same one he'd spoken to earlier.

"Greetings, General Cohen. I am Ekrani Garl-Torin. I present our supreme leader, Iskv-Selagan." He gestured to the being to his left.

That Admari took a step forward and slowly inclined its head. "I greet you as one leader to another." The translator had a masculine tone.

David wondered if they had similar genders to humans. While advanced beings that reproduced via advanced cell replication did exist in the Milky Way, virtually all known humanoid races functioned similarly to humans. "Welcome aboard the CSV *Lion of Judah*, Iskv-Selagan. Allow me to introduce some of my senior staff. Colonel Aibek, executive officer of the *Lion*; Major Merriweather, one of our top engineers; Dr. Tural, our chief medical officer; Dr. Hayworth, one of the leading minds of the Terran Coalition; and finally, Selina Bo'hai, linguist and de facto leader of our Zeivlot scientific contingent."

Iskv-Selagan said something in what appeared to be the Admari tongue that wasn't translated before speaking through the vocoder. "I have the shipmasters of our three largest vessels with me. You have already spoken with Garl-Torin. Garl-Wrin and Garl-Marjun are also here. We speak for all Admari."

"Please, be seated. Can we offer you refreshments?"

The four aliens exchanged glances before pulling the chairs before them out and sitting.

"I observed many heavily armed warriors between our transport and this congregation abode."

David parsed what Iskv-Selagan had said. *Guess they don't want anything.* "Since we've arrived in this galaxy, we've encountered a few hostile races. I believe in being prudent with my ship. I'm sure as a fellow ship commander, you can understand."

Iskv-Selagan blinked. "Yes, this meets with my recognition."

"Garl-Torin mentioned that your people had been attacked by the nanite swarms."

"They devoured our world and sent what few remained into the void, never to return. The great pestilence has done the same to many planets in this galaxy. We have no weapons able to stand against them, and until we observed your people successfully fighting the pestilence, the Admari knew of no race that could."

"I can't imagine what it was like for your people to suffer such a devastating loss. When did this happen?"

"That is unknown. We have been dwellers of the void for so long that our records no longer tell us of a time when we lived on our home world. What stories we have are passed down from generation to generation. All we know now is the harshness of the vacuum."

Hayworth raised an eyebrow. "If I may, why don't you find another planet to settle on? This galaxy appears to have many inhabitable worlds, unless your species has specific gravity and atmosphere requirements, which, given your presence here, doesn't seem likely."

Garl-Wrin, one of the other shipmasters, replied, "After so many generations, we're unsure whether our bodies could survive on the surface. Regardless, as long as we lack the means to defend against the pestilence, it is the will of all Admari that we remain in the safety of the great night."

It must've been hundreds if not thousands of years since this species fled into space. A million questions raced through David's mind as he pondered what their lives must be like. *I can't believe they do anything more than survive.*

"General Cohen, we believe you possess the means to help us achieve the dream of all Admari... to once again have the choice to colonize a new home. Even if it means only some of our people could live on it, anything is better than what we endure now," Iskv-Selagan said.

They want our neutron-beam technology. David's heart sank, as he would do almost anything to help them. *Transfer of weapons tech is strictly forbidden by Coalition law, and moreover, I can't take the risk of what they'd do with it.* "And what means is that, Iskv-Selagan?"

"The powerful energy-based weapon you used to defeat the pestilence. Give it to us so that we might live again."

David licked his lips. "It's not quite that simple. We can't just rip one of them off our ship to give you. Besides, we overloaded our neutron beams to get the effect you saw. It can't sustain repeated firings."

"That is no matter. If you work with our engineers, I am sure a solution could be found. If there is something we possess that would induce you to make the trade, we will give it."

Hayworth began, "We can't give—"

David held up a hand. "I'm well aware, Doctor." He met Iskv-Selagan's big black eyes. "There are specific laws by which I am bound that prohibit me from giving our technology, *especially* our weapons, to anyone. I'm willing to do anything in our power short of transferring a neutron beam or the schematics to one to your people."

Iskv-Selagan sat perfectly still for what seemed like an eternity. The Admari didn't seem to communicate emotion via their faces, probably due to a lack of facial features. Yet it was easy to conclude he didn't like the answer. "We are in great need. You possess the means to save us. It is uncomplicated."

Well, he doesn't want to hear the no. I can understand that. "I suggest that perhaps we could start by examining your energy-based weapons, if your species has those. Doctor, explain how we were able to damage the nanites."

Hayworth's face blanched. "The alloy used by the nanites is extremely resistant to thermal and physical damage, but if you can increase the temperature of a particle beam to close to the surface of a star... Constructs made of matter in the universe must obey the laws of physics."

Before David could pick up the thread, Dr. Tural interjected, "Excuse me, but I can't help but wonder what the devices you're wearing on your chests, arms, and legs are. Is that an exoskeleton?"

The four Admari exchanged looks and spoke in their native language briefly before the leader turned back to Dr. Tural. "Yes. Our bodies are not optimized for gravity any longer. These exoskeletons, as you call them, allow us to walk and interact with comfort."

"Don't your ships have artificial gravity?" David asked, shocked. "You have Lawrence drives. Those two go hand in hand."

"Our vessels once had uniform systems, General. They are old. We are old. Our civilization, what's left of it, is dying. That is why we seek the weapon, so that before there are no Admari left, we might have a chance to rebuild."

Most situations David Cohen found himself in were easily definable as right and wrong. Reducing complex problems to moral questions was something he'd mastered over the years because, as a Jew, he had a duty to make choices that kept the Mitzvot. *Even when the answer isn't obvious.* On the surface, while the law was clear, there was a gray area. David tried to put himself in the Admari's shoes. *I wonder how bad it is over there. Perhaps we could alleviate some of their suffering.* "I'm prepared to offer engineering support, spare parts if we can fabricate them, and humanitarian supplies along with our guidance on adjusting your weapons to fight the nanites."

"That is not sufficient." Iskv-Selagan brought his hand up and slammed it onto the table. "You can bolster... help us."

While the speech reproduced by the vocoder lacked inflection and emotion, the pain in the Admari's voice as he spoke in his native tongue was evident. David felt nothing but compassion and sympathy for their plight. *But that doesn't change the fact that I can't give out some of the most potent weapons we have.* "Iskv-Selagan, we'll do anything we can beyond the transfer of lethal technology."

"Repugnant!" Iskv-Selagan replied then added a stream of Admari words that the vocoder apparently didn't get.

"Those who would withhold lifesaving technology from others are offensive."

David set his jaw. His empathy for their plight had its limits, the first of which was a lack of respect. He refused to tolerate disrespect. "Iskv-Selagan, you would do well to remember you're on my ship, surrounded by my crew and Marines. You are free to disagree with my decision, but it is final. Losing your temper will get you nowhere except being asked to leave."

The four aliens once again turned to one another and conversed before their leader turned back.

"We will depart."

They stood at once.

Okay, then. David sprang to his feet and gestured toward the Marine sentry. "Very well. You'll be escorted back to your vessel. If you'd like our help, it's still on offer." He extended his hand.

Iskv-Selagan stared at the outstretched appendage for a moment before turning and walking through the hatch without another word.

"Lovely fellows," Hayworth said as they disappeared into the reception area, and one of the Marines closed the aperture.

"Put yourself in their shoes, Doctor. You'd be angry too."

"Please tell me you're not considering—"

David cleared his throat. "No. Not on the table."

"Whatever we do feels so inadequate," Dr. Tural interjected. "By Allah, their entire race needs healing."

"Sometimes, I hate sitting in this chair," David mused. "This is one of them."

Aibek raised an eye scale. "I believe there may be more risk than currently realized."

"How so, XO?"

Valor 147

"These beings are desperate. Desperation makes people do illogical things. I recommend we jump away and avoid the Admari. They do not want the help we have offered, and they might try to take what they do want by force."

Silence and a sense of melancholy followed as the others considered his words. David felt it, in that he wanted to make right what was wrong but lacked the means. *Aibek's right, though. If you push anyone far enough, they'll react.* "That's a good point. Perhaps it's time for us to move on."

"They seem to have decent sensors," Hayworth replied.

"Yes, that's valid, too, Doctor. We've got antimatter power, though. I'll have Lieutenant Hammond pick a destination at the far end of our range. We'll lie low for a bit then see about reconning the system we discovered the nanites in."

Aibek nodded. "A prudent course of action, sir."

"Saved rounds, anyone?"

Bo'hai turned her head, and her purple hair caught the light so that it sparkled for a moment. "May I ask a question?"

"By all means."

"Why not give them your weapon?"

Hayworth grumbled loudly. "Do *not* encourage him. Our good general here always has a complex about saving everyone we come across."

"You gave my people fusion-reactor technology and left soldiers behind to help us build starships," Bo'hai replied. She glanced at Hayworth out of the corner of her eye but didn't comment on his statement.

"It's not the same thing, Salena. What we gave your people came after I took direct action to intervene in a military situation. When I was a kid, my mother used to go to this shop that had small figurines. Hundreds of them. There was a sign on every shelf that read 'Nice to look at, nice to hold, but if you drop it, we say sold.'" He smiled at the memory.

She tilted her head. "I do not understand the context."

"When I intervened at Zeivlot, I broke the situation. That's why we had to help you rebuild. Because it was our mistakes that almost left your planet destroyed. And yes, both worlds were well on their way to blowing themselves apart without us, but the fact is *we accelerated it*. It's also worth noting that our personnel ensure those fusion reactors aren't used for ill. I'm sure Colonel Demood along with the fleet assets deployed in system are keeping the peace."

"You can't monitor what the Admari do."

"Exactly." David shook his head. "It's a crap situation. Everyone in this room recognizes that. But giving them advanced, lethal weapons tech? No. I can't get my head around that with the facts at hand. Still, I intend to talk to Zupan Vog't when we return to Zeivlot. Perhaps I can convince her to let these aliens settle in your system."

"That would be admirable."

David inclined his head. "It's the best we can do for now. Anything else, folks?"

Silence was the only reply, to which David nodded. "All right. Let's get back to it. Dismissed."

Bo'hai, Merriweather, Dr. Tural, and Hayworth filed out, leaving only Aibek and David behind.

"Are you returning to the bridge?" Aibek asked.

"Well, I was going to hit my quarters and get out of this dress uniform then head up there."

"Would you care for some company on the walk to the gravlift?"

David nodded. "Of course. What's on your mind?"

They exited together, and Aibek kept quiet until they

Valor

were past the gauntlet of Marines and into the open passageways beyond. "I am concerned by how many ships the Admari may have."

"It would be nice to have some idea, wouldn't it?"

"One vessel found us. Three more showed up within hours. It seems reasonable to extrapolate there could be dozens if not hundreds."

"Goldberg doesn't think they're all that powerful based on her deep scans."

Aibek depressed the button to call the gravlift. "Even the most powerful warrior can be swamped by inferior foes."

The doors swished open, and they stepped inside.

"I realize that, XO." David closed his eyes for a moment. "Allow me to tell you how tired I am of war."

"Saurians live to use our blades and prowess in battle to uphold the will of the Prophet and defend the weak. Yet we enjoy the fruits of victory and a time between combat."

David chuckled. "You've been hanging around us too long."

"While that may be a true statement, I have noticed many humans relish fighting. Including those wearing our uniform."

"True." David stretched his neck. "Staring down someone trying to kill you and coming out the victor is invigorating. I won't deny that. But I can't let myself enjoy it."

"I respect your ideals. Even if I find nothing wrong with delighting in the destruction of my enemies."

"Takes all kinds, my friend."

The door swished open.

"And on that note," David said with a grin, "I am going to get out of this overstarched uniform and back into my space BDUs, and I'll see you on the bridge in twenty minutes."

"I will be there."

As David strode toward his cabin, with enlisted crewmen melting away to either side and stiffening to attention as he passed them, his mind was alive with gaming out what could happen next. *One thing's for sure. We'll need to be on our toes. Aibek's right. Desperation breeds, well, desperation.*

18

THE NEAR LOSS of the space elevator so soon after its completion had sent tidal waves through Zavlot and Zeivlot society. Calvin had been sucked into numerous high-level meetings, some of which involved Zupan Vog't. To say she was unhappy was an understatement, especially after they'd declared victory over the terrorist organizations that had plagued the planet for so long.

Early in the afternoon, he trudged through the hallways of the combined military and intelligence complex in which the Marines had taken up residence. He pushed open a door marked Analysis Unit and strode in to find a small team of Zeivlots focused on banks of large screens, reviewing SIGINT.

"Colonel on deck," Susanna said as she jumped out of her seat and came to attention.

The rest, who were all uniform-wearing members of the Zeivlot military, followed.

"To what do we owe the pleasure, sir?"

"I've spent the last few days having my rear end chewed to the point that it's no longer recognizable by political types, alien generals, and civilians who want me to perform miracles as if I'm the second coming of Jesus Christ." Calvin smirked. "I keep trying to tell them He was a pacifist, but I don't think it took."

Susanna chuckled. "You want a target package?"

"Got it in one."

She gestured to one of the screens. "Then your ears were burning, because we're wrapping one up now."

"Walk me through it." They'd discovered hard evidence of the asteroid strike being deliberate, but Calvin hadn't bothered to read through all the science crap. *Just give me a door to kick, please, with a cherry on top.*

"We backtracked the rock's path and identified it as being from the primary asteroid belt beyond Zavlot." Susanna worked the screen, changing the view to show a rendering of the solar system. "While there isn't real-time sensor data of the entire belt, scans from the *Magen* and the *Yulia Paievska* confirm that as of at least a month ago, it was still in orbit around a larger asteroid, roughly here."

Calvin stared at the box that appeared around the former location of the offending hunk of metal and dust. "Is it possible that one of the mining ships knocked it out of position by accident?"

"No." Susanna crossed her arms. "It was propelled at precisely the right speed and direction, with high-quality and advanced mathematic predictions required to get it on target. We would've been proud to pull this off, frankly, sir."

"Okay. So that's the how. Who did it?"

A bunch of lines appeared after a tap of her fingers on the keyboard, superimposing over the solar system display. "I've pieced together, as best as possible, the courses of the mining fleet from the last sixty days." She zeroed in on the

Valor **153**

suspect area. "Once I filter down to the time frame in question, these jump out."

Two lines remained after a few more strokes.

Calvin's lips curled up. "Gotcha."

"Yes, sir. One or both of those two is likely to be the culprit. As I said, your ears must've been burning."

A million thoughts ran through his mind. *Okay, we've got some doors to kick in. But how?* None of the CDF ships within the system had any stealth breaching pods, nor were tier-one special operations teams at the ready. *We don't need them. A single shuttle full of power-armored Marines is enough to take either of these guys, and our vessels are seen patrolling constantly. They won't raise suspicions out in the belt.*

"Sir?" Susanna prompted.

"Oh, sorry." Calvin grinned again. "Whatcha feel about a field trip, Corporal? I could use your skills for what I just planned."

Susanna's face lit up. "With pleasure, sir."

"Pack a space bag, and meet me at the shuttle pad in thirty mikes."

"Yes, sir."

Calvin turned on his heel and set off to find Master Gunnery Sergeant Menahem and a couple of platoons of Force Recon Marines. *Knowing Master Guns, I bet they're down at the range.*

———

SHIP-CAPTURE ACTIONS WERE a staple of the Terran Coalition Marine Corps, but Calvin wished they had more equipment with them. They were limited to assault shuttles and basic power armor, but higher-tech toys like boarding pods or the hyperflexible suits the tier-one commandos sported would've come in handy.

A platform like the *Lion of Judah* would've also had far better command and control for the effort they were about to undertake, but none of that mattered. Calvin was only concerned with getting on the mining ship, taking out the hostiles, and figuring out who was behind the plot to destroy the space elevator. *Then I can kick down that bastard's door and shoot him in the face.*

"You look like you're a million kilometers away, Colonel."

Jolted from his thoughts, Calvin replied, "Ah, yeah. Kinda was, Master Guns."

"Thinking about the family back home?"

"No. More so wanting to put whoever's behind this down with extreme prejudice and end this violence once and for all."

"I'm not sure I think that's possible anymore." Menahem slid on his power armor's central breastplate and locked the piece into position. "When we got here, I really thought staving off Armageddon for these two worlds would do the trick."

He had a point. "Yeah, me too. But it's also true that most of the population doesn't want this insanity to continue."

"Then why don't they turn the terrorists in?"

"You sound a bit weary, Master Guns."

Menahem attached one of the armored gauntlets and tested the servos. "Frankly, I am, sir. I've fought the good fight for decades. I didn't mind helping these folks, but I'm sick of seeing one more terrorist every time we turn around. One more nutcase who thinks it's his or her God-given mission to go out and kill innocents."

"Eventually, they'll run out of warm bodies."

"Will they?" Menahem snorted as he put his helmet on and popped up the faceplate. "Somehow, I don't think these people will stop killing one another in our lifetimes."

Calvin put a hand on his friend's shoulder. "Maybe, maybe not. We're still doing a good thing here, and besides, what else are we going to do? Sit back on a military base and train Zeivlots?"

Menahem chuckled. "That does sound boring."

"We're going to do what we do best in the next couple of hours and be one step closer to not having to deal with these assholes anymore."

"Yes, sir." His tone might as well have been a blinking red light that Menahem wasn't buying what Calvin was trying to sell.

"Okay. Let's roll." Calvin set his helmet into the locking ring and turned. It sprang to life with a heads-up display that provided augmented-reality views of the world around him along with integration into his weapon and the tactical network. As Calvin finished the boot-up sequence, he pushed thoughts of his wife away and focused solely on the mission—because putting down bad guys helped keep his mind off everything he'd lost.

———

While the *Magen* was a small ship, it excelled at finding things, primarily because that was its job as a picket-and-escort vessel. Susanna and a few other analysts had set up shop down in the vessel's bowels, in the only secure compartmentalized information facility aboard. The place was spartan, with real-time sensor network feeds from all CDF assets plus a few selected Zeivlot military craft that had covertly moved into position.

She'd configured the gigantic floor-to-overhead displays with helmet-cam views from each of the sixteen Marines in Calvin's platoon and a top-down rendering of the mining vessel's interior. As long as it adhered to the published design used by that particular model, there shouldn't be any surprises.

Most of the screens showed the closed aft hatch of the Marine assault shuttle while a timer counted down the seconds to contact. An exterior view of the targeted mining vessel came into focus, and the shuttle latched on without incident. From that moment on, they were on the clock.

A gnawing divide grew within Susanna's soul. Part of her wanted to be right next to the Marines, sweeping through the enemy and looking for actionable intelligence to aid their efforts. Yet she couldn't set aside the feeling that she'd turned her back on her faith and upbringing somewhere along the way. Each day was an exercise in living two separate lives that weren't compatible with each other. And at some point, there *would* be a reckoning.

Her gaze went to a monitor that showed activity as the interior hatch was opened, revealing the pockmarked hull of a Zeivlot mining vessel. They'd extended the docking collar on top of an exterior airlock, and a Marine fiddled with the door, using a piece of tech, before it swung open. Since it was used to bring in loads of ore, the airlock was larger than one on a CDF vessel, and six Marines fit inside, even with bulky power armor.

They cycled in and spread out through the interior of the ship. Susanna switched her viewpoint to Calvin's helmet camera as he took point. Moving swiftly, the fire team of Marines pushed forward toward the cockpit of the vessel even as more of them poured through the airlock. The mining ships weren't big when compared with anything human-built and checked in at a quarter of the size of even the *Salinan*.

A Zeivlot rounded a corner and screamed something before Calvin put a trio of stun rounds into the man. He collapsed in a heap without a weapon visible. Less than a minute later, three more crewmembers appeared, but they were armed. Snub-nosed fully automatic slug throwers came up, and the Zeivlots opened fire in unison.

The image coming from Calvin's camera jerked to the right as he grunted in pain. Real-time displays showed multiple rounds hitting his chest armor before he and the other Marines returned fire. All three hostiles went down, twitching on the deck. One private paused to zip-tie the enemies' hands before rejoining the formation.

A weight lifted off Susanna as the squad methodically advanced, for she'd expected far more energetic resistance. *Lord, please keep them safe.*

———

"YOU SURE WE need these guys alive?" Calvin asked as he exchanged fire with a Zeivlot woman who was smart enough to stay crouched behind a bulkhead.

"Probably, Colonel. Otherwise, we won't be able to figure out the brain behind this particular operation—because it sure as heck isn't *these* folks," Menahem replied.

A burst of stun rounds caught the Zeivlot in the neck, and she pitched forward. Her rifle dropped to the deck as she released a bloodcurdling scream that turned into gurgling.

"Corpsman! Get the corpsman over here!" Calvin yelled as he pressed forward. He was less than ten meters from the cockpit. To call the thing a bridge was insulting to actual military space vessels, as the mining ship only had a small area with four chairs. Coming to a halt in front of the final hatch, he tried the control.

Nothing happened.

"They've locked us out."

Menahem appeared at his side with a string of det cord. "Allow me, sir."

Calvin snickered. "You're having way too much fun with this, Master Guns."

"Well, what's your line about God judging people and it being our job to arrange a face-to-face meeting?"

"That's pretty much it."

"This particular group, I think, needs judgment more than others, straight from HaShem," Menahem replied as he taped down the explosive material.

As they stepped back to a safe distance, alarms blared. Calvin froze, trying to decipher the warning. Insistent, it was unlike any klaxon he'd heard before. He felt sick to his stomach.

"Should we blow it, sir?" Menahem asked.

"No." Calvin turned and flipped a mental coin. "Back to the shuttle! All Marines, forget what you're doing, and *haul ass*, now!"

Menahem grabbed his armor-gauntleted arm. "Sir, are you sure?"

Calvin grunted. "Got a bad feeling, Master Guns. Now, are your ears filled with wax or something? Because I said move it!" He pushed Menahem forward as the other squad members turned and ran as fast as they could. While the power armor was heavy, it also had integrated servos and a mechanical assist, making moving in it effortless.

They gained speed as the distance to the shuttle

Valor

decreased rapidly. Calvin reconfigured his commlink as he ran. "Demood to shuttle alpha."

"Go ahead, Colonel," the pilot replied.

"Stand by to dust off the moment we get aboard."

"Sir?"

Meanwhile, the alarm continued blaring loudly enough to wake the dead.

The airlock came into focus as Calvin turned a corner. Six Marines were already inside, cycling through. The process took roughly sixty seconds, after which the chamber was repressurized. It only had room for six, and nine Marines stood outside. "I'll stay behind with Nunez and Baker." He pointed at the closest privates. "We'll post security until the rest are out, Master Guns."

"Sir, I can—"

"Now!"

Without another word, Menahem stepped through the hatch, followed by five squad mates.

Again, the depressurization cycle executed, seemingly slower than the last time. Each second was an agonizing wait. Calvin was pretty sure the crew was about to blow up the ship, though how they planned to accomplish it, he didn't know and wasn't willing to stick around to find out. *It'd be so much easier if we had actual tier-ones about. A comms geek would come in handy right about now.* Once a reactor was set to overload, stopping it without an engineering expert was next to impossible.

The six Marines in the airlock exited the ship through the docking collar and disappeared into the shuttle. That left sixty seconds to repressurize, and they would be out of there. Calvin let out a breath, thinking everything would come together.

All at once, the klaxon ceased. A split second later, an

ominous rumbling tossed all three power-armored Marines into the overhead.

Calvin screamed into his commlink, which was still set to the pilot's channel. "Undock! Now! Get outta here!" Pain shot through his body, seeming to radiate from several locations at once. The suits protected them from weapons fire, but kinetic energy still transferred through with enough force to break bones in extreme cases.

The shuttle disconnected, and its thrusters flared to life. In the time it took for them to crash back to the deck, the rumbling increased, and orange flames came into focus, racing down the passageway. *Well, damn. This is it.* Before the fire could reach them, the concussive blast wave got there instead. It blew the airlock door outward, and the rapid change in pressure left the outer door weakened so that it crumpled and gave way.

Things happened at a speed that was impossible for the human mind to process as the vacuum of space sucked everything in the corridor into the void. One moment, Calvin was grasping in vain for any handhold he could find. The next, he was tumbling through the void and registering pain from more parts of his body than before. *Shit.* As his heart pounded, Calvin worked through a mental checklist. *Suit's intact. Okay. I'm still alive. Where're Nunez and Baker?*

One Marine was relatively close to him, but the other was nowhere in sight. The shuttle was a tiny dot in his field of view, and he was rapidly moving away from it. Then the mining vessel went up like a roman candle, blowing debris in all directions, and when *that* shockwave hit a few seconds later, it felt like being kicked by an elephant.

Reality spun in circles as Calvin cartwheeled through space. He wondered if the end had finally come. *Damn. I really should've listened to my wife and retired when I could.*

19

Panicked, Susanna watched in real time as Calvin, Nunez, and Baker were shot into the void. Their life-signs detectors, integrated into the power armor, kept working along with the tactical link. It provided a solid homing ping that the *Magen* locked onto. She forced herself to take a deep breath, though an involuntary squeal left her lips after the mining ship blew apart.

Colonel Demood says to always work the problem. Susanna bit her lip and forced her brain back into the mode of a professional CDF soldier. *This is just another problem.* She turned to one of the comms ratings next to her. "Contact the bridge. See if they have any rescue craft on ready five."

He nodded before picking up a commlink interface. A few moments later, he shook his head. "Negative, Corporal."

Susanna let out a sigh. *An oversight that could cost us dearly. What other assets are in range?* She scanned the sensor board, hoping a Zeivlot patrol ship was on a suitable vector. Some of them had rescue teams aboard because of the dangerous nature of mining asteroids. She had no such luck, however. None of them could reach the stricken Marines in time, and Susanna worried they would either lose contact or develop severe issues at any moment. No CDF armor tech could survive what those suits had gone through without taking damage.

Work the problem. Nothing else was in range, no magic bullet to deploy at the last second. *Unless...* Susanna's hands flew over her input device, and she locked on to the CSV *Salinan*, which was in orbit of Zavlot but crucially outside the Lawrence limit. She toggled the command emergency override channel and prayed it would go through as she requested a vidlink with the commanding officer. *Lord, please let this work. Please. I can't have sent them to their deaths.*

———

MOST DAYS on the *Salinan* were pretty similar. Wilson spent them in his chair on the bridge, overseeing the construction of the Zavlot space elevator or doing whatever CDF paperwork was required in his day cabin. Lately, there'd been an increasing number of reports, forms, and information requests from both the Zeivlot and Zavlot civilian governments. It seemed fitting, in some way, that the aliens would discover how to do things in triplicate, just like humanity.

"Conn, Communications. Flash traffic for you, sir. Priority-one distress call coming from CDF Intelligence unit two, Corporal Nussbaum. She's asking for you by name."

Wilson exchanged glances with his XO. "That's mighty peculiar."

"I suppose we should see what's going on," Khattri replied.

"Put her on, Lieutenant."

"Aye, aye, sir."

The viewer above Wilson's head snapped on with the image of a young woman, her brown hair coiled in a tight bun. He didn't recognize her, but that was to be expected with nearly thirteen thousand soldiers and Marines in the fleet. "This is *Salinan* actual. Now, what's going on over there, Corporal?"

"Sir, Colonel Demood and two others are lost in the void following an explosion during a VBSS evolution. No rescue craft are in range, and the *Magen* doesn't have one on ready five. Are you able to help?"

Wilson ran the possibilities. *We've got our SAR bird active, and void jumpers are always on deck during construction, just in case.* "Do you have their location, Nussbaum?"

"Yes, sir, but they're headed away from one another. I have optimal XYZ coordinates for your jump."

"Send them to us immediately. We'll jump within sixty seconds." A glance at the nav comp confirmed the *Salinan* was past the Lawrence limit. "Oh, and Corporal? Tell Demood he owes me one."

Susanna cracked a hint of a smile. "Yes, sir."

The screen went dark.

"Navigation, plot the jump as soon as we receive those coordinates." He turned to Khattri. "Get the rescue team warmed up. We'll need the antigrav sleds and both SAR craft."

"We've only got one on ready five, sir."

Wilson scrunched up his face. "Tell them to move heaven and earth to get the other one ready. Fly it without a preflight if you have to, but there's no way one craft can pull in all three Marines."

"Conn, Navigation. Coordinates received, confirmed, and plotted, sir."

"Execute emergency jump."

Moments later, the *Salinan* emerged from its brief wormhole transit. The deck plates shook, jostling Wilson's feet. "Launch the SAR birds. TAO, lock on to the closest Marine signal, and transmit it to the tactical network."

"Aye, aye, sir."

———

CALVIN ATTEMPTED to manually fire his power armor's thrusters, hoping to slow his spin rate. He was seeing things cross-eyed and felt blackout or worse was ahead. The first burst only made him go faster, but the second and third slowed things down enough for him to be able to focus. *Okay. Suit's pressurized and intact. But emergency thrusters have twenty percent fuel left.* Power armor wasn't designed for extended operation in the void but accomplished it as more of an add-on.

"Rescue One-Five calling any Marine stations."

It took him a moment to filter through the commlink channels and engage the universal guard frequency. "This is Demood. I read you."

"Confirmed, Colonel. We're two mikes out."

"I got two other Marines out here. Get them first."

"Private Nunez is already secured. You're next on our pickup list, while the other SAR bird is chasing down your third man."

Calvin licked his lips and tried to focus on slowing his heart rate. "Roger, Rescue One-Five."

Sixty seconds passed, during which Calvin continued to tumble through the void.

"Colonel, our sensor links show you're spinning at roughly thirty degrees a second. Can you slow it?"

"I'll try." Calvin triggered the thrusters in a pattern that

Valor 165

should've slowed him down. Instead, he sped up. *Ah shit.* "Uh, Rescue One-Five, negative. I'm going faster now. Got a suit fault here."

"Roger, Colonel. Hang tight."

For Calvin, waiting for help was among the most challenging things in the universe. It went against everything in his nature, but even he had to admit when he was dependent on others. As Calvin counted the seconds, he prayed silently.

The rescue shuttle was only a few meters away, and its aft airlock was open to the void. A brightly lit figure in a type of space suit he didn't recognize accelerated toward him.

They're going to try to grab me.

The realization hit Calvin a split second before the hard-suited figure smacked into his power armor, and both of them spun away. After ten meters, he jerked hard, and the spin stopped. The effect made him feel like someone had slammed his chest with a five-kilogram sledgehammer.

Slowly, he started moving toward the other figure. "You okay, Colonel?"

"Uh..." Calvin coughed and realized the wind had been knocked out of him. It took more than a few seconds to recover from the diaphragm spasm.

The other figure came into complete focus. He was from the *Salinan*, according to the patch on his hard suit. "Hang tight. I'm going to pull us back into the shuttle, okay? Any leaks?"

"No," Calvin replied, slowly regaining his breath. "I'm good."

A couple of minutes later, they were back in the aft airlock, safe and sound, as the pressure cycle completed.

Calvin stumbled into the cargo area and removed his helmet. "Thanks for the assist."

"Senior Chief Stokes at your service, sir."

"I thought you were a salvage guy."

Stokes shook his head. "Master void jumper, salvage expert, zero-g construction specialist. We do a little bit of everything, Colonel."

Calvin chuckled. "I see. No complaints here." He glanced at the other Marine. "You okay, Private?"

"Yes, sir," Nunez replied. "Ready for another crack at those asshole terrorists."

"Amen." Calvin's eyes went back to Stokes. "What about Private Baker?"

Stokes bit his lip. "Sorry, sir. By the time Rescue One-Six got to him, there was nothing they could do. Total loss of pressure."

Calvin flexed his armored gauntlet several times before flinging his helmet across the compartment into the exterior hull. With rage still coursing through his body, he punched an alloy pole repeatedly before dropping into one of the empty seats. "Did they recover his body?"

"Yes, sir."

"Good."

The anger abated, and Calvin no longer saw red. *Now is the time to plan.* Another ship was out there, and he would find a way to make them pay. *In blood.*

I hate being poked and prodded by the docs. Calvin reflected on being cleared for duty, though he'd forced the issue by daring the *Salinan*'s medical personnel to try to keep him on bed rest for the day, even though the doctor felt it prudent.

Valor 167

Sometimes, what was best for the human body didn't comport with his required duties.

Calvin stepped off the deck-one gravlift and pushed the hatch open to its conference room a few steps later. The layout was similar to that of the *Lion of Judah* and every other fleet vessel he'd been on but much smaller. Instead of the dozen chairs at the main table and a couple dozen more lining the walls on the *Lion*, the room barely seated ten.

Susanna and Menahem were already present, and both rose as he stepped in.

"Sir, it's good to see you in one piece," Susanna blurted out.

"Well, I guess the Almighty wasn't interested in my sullying up his nice afterlife, so I got kicked back," Calvin replied with a snicker. "Heard you had a lot to do with the rescue, Corporal."

"I only wish I could've saved all of you."

He put a hand on her shoulder. "Listen, all three of us should be dead, okay? We'll get some payback for Baker. I promise you that."

"Yes, sir."

While Calvin didn't consider Susanna the model of a CDF soldier and certainly not that of a Marine, her quiet diligence demanded his respect. *Unless she tries to hug me. Nobody hugs a Marine.* "Master Guns, everyone else okay?"

"Squad's back on the *Magen*. I've got them preparing for another run, since that other ship is still out there."

"Which may or may not be involved," Calvin replied. "I mean, we know the one we just boarded is. The bastards blew themselves up to avoid capture."

"My gut says that given the size of the asteroid belt and that two ships traced back to the exact area the rock came from, we'll probably find something on the other one too," Susanna interjected.

Calvin eyed her. "I don't usually trust gut instincts unless they're my own, but you've got a good track record so far. Don't let me down now."

"I'll try not to, sir." A trace of a smile came to her lips.

The hatch behind Calvin swung open, nearly hitting him in the backside. Major Wilson and two other men strode through. Even though he outranked the *Salinan*'s CO, Calvin came to attention. *It is* his *ship, after all.*

"Oh, no need for that, Colonel. I'd be saluting you if we were on the bridge," Wilson said with a grin. He gestured toward the chairs. "Please, let's get started. Glad to see you're up and about. I thought they might keep you in the doc shack for a bit."

"I checked myself out," Calvin deadpanned.

Everyone snickered at that but none more loudly than the two newcomers, both of whom were senior enlisted personnel.

"Let me introduce Senior Chief William Stokes, deep space recovery, and Chief Nicholas Nguyen, void jumper."

Calvin reached out and shook both men's hands. "I take it I've got you to thank for Nunez being alive, Nguyen?"

"Ah, I'd probably thank the good Lord, Colonel, because that was the most insane stunt I think we've pulled." Nguyen eyed Wilson. "And we do some crazy stuff on this ship."

Wilson smirked but didn't reply. Instead, he sat at the head of the table while again gesturing to the others. The rest took their seats, as did Calvin, Susanna, and Menahem.

"Before we get started, again, thank you and your entire crew, Major," Calvin said. "But the job isn't finished. There's still another mining ship out there. We think it has tangos on it and, hopefully, actionable intel."

Valor 169

"Well, I'm glad to hear the well isn't dry, Colonel. But what can we do for you? The *Salinan* isn't a fighting ship."

"My thought is we need to hit these guys from multiple directions at once. Engine room, cockpit, central ore processing. Shock and awe. They won't have any idea what hit them. If we had access to the equipment on the *Lion of Judah*, it wouldn't be an issue. But we don't. I was hoping your salvage experts here might have a solution."

"What are you thinking, sir? Even if we cut into, say, the cockpit or right outside it, explosive decompression would kill anyone we wanted to take prisoner."

Stokes narrowed his eyes. "We have rescue pods designed to go over a ship's hull while we use plasma torches to slice through the alloy. They're made of a hardened polymer and can hold ten people in soft suits. Integrated airlock, even."

"It's an asteroid belt, though," Nguyen interjected. "Micrometeoroids will be *everywhere*."

"Yeah, but it doesn't have to be perfect. They just need to get into the ship and secure it. We can be standing by with hull patches to reseal the holes." His eyes went to Wilson. "If you approve, sir."

"What's that bit about recovery specialists not being heroes?"

Stokes grinned. "We're salvage experts, Colonel."

"Well, here's your chance to be a hero."

"Aw, hell, put it like that, and I have to sign up. By your leave, of course, Major."

"You could've had the same effect by promising them a case of beer," Wilson replied with a snicker. "We're not sporting the Battle E for playing it safe, Colonel Demood. If your people and mine devise a solid plan, we're in."

"Outstanding, Major." Calvin leaned back. "I learned my

lesson from last time. We'll have SAR and *all* fleet assets standing by. Hate to say it, but I'm a newbie at fleet ops. It cost us dearly."

Wilson nodded. "Anything else, Colonel?"

"Negative."

"Then let's get back to it. I'll have the master chief show you to temporary quarters and clear a space for your team to work belowdecks."

"Excellent." Calvin rubbed his hands together, eager to get back at it.

Wilson stood. "Carry on, ladies and gentlemen."

"Ah, might I have a word in private?" Calvin asked.

"Sure, Colonel." Wilson jerked his thumb toward the exit. "The rest of you, get moving."

Everyone else filed out, and the hatch clanged shut.

Calvin put his hands on the table. "I want to thank you for coming to get us. Putting your people at extreme risk in a multipronged rescue mission at a moment's notice couldn't have been easy."

"It's all part of the service," Wilson replied. He licked his lips then grinned. "Besides, all I hear about Marines is how ballsy they are. Had to represent for the CDF."

Calvin snickered. "Floating through the void, I kept thinking, 'I'm getting way too old for this crap.' The allure of performing death-defying stunts like a holo-vid character is waning. Quickly."

"We don't get to do such things often, so the *Salinan* has to make up for lost time when there's an opportunity." Wilson let out a sigh. "The truth is, Colonel... I was supposed to be on my last tour."

I wonder how many of us felt the same way. "Me too. Thirty-two years in the TCMC. Felt like I earned that retire-

Valor 171

ment package, with the League being defeated and all, if not quite the way I wanted."

"We should've run those commie bastards all the way back to Earth before erasing them from the universe," Wilson replied. "But, you know, politicians."

Calvin snorted. "Hey, at least Spencer's one of the decent ones."

"Yeah, well, almost anybody would be better than Fuentes and Jezebel."

"Not a Rhodes fan, I take it?"

"I'd rather hot drop onto Earth with a battle rifle than spend five seconds with that—" Wilson snarled. "Too many friends got swept up in her purges, and unlike Spencer, I'll *never* forgive Fuentes for not having a set."

Former Vice President Jessica Rhodes—known as Jezebel as an insult within the military—had nearly single-handedly destroyed CDF readiness before the third battle of Canaan. Calvin regarded it as a miracle from God that they'd survived—and won. "Amen, brother."

"You read about times in the history books when we racked and stacked one another based on characteristics like skin color. I never could wrap my head around how that happened. Or continued. Until I saw how rabid Jezebel's supporters were. No matter what she said, they'd go along with it. Dividing us by every imaginable difference. Personality cults are about the most dangerous thing in the universe, outside the Leaguers."

"Still some that think like that," Calvin replied. "I wouldn't be too welcome on New Oranje." He gestured to his arm, bearing dark skin.

"Neither would I because I'd be right there with you, beating them down."

"Amen." Calvin narrowed his eyes. "Don't take this the

wrong way, Major, but you don't exactly come across as the polished CDF officer type."

"Neither do you, Colonel."

"Suppose you've got me there. Mustang, here."

"Same," Wilson replied. "And an LDO to boot."

Calvin raised an eyebrow. "What's an LDO?"

"Limited-duty officer." Wilson shrugged. "It means I don't have a degree. Didn't have a high school diploma, either, when I joined. I'm from Lindstrom. Border world and not quite as tightly integrated into the GalNet and records systems back then as it is now. But I wanted to fight Leaguers and found a way to fake my birth certificate at sixteen. Then I enlisted. God, it was a simpler time back then."

"I think we all get toward middle age and think that." *I like this guy. Anyone who fakes his age to go fight gets my respect.*

"Got any family back home?"

Calvin waggled his ring finger and the simple gold band on it. "Wife. Baby was on the way when we disappeared." He chuckled bitterly. "I'd put in my retirement papers too."

"First one?"

"Yeah." Calvin licked his lips. "A little old, I know, but we didn't want to have kids with the war on. My wife wanted me there to help raise them rather than being gone so much. Marine tours are pretty brutal, you know? Three years of straight combat."

"Got three myself. Two boys and a girl. God, I miss 'em."

"Had you mapped out life post-CDF?"

"Yeah. My wife and I wanted to move to Bounty."

"Isn't that a farming world? The new breadbasket of the Coalition? Pretty sure I saw an ad offering free land on it."

Wilson nodded. "One and the same. I was going to raise chickens."

Valor

173

"Chickens?"

"What can I say? I worked in a frontier store as a kid. Got really good at handling chickens."

Calvin blinked. "Handling, as in...?"

"Cutting them up for customers."

"That's an unusual skill, Major," Calvin replied as he laughed loudly. "You're all right for a squid."

Wilson grinned. "Hey, it's been an unusual life, to use your word." He turned somber. "Wouldn't trade it for anything, though. I've loved my time in the CDF, and while I might want to be home with my wife, doing something besides figuring out how to kill terrorists, this is where God wants me, for whatever reason."

Calvin's eyes were drawn to the major's left shoulder. Beneath the Terran Coalition flag sat another emblem. Rectangular, it had a white base color, a blue square in the upper left corner, and a red cross superimposed. The patch was the flag of Christianity. "You know," he began, pointing at it, "not everyone who wears one of those actually follows the faith."

"Is that a personal observation?"

"You could say that." Calvin gritted his teeth. "Haven't exactly lived up to it myself."

"It was an exceedingly long war, Colonel." Wilson pursed his lips. "And I'm not exactly proud of everything I did in it, either. Anyone who can say they are hasn't been in real combat."

"Truer words were never spoken. I'd toast them if I had some beer."

"Amen." Wilson chuckled. "But we do this so that our children don't have to, right? I sure don't want my boys slogging away in some Godforsaken swamp twenty years from now."

The idea of a Terran Coalition not at war was something Calvin wasn't even sure how to process. They'd fought the League for almost two generations, and with the war ending in a less-than-complete victory, he had no idea what would happen next. "Yeah. I wonder how our absence is affecting the postwar period. I'm sure our communist *friends* have celebrated the *Lion*'s disappearance."

"We'll find out soon enough."

Calvin raised an eyebrow. "You think we're getting home?"

"Don't you?"

"Maybe. I dunno." Calvin shrugged. "Frankly, I try not to think about it. If I stare at a picture of Jessica—my wife—too much... well, it's depressing."

"So avoid it, and focus on knocking down bad guys?"

"Pretty much."

Wilson snorted. "Well, not exactly the healthiest way to deal with it, sir... but I'd be lying if I said I was doing anything different. Except my focus is on building space installations."

"And insane plans to use salvage equipment to board terrorist-controlled spaceships."

"Well, this is the Coalition Defense Force. Absurd uses of stock equipment are part of the job requirements."

"Apparently, the Marines don't have a monopoly on creative uses of a given thing."

"No."

They both snickered, and Wilson shook his head.

"Well, I'd better get out of your hair, Major. Lots of planning to do. I'd like to use your shuttle bay to train, if that's amenable."

Wilson nodded. "Seeing as you outrank me sir, it'll have to be."

Valor **175**

Calvin smiled thinly. "Yeah, but we're different branches, and I don't want to feed that myth about Marines disrespecting the CDF."

"Then I appreciate the request. Granted. You know, for what it's worth, Colonel, I don't care for hypocrites. And I try to follow my faith. Sometimes it takes being a sinner to realize that."

"Truth, Major." Calvin stood. "So, what are you doing being an officer if you don't like hypocrisy?"

"Oh, they barely accept me as such. Mustang, strike one. LDO, strike two. Still... I got my dream. Command of a ship." Wilson rose as well.

"Then I'd say it all turned out well, and to hell with what anyone else thinks." He stuck out his hand. "Again, thank you and your people for saving me and Nunez."

"I only wish we could've saved everyone," Wilson replied and shook Calvin's hand.

"Something tells me there will be more opportunities, Major. I've put down a lot of these damn terrorists, but they keep popping up."

"We'll do whatever we can to help." Wilson narrowed his eyes. "I promise you that."

"I'll hold you to it. Godspeed, Major."

"Godspeed, Demood."

Calvin turned and strode out of the conference room. *Gotta respect anyone who served as enlisted.* Calvin had taken the same road, but it came more naturally in the TCMC, especially during wartime.

The rest of the day would be dedicated to building a training area, and the next day, they would drill. He wasn't going to rush, because while the other ship was probably alerted to the attempted boarding, it had made no deviation from its course. *Bastards are probably trying to blend in and hope they were overlooked.*

As the gravlift doors closed, Calvin wondered what passed for chow on the small vessel. *Probably more of that Zeivlot crap. I'll be glad when we get some human food again.* Something in the back of his head said he should be thankful to have sustenance in the first place, but he paid it no heed. Soon, the terrorists would pay.

20

————

WITH THE LION of Judah safely jumped away from the Admari vessel and holding in deep space, David had time to do what mattered most: plot their next move. He'd called a staff meeting with the senior officers and Dr. Hayworth, searching for a consensus and to explore all options. As he strode into the deck-one conference room, all came to attention.

"General on deck!" Tinetariro said as she stood.

"As you were. Please, be seated." David slid into the chair at the head of the table. "I know you've all been working nonstop the last few days. And I'm eager to hear what the science team has come up with in conjunction with engineering and tactical."

Hayworth cleared his throat. "I think it's clear we need to return and gain access to the distress signal. Even if all we accomplish is proving a negative, it suggests that something is still functional and is likely technology from the precursors."

"Doctor, I get what you're saying, but we're talking about technology that's absurdly old by our standards. Frankly, it defies logic that any of the devices we've found so far still work," Hanson interjected. "Can you imagine what would become of even the *Lion* if we left her in space for ten thousand years and came back?"

"And? Comparatively speaking, every human space vessel is a child's toy. The material composites used are so far beyond us... I can barely comprehend it, Major." Hayworth smirked. "And I'm one of the smartest humans alive."

David smiled thinly. "To the doctor's point, the why matters little to me. Only that it is. What I'm unwilling to do is engage in another head-on fight with the nanites. Using the *Margaret Thatcher* for recon came to mind, but I don't think it would have any more success than we did."

"Stealth recon fighters, sir?" Amir asked. "In low-power mode, we could jump in above the elliptical, take a parabolic course through the system, and, I hope, avoid whatever those things have for sensors."

"It's the 'hope' part that bothers me," David replied. "I'm not willing to ask pilots to knowingly risk death because there's nothing we could do to help them."

Amir spread his hands out on the table. "Sir, it is a risk we're willing to take. And I would be the first in line."

Before David could respond, the alert klaxon sounded its piercing wail, and the intercom came to life. "General quarters. General quarters. Set condition one throughout the ship. All hands to battle stations. I say again, all hands, man your battle stations. This is not a drill. General Cohen to the bridge." First Lieutenant Shelly Hammond's voice echoed from speakers in both the conference room and the passageway outside.

David sprang to his feet. "Major Hanson, get down to engineering. Colonel Amir, to the hangar deck. Everyone else, with me." His mind swam with a million possibilities, the first being that either the nanites or the Admari had found them. One seemed a far more daunting prospect than the other. He cleared the hatch and turned left toward the bridge then pulled his cover on as he entered.

The *Lion*'s control center was a beehive of activity, though it was somewhat difficult to see with the dark-blue lighting. Hammond sat in the CO's chair, while the second-shift tactical and navigation officers manned their respective posts.

"Situation, Lieutenant?" David asked as he made his way across the bridge.

"Several dozen Admari vessels have appeared in a spherical formation around us, sir," Hammond replied. "Their shields are up, and we're detecting power readings consistent with an energy-weapons capacitor. They're not responding to a broad-frequency warning."

"Conn, TAO," Second Lieutenant Victoria Kelsey interrupted. "All sections report battle stations manned and ready. Condition one set throughout the ship, ma'am."

Dread in the pit of David's stomach made him feel uneasy. He blew out a breath. "Lieutenant Hammond, I have the conn."

"Aye, aye, sir. General Cohen has the conn."

"Take your station, Lieutenant." David motioned toward Aibek and the others. "Captain Goldberg, tactical, please. And get Taylor up here. We might need his cryptography services."

As David lowered himself into the CO's chair, his mind raced. *It's obvious what they want, but how did they find us?* "Communications, tell the Admari I want to speak with their leader. Emphasize it's coming directly from me."

"Aye, aye, sir," Second Lieutenant Jackson Bell, the second-watch comms officer, replied.

David pulled up the tactical display on his monitor and examined the plot. *They've got us pinned in.* The sphere enveloped the entire battlegroup and left no avenue for sublight escape that didn't take them within weapons range of multiple Admari vessels. *I see they have different kinds of ships too.* Most were the same class, but a few appeared larger and, David assumed, more capable.

"Sir, I have Leader Iskv-Selagan for you," Bell interjected.

"Let's see him, Lieutenant."

A few moments later, Iskv-Selagan appeared on the screen above David's chair. Unlike before, the bridge of his vessel was darkened, and purple light backlit everything. "It is regrettable we meet again under these circumstances, General Cohen."

David raised an eyebrow. "And which are those, Iskv-Selagan? Because where I come from, dropping in unannounced with this much firepower is considered a hostile act."

Iskv-Selagan blinked and adjusted his skinny gray body. "We have no desire for combat, General. But my people cannot abide knowing a method to fight the great pestilence is so close yet not being allowed to have it. We have been sentenced to the void for too long. We are *dying*."

"Again, I am not indifferent to the Admari's situation, and I'm willing to share information that should put you down the road to developing a counter of your own."

"No! You have a weapon now. Give it to us. Or we will take it by force."

"Iskv-Selagan, listen to me very carefully. Right now, I view you as a sympathetic individual and want to help your

Valor 181

race. The moment you attack my people, that changes. Do not make an enemy of the Terran Coalition."

"It is you who makes an enemy of us."

The feed abruptly cut out, leaving silence behind.

"TAO, what weapons capability are you seeing on those ships, especially the larger ones?"

Ruth shook her head. "There's some pretty heavy armor on them, sir. I know they have ports for directed-energy weapons, but until they fire, no idea what type."

Great. "I have no interest in fighting these people," David said with exasperation. "Navigation, plot a Lawrence drive jump. Deep space, maximum range. We'll hold the hole open for the escorts."

"Aye, aye, sir."

"Communications, direct the destroyers to jump as soon as we engage our drive."

The Admari vessels began to compress the sphere as Hammond obeyed her orders. In short order, they would be within nominal range for Coalition weaponry.

"Conn, Navigation. Jump coordinates set, sir. Lawrence drive ready to activate."

"Engage Lawrence drive, Lieutenant."

Moments later, the lights on the bridge dimmed.

"Perhaps we should stand our ground," Aibek hissed.

David shook his head. "I'd rather get out of here without a fight and have Hanson figure out how these guys can find us in the middle of nowhere. We have no quarrel with the Admari."

"They apparently have one with us."

As usual, the XO cuts straight to the point of the matter. David double-checked the nav readout a moment before Hammond offered her report.

"Conn, Navigation. Wormhole fully formed, sir."

"Send the escorts through first, then take us in, Lieutenant."

A few seconds later, the four Ajax-class destroyers accelerated as their engines flared to life, and they crossed into the maw of the swirling mass. The *Lion* followed and emerged on the other side. The transit was routine, and David breathed a sigh of relief. Since the jump that had brought them to Sextans B, FTL was no longer as carefree as it had once been.

David counted out five seconds—the time a starship's sensors would be down following an FTL jump.

"Conn, TAO. Our escorts are present and accounted for, designated Sierra One through Four. No other contacts in range."

The report did much to calm David's mind. He nodded. "We'll stay at condition one for thirty minutes, just in case."

"Major Hanson must begin determining how they tracked us immediately."

Hayworth spoke up from the science station. "I'll assist."

"Thank you, Doctor." David tilted his head. "Let's have a contingent from the masters-at-arms go over every inch of the ship the Admari had access to, which isn't much."

Aibek raised an eye scale. "That was done once they left, sir."

"No reason not to do it again."

"I will see to it personally," Aibek replied.

One more problem we have to deal with. David wasn't sure what straw would break his back. *Maybe it's time to head back to Zeivlot and see what Calvin and his people have accomplished.* There'd been no comms, as there were no buoys or orbital q-comms, unlike in the Milky Way. He trusted that if there'd been a severe emergency, the vessels still there would've

Valor 183

tracked the *Lion of Judah* down, but he still worried about the tough Marine.

"Conn, TAO," Ruth blurted out, cutting into David's thoughts. "Aspect change, inbound wormholes. Admari signature, sir."

A growl escaped David's lips before he could cut it off. *This is bad.* To his knowledge, no race had technology that could track a vessel through the void in real time. With its vast PASCORE sensor network, even the Terran Coalition could only give educated guesses. "If retreat isn't an option, then we stand our ground."

"Couldn't agree more, sir," Tinetariro cut in. She'd appeared at her usual perch at a console behind the CO's and XO's chairs. "Apologies. I was out of uniform when general quarters was called."

David allowed himself a grin. "Our alien friends had the good sense to wait for you, Master Chief." He turned toward Bell. "Comms, warn the Admari off. Tell them if they close within ten thousand kilometers, I will consider it a hostile act."

"Aye, aye, sir," After a pause, he continued, "Text-only reply. 'Give us the weapon, or we will take it ourselves. This is the final request.'"

In the lead-up to every conflict, a point came when David knew the die had been cast, and there would be no way to avoid hostilities. *The Romans called it crossing the Rubicon. HaShem, if it is your will, please spare the lives of those under my command, and help the Admari to see we are not their enemies. Amen.* "XO, get the air boss to warm up every combat spacecraft we've got. I want Amir's wing on ready five ten minutes ago."

"It will be done," Aibek rumbled.

"Conn, TAO. We're getting lit up like a Christmas tree by

targeting scanners. Now showing forty-seven Admari vessels."

"TAO, redesignate Sierra Five through Fifty-One as Master One through Forty-Seven. Keep our escorts close, and use formation bravo-six for interlocking point-defense support."

"Aye, aye, sir."

"Thoughts, XO?"

"Do you plan to wait for them to shoot first?" Aibek hissed.

"We don't start fights... but we do finish them."

Aibek's cheeks twitched. "Striking first with the most power is our way."

"I know." David watched the tactical plot, wondering what the Admari were thinking. *Probably hoping we'll cave.* It gave him hope that perhaps sanity would prevail.

"Conn, TAO. Aspect change. Weapons launch detected, all hostile vessels. Looks like missiles of some sort, sir. Pulsed plasma thrust and radiologics confirmed." Ruth turned. "They've acquired us and are homing."

"Navigation, all ahead flank. Come to heading zero-seven-five, negative declination twenty degrees, then commence evasive maneuvers, pattern alpha-charlie-seven. TAO, firing point procedures, neutron beams, Master... Six, Thirteen, Twenty, Thirty-Two, and Forty-Six. Target engines and weapons emplacements *only*, Captain." As the closest hostile vessels, the five ships made decent first targets.

"Firing solutions set, sir."

The pique came through in Ruth's voice, and he figured she wanted to light the Admari ships up. *Perhaps we can stop this before it goes too far. I'll cling to that until proven otherwise. There's also the small matter of how sophisticated their vessels are.* "Match bearings, shoot, neutron beams."

The dozens of neutron emitters across the hull of the *Lion of Judah* came to life. Blue spears of directed energy shot out in every direction as Ruth plied her trade. The deflectors on the Admari ships became visible momentarily, their orange spheres stopping the attacks, at least for a time. Meanwhile, the incoming missiles plowed toward the aft quarter of the *Lion*. Automated point-defense emplacements tracked them before lighting up the void in a spectacular light show. Small explosions as the warheads detonated from direct PD strikes dotted the inky blackness of space, but some of them got through.

David gripped the handrests of his chair as he and the rest of the bridge crew jostled in their harnesses. *Six direct hits, maybe seven?* It was difficult to tell only from a count of the individual shakes.

"Aft shields holding but weakened, sir. Fusion warheads," Ruth said. "Negligible damage to hostile contacts. I got a few energy-weapon turrets and missile tubes. All targeted vessels still combat capable."

Aibek leaned closer. "Perhaps you should allow Captain Goldberg to expand where she attacks. Structural bracing and the reactors of these vessels, if hit, would likely disable them."

"If we hit a reactor, that'll take out the entire ship," David replied.

"Which was how we took out so many Leaguers, if my memory is accurate."

"Killing large numbers of these aliens is not something I'm interested in, old friend. I understand *why* they're doing this. And I have a feeling that were *we* in their place, I'd probably reach similar conclusions."

"They have made themselves our enemy. Nothing else matters once blood is shed."

David blew out a breath. "Which is precisely why I'm attempting to avoid killing. If we can drive them away without loss of life, there's still a chance to end this without it degenerating into slaughter."

"If that strategy is unsuccessful?"

"Then I'll shift to stronger methods." David met Aibek's eyes.

"Conn, TAO. Getting energy buildup within the Admari ships. I think they're warming up energy weapons."

"Firing point procedures, neutron beams, same targets. Bloody their noses." David gritted his teeth. *Back off before we reach the point of no return.*

———

DOWN IN THE *Lion of Judah*'s engineering reactor control area, adjacent to the massive, multideck matter-antimatter reactor that powered the mighty warship, Hanson, Merriweather, and dozens of other officers and enlisted ratings kept watch and, more importantly, responded in real time to threats.

Hanson steadied himself as the ship shook yet again. The port shield quarter dropped precipitously, drawing further attention. The problem wasn't so much that the enemy concentrated their fire on it. To him, it was more the type of weapon.

"Stress on the port-side deflector generator is rising," Merriweather said. "I don't recall seeing that effect before."

"Well, not with the shields above eighty-percent cohesion, anyway," Hanson replied. "What the heck do you make of that energy signature?"

Merriweather shook her head. "I've never seen anything like it. My best guess is it's something that overloads

Valor 187

deflector grids to short out the generator. Or... just a fluke of how this species's tech matches up against ours."

"It's developing a feedback loop." Hanson watched as the overload built further in the port generator. "They must be observing this, because most of their shots are going directly on that quadrant."

Merriweather stood and bent over his console. "There's nothing we can do, either."

"Well, that's not exactly accurate, Major."

She affixed him with a stare. "We're in combat."

"Yeah, well, the only solution is to drop our port-quadrant screens, let the generator recharge, and raise them again." Hanson pulled up the intercom app and engaged it for the bridge. "I'd better let the general know."

"You want to *what*?"

"It's either that or have the generator blow up, sir." Hanson's voice crackled through the speaker built into the CO's chair.

David couldn't believe what he was hearing. "I'm not sure if you noticed, Major, but we've got nearly fifty hostiles shooting at us right now. Without shields, our armor will be taking those blows. Give me a better option."

"There is none, sir. At least not with the time I've got to work with."

This isn't happening. David balled his right hand into a fist and exercised every ounce of self-control he had not to slam it into the armrest. "All right, Major. I'll figure it out up here. Cohen out." The commlink channel closed with a click.

Aibek hissed. "The Admari warheads are powerful

enough to cause considerable damage to our hull." The XO left unsaid that the *Lion* was still fighting with one hand behind her back.

"Conn, TAO. Existing targeting is ineffective, sir."

Pouring accelerant on the fire, Ruth? David thought back to the engagement with the Jinvaas Confederation. He'd taken every possible precaution to avoid Vogtek casualties during the ritual combat with their cruisers. *But this situation isn't the same. We were in the wrong then. Just cause or not, the Admari are attacking us, and they'll kill my people if I let them.* As abhorrent as killing another one of HaShem's creatures was, allowing the men and women who served under him to die was far worse. "Forward-magnetic-cannon status?"

"Double loaded with EMP and high-explosive shells, sir."

Setting his jaw, David tugged his black space sweater down. It went over his khaki uniform shirt and helped combat the cold he usually felt. "TAO, firing point procedures, magnetic cannons and neutron beams, Master Six and Twenty."

"Firing solutions set, sir."

"Match bearings, shoot, magnetic cannons and neutron beams."

The main armament of the *Lion of Judah* was its five-hundred-millimeter magnetic cannons. They hurled shells that weighed as much as small helicars through the void at ten percent of light speed. While mag cannons were a mainstay on most noncarrier CDF vessels, the *Lion* mounted the largest ones in service. Dozens of EMP and HE projectiles erupted from the long barrels and, seconds later, slammed into the Admari's defensive screens.

Ruth followed up the initial hits with a series of neutron-beam strikes, which broke through the enemy's shields and

Valor 189

flayed the hulls of their vessels. One Admari ship lost half its engine pod, while the other suffered an energy spear slicing neatly through ten decks of the superstructure, leaving a molten hole that vented atmosphere.

"Conn, TAO. Master Twenty disabled, sir. Master Six is no longer combat capable, though she's still maneuvering."

"It stands to reason that our Hunter missiles would be effective as well," Aibek said.

David nodded. "Probably, but since we can't make more, I'd rather save them. Besides, we just sent a direct message to the Admari fleet commander." He glanced at Bell. "Communications, send text-only message: We will continue to defend ourselves until you break off your unprovoked attack."

The *Lion* shook as another barrage of energy-weapons fire found her.

David gritted his teeth. "Guess that's our answer. Time to drop the gloves. TAO, synchronize firing patterns with the *Margaret Thatcher* and the rest of our escorts."

"Aye, aye, sir."

"Navigation, come to heading—" David rechecked the tactical plot overlay. "Two-six-three, positive declination seventeen. Maintain flank speed." *We should have a small opening to drop our port shields, take the pressure off that generator, and get them back up before we're blown apart. I hope.*

21

———

SPARKS from an electrical control console rained down on several engineering ratings who were busy with damage-control efforts.

Hanson stopped what he was doing and ran to help. "Lock down the port-side grid, or we're going to lose half our conduits and junction controls!" he bellowed.

While the enlisted personnel rushed to comply, he turned back to resetting the port deflector. Most of the recharging process was computer controlled, but Hanson knew better than to leave everything to a machine.

A high-pitched whine unlike any Hanson recalled hearing filled the air of the central engineering space. Thinking that yet another problem had developed, he looked up from the console he was bent over just in time to see a group of ten extra-tall, thin gray humanoids shimmer into being.

Hanson blinked, thinking he'd gone insane. But the aliens spread out, and another group appeared, accompanied by the same high-pitched whine. Each wore an exoskeleton and carried a weapon that reminded him of a

Valor 191

rifle. His combat training kicked into high gear as he slapped his handcomm. "Intruder alert! Alien intruders in main engineering. We need masters-at-arms and the Marines now! Hostiles possess matter-transportation technology."

"Catch, Major!" Merriweather yelled.

An energy pistol flew toward him. He turned and grabbed it then moved to the railing of the control center. After confirming the weapon was set to stun, he fired a beam at the nearest creature. *These must be the Admari. The description tracks with what General Cohen said at dinner the other night.*

The beam sizzled as it connected with the being, though it appeared as if the exoskeleton absorbed its energy. The Admari kept moving forward and raised its weapon. A bolt of purple energy shot through the air and buried itself in the overhead, where it left a scorch mark as proof of its presence.

Hanson dived behind a nearby rolling cart and dialed up the intensity of the particle weapon. The particular Admari he'd shot was out of sight by the time he tried to shoot him again, but there were plenty of targets to choose from. Hanson picked an alien in the middle of the open area around the antimatter reactor and squeezed the trigger.

This time, the beam had an effect. It drilled through one of the exoskeleton joints and the gray skin of the Admari boarder. The alien screamed, its piercing wail seeming to reverberate off the alloy surfaces around them.

Meanwhile, Merriweather had distributed most of the contents of the emergency-weapons locker on the second level of the control center, while other engineering ratings got whatever they could to fight back.

A few enlisted personnel even tried to beat the Admari

with large spanners and, in one case, used a laser drill on an unlucky hostile. For all the engineers' spunk, however, the aliens were using pulse-energy weapons to great effect. Ratings lay collapsed on the deck. Hanson prayed they were still alive.

Merriweather slid to a stop next to him and passed over a battle rifle. "Stun rounds aren't effective. Those exoskeletons seem to have energy shields, so I loaded EMP rounds. Only two mags of those, though."

Hanson nodded and hefted the weapon. "Thanks. Any ETA on backup?"

"Major Almeida said the rapid reaction force for the aft section is on the way, so I hope no more than five minutes."

Bursts of purple energy smacked all over the place, melting surfaces the engineers had taken cover behind, while continuing to drop ratings in their tracks, though most were no longer exposed.

Hanson sent several shots into the melee, felling two Admari, who collapsed on the deck. Dark-green blood from a gaping hole pooled around one of them . He felt no remorse. *It's them or us.* Adrenaline pumped through his veins as he fired again and again.

After Hanson and Merriweather had taken down several hostiles, the remaining Admari tracked the source of their shots. They keyed in on them and filled the air with purple bursts of energy. The concentrated barrage melted half the cart they were hiding behind and sent both of them scurrying toward more solid cover.

Even as Hanson poked his head up and pointed his pistol toward the bottom level in hopes of taking out another hostile, the whine of the matter-transportation technology sounded once more, and another twenty aliens flooded into the engineering compartment. *There're more of them in here than my people.*

"Should we try pulse grenades?" Merriweather whispered.

Hanson shook his head. "I don't even want to think about what could happen if a grenade hit the wrong piece of equipment." He peered over the console to see the gray aliens hooking up a device to a computer terminal and sent another burst of energy in their direction.

"What's the plan, then?" she asked as a dozen return shots smacked around them, forcing them both to keep their heads down.

"Slow 'em down as much as we can until the Marines arrive."

Merriweather took a peek down at the activity below. The Admari controlled the bottom level, outside a few engineering ratings who'd gotten a weapons locker open and were holed up in the control area where the fuel-intermix panels resided. "Not good. I don't know what they're doing, but if you mess with the wrong things down there, you could blow up the ship."

Hanson put his handcomm back to his lips. "Major Almeida, if that RRF is coming, now's the time. We've got hostiles attempting to interface with the *Lion*'s systems."

The device crackled with static. "Two minutes."

"Roger that." Hanson blew out a breath. "If they're not here on time, I'm open to using pulse grenades."

Merriweather nodded. "Whatever it takes."

"Amen."

"They're *what,* Master Chief?" David asked.

"Hostile boarding parties are teleporting into engineering, sir. Masters-at-arms and the nearest Marine RRF are en route," Tinetariro replied. "Engineering reports the Admari are attempting to download information from our central computer system."

David gritted his teeth. *Teleportation tech. What other surprises do these guys have?* He wasn't quite sure how the aliens, who apparently lived in the void, had such wonders at their fingertips. *But they can't take on the nanites?* It seemed reasonable to assume that perhaps their understanding of the original technology had faded over time. *Without an industrial base to build more vessels and higher education to train the next generation of scientists and engineers. Eventually, knowledge would be lost.* However, such considerations mattered little as the *Lion* shook from repeated energy-weapons hits. "TAO, status of magnetic-cannon reloads?"

"Thirty seconds, sir. Energy-weapons capacitor almost back to full as well. Two minutes to port-shield-generator recycle."

"Comms, transmit to commander, Admari fleet. There is no reason to continue this pointless engagement. Cease fire, and we will return your personnel after debriefing them."

Moments later, Bell replied, "Text-only reply, sir. 'We will fight until the weapon is retrieved or no Admari remains.'"

David all but snarled. If he used curse words, many of them would've been dropped on the deck. Instead, he shook his head. "Got any advice here, XO?"

"The enemy is unwilling to yield yet can pursue us. Defeating them by force of arms is the only option," Aibek replied with a hiss. "We could attempt to capture their flagship and force Iskv-Selagan to surrender."

Valor 195

"I thought of that."

"But?"

"We don't know what the interior of their ships looks like, what boobytraps they might have in store... or if it would even make a difference." David shook his head. "Too much risk to our Marines."

"Then the solution is obvious... keep disabling or destroying their vessels until they realize they are outmatched and cede the field."

David turned, staring back toward Hayworth at what passed for a science station. "Doctor, anything on how they're tracking us?"

"Only that I'm reasonably sure there's no device inside the *Lion of Judah*, after repeated searches of the area the Admari delegation had access to. We can't rule out something attached to our hull, however. Micro QETs accomplish that purpose quite well within short to medium ranges."

David was familiar with the technology, which was typically used by intelligence agencies, to track vessels. *But they must be shot into the hull with a small handheld launcher or placed on an EVA. I don't think the Admari used that method, because we would've detected it.* "Keep searching."

Hayworth nodded. "What else would I be doing?"

"Touché, Doctor." David forced a thin smile before returning his attention to the front of the bridge. The killing seemed senseless, but he supposed it made a bit of sense from the Admari position. *If we'd been sentenced to the void for untold years, I might resort to extreme tactics too.* Understanding their point of view mattered little, however. *There're still several dozen ships trying to disable or destroy us.* As the sleek vessels charged forward, back into firing range, David set his jaw. "TAO, firing point procedures, magnetic cannons and neutron beams, Master Twenty-One, Thirty-Eight, and Fifty-Two."

"Firing solutions set, sir."

"Match bearings, shoot, magnetic cannons and neutron beams."

As the Admari vessels filled the void with their infernally accurate energy blasts, the *Lion's* primary batteries spoke in reply. The helicar-weight projectiles flung out of the mag-cannons raced through space before slamming into the enemy's protective energy screens, followed quickly by neutron beam strikes. The blue spears of death blasted through the ancient hulls of the Admari warships and back into the inky blackness. Bursts of orange and blue flames shot out of the holes before quickly extinguishing in the vacuum as all available oxygen was used up.

David hung on to his armrests as the ship heaved.

"Significant armor damage on the port quarter," Aibek said as he pointed at a status display flashing red.

We'll have to risk raising the shield a few seconds early. "TAO, energize the port shield generator."

"Aye, aye, sir."

Strike and parry. We're the superior combatant, but can we hold the line without using up most of our consumable munitions? Keeping a close eye on the forward and aft mag-cannon-shell magazines, David prepared to order another strike. All the while, the butcher's bill weighed heavily on his conscience. *HaShem, give them the wisdom to stop this.* He grimly formed the words for another combat evolution.

———

HANSON SENT another beam into the mass of Admari boarders clustered around a set of terminals at the bottom

Valor   197

of the antimatter reactor. He didn't know whether the shot landed, but he only had a split second to try to aim, thanks to the impressive number of particle-beam blasts they were sending his and Merriweather's way. She was a meter away, crouched behind a console and trying to keep them occupied.

"I can't tell if they've managed to get into anything important," Merriweather whispered. "But if nothing else, the language barrier should slow them down."

"Yeah, I was counting on that," Hanson replied as he aimed his pulse pistol in the general direction of the aliens and squeezed the trigger. That time, the familiar cry of a wounded Admari told him he'd gotten lucky.

"The Marines need to get here."

Hanson was about to make a smart remark when a loud explosion echoed, and both hatches into the main engineering space blew inward. Pulse grenades clattered to the deck plating and erupted in bright flashes of light and sound that disoriented anyone nearby. *Well, I guess that answers whether the reactor housing can handle small blasts.*

Power-armored Marines charged through the openings and opened fire on the Admari with well-aimed three-round bursts. Half a dozen went down instantly while the others tried to react. A smattering of energy beams went in the general direction of the Marines, but the aliens were still too stunned to effectively aim.

As the Admari started to get their wits back about them, Hanson popped up and put a beam into one of the beings, who had gotten behind cover in relation to the QRF but was exposed to the overhead. The shot hit the alien's center mass, and it collapsed to the deck.

More than thirty Marines had flooded in, and multiple fire teams were taking up flanking positions on the remaining Admari. Meanwhile, the *Lion*'s port shield had recharged, and since the boarding parties had quit teleporting in, Hanson assumed the technology was useless when the deflectors were up.

Hoping to avoid any further damage to the delicate engine and reactor controls, Hanson stood and shouted, "Hey, you're surrounded! Drop your weapons, and come out with your hands up!"

One of the thin gray aliens stared at him before screeching something in its native tongue. As one, they rose from their positions and charged at the Marine force.

Thirty battle rifles spoke as one as the piercing whine of energy weapons filled the air. Moments later, it was over. Dozens of Admari lay on the ground, still twitching as their green blood flowed freely on the deck. One power-armored Marine seemed to have been hit seriously, and several others stood over him, administering first aid. Several engineers who'd been stunned by the alien weapons slowly stirred, and more medics came in to assist.

The scene shocked Hanson to his core. Bile rose in his throat as the smell of propellent mixed with the scent of alien blood reached his nose, and for a moment, he thought his breakfast was going to come roaring up. At the last moment, Hanson fought the impulse down and stared at the dozens of bodies instead. *Why'd they do that?* There was no way for the Admari to win the engagement, and they had to know it. *Perhaps in their culture, surrender is dishonorable.*

"You guys good up there, Major?" a Marine yelled.

"Casualties all over the place on the bottom deck. Take care of them first."

"On it, sir."

Hanson turned to Merriweather. "Round up as many ratings as you can, and check every inch of the reactor, especially the coolant and fuel lines. God help us all if that's damaged."

"Yes, sir." She turned to go before glancing over her shoulder. "Nice work with the pistol."

"Thanks." Hanson grinned. "Just because I'm a nerd doesn't mean I can't fight."

22

DAVID STUDIED the tactical plot as controlled chaos reigned around the bridge. Orders, replies, and information flew between the enlisted ratings, feeding up to the watch officers and finally to him. They'd taken out almost a dozen of the Admari cruiser-sized vessels, with roughly half being destroyed. The rest were disabled and floating in the void. The enemy had switched up their tactics. No longer targeting a specific shield quadrant, they just flung the shield-draining energy bolts at the *Lion* from all sides. *Which will make recharging our deflectors that much harder.*

"Conn, TAO. Magnetic-cannon reload complete, sir."

"Firing point procedures, magnetic cannons and neutron beams, Master Eight, Eleven, and Thirty-Six."

"Firing solutions set, sir."

"Match bearings, shoot, magnetic cannons and neutron beams."

Another salvo of mag-cannon shells followed by blue spears of concentrated particle energy shot out of the *Lion*. The *Thatcher* and other destroyers added their fury to the mix, matching targets and timing. Ruth had quickly determined the optimal firing patterns for inflicting maximum damage on the Admari vessels. It showed when two of the contacts blew apart from direct reactor hits and the third lost all power.

All the while, incoming blasts from the alien ships lit up the *Lion of Judah*'s shields while overstressing her deflector generators. David stared at the status display showing all four of them careening toward the red line of an overload. He decided to open the playbook a touch more. "TAO, make tubes one through twelve of the forward VLRS ready in all respects, and open the outer doors."

"Tubes one through twelve ready in all respects. Outer doors are open, sir. Awaiting targeting instructions."

David checked the tactical plot. "Firing point procedures, tubes one through twelve, Master Forty-Eight." The vessel was the closest hostile to them at that moment.

"Firing solutions set, sir."

"Match bearings, shoot, tubes one through twelve."

Every half second, a Hunter missile erupted from the launch cells behind the bridge, making the deck shake enough that it seemed as if the ship were coming apart for six seconds. Spreading out from the *Lion*, twelve icons appeared on the plot and accelerated toward the Admari vessel. Typically, David would've expected to see at least a couple of the advanced shackled AI warheads shot down by opposing point defense, but all twelve hit the target, erasing it from the void in a series of violent explosions.

David's jaw dropped. "TAO, can you confirm all of our Hunters detonated without interception?"

"Not only that, sir, but I didn't detect *any* outgoing point-defense fire."

Aibek blinked a few times. "How is that possible?"

"Captain, cross-reference the sensor scans from Master

Forty-Eight with another contact that matches its design silhouette."

Ruth turned. "It's identical to another vessel of the same design, sir."

David's first thought was that they had a decisive advantage over the Admari. *Forget decisive. All I have to do is launch Amir's bomber squadrons, and that's the end of their entire fleet with little risk to us. All we'll have to do is keep those boarding parties at bay until the job's done.* "Either they can't track our missiles, or that's one heck of a glaring hole in their defensive capabilities."

"Those ships are, well, ancient. Who knows? Maybe they once did." Ruth turned back toward the front.

"Communications, get me Colonel Amir."

"Aye, aye, sir," Bell replied.

The intercom on the CO's chair crackled to life. "This is Amir."

"All strapped in?" David asked.

"Nothing like a good scramble drill, sir."

David couldn't quite tell whether his old friend was enjoying himself. *Flyboys do live to paw the vacuum, after all.* "Keeps the nuggets on their toes, anyway. We've determined that most if not all the Admari ships lack integrated point-defense systems."

"That is astonishing, but our bombers will make short work of their fleet."

As David opened his mouth to give the order to launch, the words caught in his throat. *If this really is the majority of the Admari fleet, and they've been honest with us, which, with the number of vessels here, seems realistic... I will be giving the order to eradicate a species.* As much as he wanted to push the thought out of his head and only focus on the military reality, there was a term for what he was about to do: genocide.

"Sir?" Aibek prompted.

Throughout his life, David had struggled with the demands and precepts of his faith and the requirements of the all-out war against the League of Sol. But even then, the conflict was defensive, and Jewish law made clear that self-defense was acceptable. *This is self-defense too.* His conscience wouldn't let it go, though. *Sentient life has supreme value. That's a core value of the Coalition Defense Force and our ethics, not to mention the Jewish faith. If the Admari wanted to conquer another species or even had the capability to, that's one thing. I know this is wrong.*

"General, are you still there?" Amir asked.

HaShem, give me wisdom. David gritted his teeth and shook his head. "Stand down, Colonel. I'll let you know if and when I change my mind."

Aibek's eyes widened. "I do not understand. We have them, as you humans say, dead to rights."

"Yes, we do," David replied more softly than usual.

"Sir, I must echo the XO. They're attacking us. We have no duty beyond defending ourselves here," Tinetariro interjected.

"Oh, yes, we do, Master Chief. We shall maintain our humanity even in combat, and every CDF soldier shall do all he can to avoid harming innocent lives, honor, and property. In case we've momentarily forgotten the CDF's purity-of-arms code."

"It's regrettable that the Admari house their civilization on those ships, but that's *their* problem, not ours."

David glanced between her and Aibek. "There's got to be a better way. Perhaps if I could get their leader to sit down and talk, we could find it." He blew out a breath and didn't wait for a response before he pressed on. "Communications, send to commander, Admari fleet. *Lion of Judah* wishes to cease hostilities and requests terms of surrender."

After a sharp intake of breath, Ruth said, "Sir, we have them on the run—"

"Lieutenant, send that message immediately." David held up a hand. "That'll be all, TAO."

Everyone's stares bored into him. He paid it no heed and instead waited for a response from the Admari. Incoming energy-weapons fire slackened quickly then stopped altogether. "TAO, cease fire. Order our escorts to as well, unless they start it up again."

"Aye, aye, sir," Ruth replied bitterly.

"Sir, they've replied with a vidlink," Bell said after a few minutes.

"Put him on my viewer, Lieutenant."

The thin gray alien named Iskv-Selagan, whom David had come to recognize after seeing him a few times, flashed on the screen. "General Cohen, why do you request terms? I know the fight goes poorly for us."

"Because exterminating your race is immoral, and I won't do it," David replied.

"Then you will give us the weapon? If not, there is nothing further to say."

"I'm willing to discuss it seriously. But only in person. I must have assurances from you. As a show of good faith, we will deploy search-and-rescue teams to look for survivors in the void if you agree."

Iskv-Selagan seemed to blink, though it was hard to tell. "What of our hostilities?"

David shrugged. "The way I see it, you can track us through Lawrence drive jumps, and if these talks fail, we can go back to trying to kill one another. But I hope that won't be necessary."

"I am willing to come aboard your vessel to parley. Know that I have no use to you as a hostage. My people will continue the fight, as my life is meaningless. You may send your rescue teams, but know that no information will be provided by any Admari."

Either he's talking a great game, or these guys are devoted to the point of fanaticism. "Very well. The same shuttle bay as last time. Your call on when. Anyone we find, we'll bring to the *Lion* so that you may take them home with you."

"That will be acceptable. I will arrive in one of your hours."

David nodded. "I'll see you then. *Lion of Judah* out."

Hayworth appeared in front of the CO's and XO's chairs as the screen went blank. "You cannot be serious."

Once more, David held up a hand. "Doctor, we've got an hour for the engineering team to figure out how the Admari are tracking us. In the meanwhile, you and the XO are more than welcome to discuss the matter further in my day cabin."

Hayworth let out a barely disguised grumble. "Then why don't we get on it so that I can go help Hanson's people sort this problem."

David stood. "Captain Goldberg, you have the conn. Alert me if anything changes out here." He gestured toward the hatch at the back of the bridge. "After you, gentlemen. Oh, and, XO, get the SAR craft moving."

———

DURING THE BATTLE, some of David's knickknacks had fallen off the desk in his day cabin. He bent over to pick up an inert hand grenade bolted to a plaque that read "Complaint Department. Please take a number." A 1 hung off the grenade's firing pin. It had been a gift from a master chief he'd worked with a decade earlier, and it always brought a smile to his face. On the other hand, the meeting that was about to occur would not.

As David moved to sit behind his desk, Aibek and Hayworth strode in through the open hatch.

Aibek slammed it shut then turned. "General, I say this with all respect, as you are not only my commanding officer but also one of the finest warriors I've had the honor to serve with. And I hope after what I must say, you still count me as a friend, as I do you." He settled into one of the chairs in front of the desk.

David sat as well. "No ranks in here. You have my permission to speak freely, as you always do, XO. And it would be a sad day if sincere advice from those I serve with would color my friendships."

"Then hear me. We cannot supply arms to the Admari. Beyond it being against the law of the Terran Coalition and the Saurian Empire, the risk of their harming innocents with those weapons is too great. The moral hazard if they were to do so... comes back on us."

David glanced between Aibek and Hayworth. "I assume you agree, Doctor?"

"I am a loud proponent of noninterference, General. But I, too, share the moral concerns brought forward by Colonel Aibek. The reason I refuse, for the most part, to work on weapons systems is that I can't control what others do with my work, and governments have repeatedly proven they will do immoral things in conflicts."

"Then allow me to explain my position and reasoning. Since you both invoked morality." David sighed. "The Admari's cause is just. These nanites appear to be a force that malevolently destroys everything it comes in contact with. Ships... planets... people. From our brief encounter with them, we suspect they're responsible for destroying the precursor race. That means they have been menacing this galaxy for what? Hundreds of thousands of years? Helping the Admari defend themselves is not only the right thing to do. It's inherently immoral to turn away when we have the ability to change the facts on the ground in their favor."

"And what if they're able to repel the nanites then use our weapons to outfit a fleet of vessels to invade another world? Or two or three?" Hayworth asked as he stared into David's eyes. "Would that be a just cause?"

"Of course not," David snapped. He'd thought about that as well. "We have to consider that the Admari will keep coming until either they get the specs, or we kill *all* of them. Not to mention they've got pretty decent anti-ship weapons. We have the edge, but in extended combat, especially if more of them arrive, they could give even the *Lion of Judah* a run for her money. Can you imagine what their fleet would do to any species we've encountered so far?"

"I don't recall anyone having a problem with killing League sailors in large numbers," Hayworth interjected. "Why here? They've attacked us."

Aibek frowned. "General Cohen makes an excellent point. If we accept that the Admari's cause is worth fighting for, which I do unreservedly, slaughtering them is not right in the eyes of the Prophet either."

As David listened to the back and forth, he realized the situation had spiraled so entirely out of control that he was flying by the seat of his pants. *Dr. Hayworth is right. We don't know what they'll do. Except they've promised to take the specs or die trying.* David could barely get his head around the idea of a race deciding to commit collective suicide to obtain a weapon. *Maybe when you step back and think about it, after who knows how long in the void, they finally have a chance to change their circumstances. I'd jump at that too.*

"Your penchant for having to help everyone you come across is going to get you into a lot of trouble one of these days, General," Hayworth grumbled. "And I know you well enough that when those unintended consequences finally show up, you'll feel guilt over it for the rest of your life. But worse than that, many sentient beings will no longer exist."

"So what, then, exactly? We keep blowing their ships apart and eliminating their boarding parties until the Admari no longer exist?"

Hayworth licked his lips. "If the Zavlots had attacked the *Lion of Judah*, demanding fusion-missile technology to destroy the Zeivlots, and refused to quit attacking... would you hesitate in defending us against them?"

"To borrow your turn of phrase, Doctor, that's not an apples-to-apples comparison. If I had any belief that the Admari were going to take our technology and attack innocents, I'd never consider giving it to them."

Hayworth shrugged. "We have no way of knowing. Which is why the laws exist."

David closed his eyes, running different possibilities through his mind. "Maybe there's a way to help them and maintain the ability to police the Admari's use of our weapons."

"Such as?" Aibek hissed. "We cannot place observers on their ships, and any electronic means of monitoring could be removed."

"Oh, I realize that. But they have a fascinating piece of technology that allows them to track ships through wormholes. If we got our hands on that, we could follow their actions."

"I doubt there's some magic tech to solve the moral

Valor 209

conundrum, General," Hayworth replied. "The military always expects us scientists to save the day for them. But you have to accept that this is a dilemma and decide accordingly."

David raised an eyebrow. "Really? I see it more as a Hobson's choice. Yes, I supposedly have free rein to decide, but committing genocide isn't on my list of possible outcomes, Doctor."

"That's probably a bluff."

"I saw no evidence of the Admari using deception," Aibek hissed. "They showed bravery in the face of a superior opponent. That is something I must respect."

Hayworth grumbled, "I sense you have changed your opinion, Colonel."

"It is a matter of perspective, Doctor. One of the tenets of my faith is that the strong must defend the weak. The points brought forward by General Cohen illustrate we would be in error. I do not like the conclusion, but caught between bad outcomes, it is perhaps the least bad."

"I don't relish the thought of killing sentient beings either," Hayworth retorted. "But I dislike fueling wars with our technology even less."

"Gentlemen, I thank you both for your perspective. Ultimately, the call is mine. XO, prepare for Iskv-Selagan's arrival. We'll do it in the same conference room near the VIP shuttle bay. I'll have made a decision by the time he arrives."

Both of them stood.

"There will be unintended consequences if you give them neutron beams, General," Hayworth said. "Hear me on this, if you never listen to another word I say."

"There will be consequences no matter what we do, Doctor. I appreciate your input. Dismissed."

David leaned back as they exited through the hatch, and Aibek closed it behind him. Part of him felt as if Hayworth had hit the nail on the head. *One of these days, something terrible will happen as we grope around, trying to figure out how to work with alien species whose cultures we can barely understand.* Most situations they'd stumbled into so far seemed to be one big morality test after another. Thoughts of why HaShem had allowed the *Lion* to end up in Sextans B were never far from David's mind, and at the moment, they were especially prominent. *Adonai, please give me wisdom, and guide me to what path I should take.* He did not relish the next forty-five minutes.

23

——————

Time for round two, Calvin thought as the Marine shuttle wound its way through the void. He didn't like losing, and he hated having his Marines die a whole lot more, which meant the upcoming action was personal. Calvin checked his battle rifle one final time, ensuring it was ready for combat. *A shame we need them alive. I'd much prefer to kill these terrorist bastards.*

"Ready over there, Colonel?" Stokes asked. "Because you're mere mortals without those fancy power-armor rigs. You know that, right?" Of all the salvage and rescue experts on the *Salinan*, he was the cockiest.

Calvin smirked. "Senior Chief, I can kill a man with my bare hands in several dozen ways. So while I might be wearing a soft suit to help us reach our time targets, make no mistake. I'll put these mothers down, no matter what it takes."

Stokes chuckled. "You'd fit in with the deep-space rescue team, Colonel. That's a compliment, by the way."

"Yeah, yeah." Calvin made sure his rifle was firmly attached to its one-point sling then moved on to ensuring his sidearm was battle ready. It held lethal rounds, as he was unwilling to go into a fight without some weapon capable of killing the enemy.

As the Zeivlot mining vessels had nothing in the way of sensors beyond the absolute basics required for interplanetary travel, sneaking up on them would be relatively easy. Their cause was aided by TCMC assault craft having a stealth coating. Though it wasn't nearly as good as a CDF Stealth Raider or some of the more creative tier-one special operations toys, against a species three hundred years behind them technologically, their edge was more than enough.

The three shuttles steadily closed the distance, each containing two salvage ratings from the *Salinan* and eight Marines.

"Colonel, we've got an optimal vector. Do you wish to commit?" The intercom crackled with the pilot's voice.

"Hit it, Warrant."

"Wilco, sir."

While Calvin would've preferred to blow holes in the side of the ship, explosively decompress it, and capture the thing that way, the rescue tents provided an option for ingress that wouldn't kill everyone aboard.

It took a few more minutes for the assault craft to line up perfectly, matching the movements of the mining ship. The green light came on in the cargo area, and Stokes cycled the air out of the cabin after confirming the cockpit was sealed off.

Stokes opened the back ramp, giving those inside the shuttle an experience they rarely had: being in the inky blackness of the void without any protections other than their pressure suits. At a thumbs-up signal from him, the salvage ratings moved out of the shuttle and propelled

Valor   213

downward with thruster packs toward the hull of the miner.

Calvin blew out a breath as they made contact with the hull and locked on with magnetic boots. "Demood to home plate. We're passing checkpoint Bravo. How copy?"

"Good copy, Colonel," Susanna replied.

A tether ran from Stokes's suit to the shuttle bay and was meant to attach to the rescue enclosure. Calvin had practiced the evolution repeatedly and guided the heavy polymer construct forward and locked it onto the cable. He gave the cylindrical rescue chamber a heave out the back of the shuttle, and it glided down the tether as it left the artificial-gravity-equipped deck plates. The *Salinan*'s crewmen fitted it to the hull and gave Calvin the thumbs-up.

"Okay, ladies, time to earn our pay. One by one, just like we practiced." Calvin gestured to the tether.

The Marines didn't need encouragement. They hooked D-rings connected to their harnesses onto the tether and pushed off single file. Within three minutes, all of them, including Calvin, were safely within the rescue enclosure. As the last man in, Calvin detached the tether from its exterior latch point.

Stokes gestured to the flap that allowed access to the void. "Close that up. We've got a tight seal on the hull and are ready to cut through on your command, sir."

Heh, he's got balls. Ordering a full bird around. I really *like these guys.* "Place the det cord, but wait for my signal. We do this in unison with the two other teams." Calvin keyed up his commlink. "Home plate, passing checkpoint Charlie."

"Roger, sir. Team three has passed Charlie as well."

"Notify me the moment team two is in position."

"Yes, sir."

It felt like the height of absurdity—eight Marines and

two deep-space rescue technicians sitting atop an alien mining ship four and a half million light-years from Canaan. *Yet this is what we do. Find the bad guys, kick their doors in, and send them off to whatever passes for Zeivlot hell.* Calvin pursed his lips. He felt naked without power armor.

Stokes fiddled with a small metallic cylinder.

"Eh, what's that, senior chief?"

"Inert gas. In this case, nitrogen. It'll keep this chamber halfway pressurized and prevent us from having to worry about explosive depression when we blow a hole in the ship."

"Ah." Calvin shook his head. He wouldn't have thought of such a thing, but he didn't do zero-G operations often.

"Colonel, team two has passed Charlie," Susanna interjected.

Calvin grinned. "You heard the lady, gentlemen. Demood to all teams. Execute, execute, execute."

A split second later, the det cord melted an oversize hole in the outer hull. In an oxygen-rich environment, sparks would have showered, but thanks to the effect of the vacuum and the inert gas, there was nothing beyond a red glow where the alloy heated and melted.

Stokes pushed the cut-out piece of alloy into the ship, where it landed with a bone-jarring thud. Air rushed into the rescue enclosure, equalizing the pressure. The thick polymer flexed but didn't break. He pulled a canister off his belt and quickly sprayed a foamy substance around the edge of the opening before standing back.

Calvin vaguely remembered that the foam would cool superheated alloy as he dropped into the ship and landed in a crouched position. The interior was identical to the last mining vessel they'd boarded. He quickly moved out of the way, and the remaining seven Marines dropped through the opening. "Home plate, this is Demood. Passing checkpoint delta."

"Roger. All teams report same."

Unlike the last time, each team had an objective and would not stop or coordinate with the others beyond reporting their status. Calvin's target was what passed for a bridge. He led the way as they moved five meters down the passageway. The reinforced bulkhead hatch to the control center loomed at its terminus.

"Shaped charges—"

The door opened, and two Zeivlots came out with slug-throwers. Calvin raised his battle rifle and squeezed the trigger. A perfect three-round burst hit one of the hostiles in her center mass, and the woman dropped to the deck, her limbs askew as she twitched.

Behind him, two other Marines engaged the second hostile, and a split second later, that Zeivlot had collapsed as well, with half a dozen stun barbs protruding from his chest.

Calvin saw the aborted attack for what it was: a chance to capture the bridge without resorting to explosives or further delay. He charged forward, knowing his Marines would fall in without being told. The cockpit was cramped by Coalition standards. He put a stun-round burst into the nearest Zeivlot, but three more loomed beyond. Calvin made sure to get out of the opening so that the rest of his squad could gain entrance, but the move put him in range of a defender.

A humanoid with a large spanner wouldn't be something a Marine classified as a threat very often, but since he was without power armor and they were in close quarters, the individual had a slight advantage, which the Zeivlot parlayed into a larger one as he brought the wrench down on Calvin's battle rifle.

Calvin's fingers stung as the harsh reverberation of the strike caused him to lose his grip on the weapon, and it clattered to the floor. Stunned, he took a step back and felt for his thigh-holstered sidearm as the Zeivlot charged.

A twenty-year combat veteran's most significant advantage was muscle memory. Calvin didn't have to think in life-threatening situations. He simply reacted. He drew and aimed the sidearm then squeezed the trigger three times.

The charging Zeivlot, whose eyes flashed hate, collapsed to the deck as blood flowed freely from multiple chest wounds. Moments later, the light went out of his eyes, and he lay still.

Calvin swung around, gripping the pistol with purpose. The two other hostiles lay convulsing as Marines zip-tied their hands together. The control room was secure, and he let himself relax a hair before engaging his commlink. "Demood to home plate. Passing checkpoint echo."

———

Unlike the Ajax-class destroyers, the *Salinan* didn't have SCIFs, which were purpose-built to handle information transfer between multiple CDF combatant platforms. Instead, Susanna and the intelligence unit had been forced to improvise. They'd ended up taking over one of the crew mess areas, bringing in a bunch of C4ISR gear, and setting up makeshift workstations. It had gone over better than Susanna thought it would, as most of the enlisted personnel had to eat in the chief's mess for the day. *Though I don't know why they all think that's so wonderful.*

With high-speed comms links operating between the ship and the Marine assault shuttles, Susanna viewed the battle in real time through the helmet-mounted cameras each boarding team member wore. She'd switched to Corporal Ahmad's feed, as his element was tasked with storming the engineering section.

Initially, the Marines had successfully penetrated the engine spaces without alerting the terrorists manning the vessel, but they'd failed to get to the reactor without being spotted. A wild firefight had ensued and was still in progress.

"Home plate to Demood," Susanna said.

"Good copy, home plate."

"Sir, your team might be needed in the engineering section. Corporal Ahmad is pinned down by multiple tangos."

"How many hostiles are still in play?"

"At least eight, sir. With good cover."

"Acknowledged. Demood out."

Susanna blew out a breath. On the monitor dedicated to Calvin's feed, the image abruptly turned and raced down a corridor so quickly that staring at it almost made her nauseated. Another screen showed the locations of all CDF personnel as they moved about a schematic of the mining vessel, and four blue dots followed him.

Meanwhile, on Ahmad's display, one of the terrorists went down thanks to a three-round burst to the chest. "They're trying to get to the reactor! Push up! Push up!" His voice was disembodied, coming through the microphone on the helmet's exterior.

One Marine tossed a pulse grenade before several more charged from cover, and the grenade thrower was hit by several bullets from a Zeivlot slug-thrower. He flatlined almost immediately.

Above all else, watching them fight and die was the worst duty Susanna had ever had. She couldn't affect the situation except by routing in reinforcements. And that didn't seem like it was enough. She flashed back to fighting with Mata back on Freiderwelt and remembered shooting a League soldier with a pistol, thinking she'd killed him, only to find out a few moments later the bullets were stun rounds.

The Zeivlot terrorists gave as good as they got, with the playing field somewhat more level, thanks to the Marines' lack of power armor—at least until Calvin's fire team blew through a side hatch and flanked most of them.

Susanna watched as stun rounds slammed into the Zeivlots, knocking several hostiles to the ground. Pulse grenades filled the space with sharp explosions of bright-white light, and when the screens cleared, the Marines had control of the engineering area. She turned away as Calvin shot one of the last terrorists as he attempted to manipulate the reactor control.

"Team two is passing checkpoint echo," Ahmad said over the commlink. His voice carried the unmistakable sound of relief.

And just like that, it was over. With every hostile on the ship stunned or dead, the Marines took control of the vessel, and the salvage personnel from the *Salinan* began inspecting the reactor. Susanna felt shocked that observing combat—and death along with it—no longer affected her as it once had. *What does the colonel say? Another day at the office.* Regardless of anything else, she was sure becoming numb to violence wasn't a good thing.

———

WILSON HAD SPENT the last two hours perched in the CO's chair on the *Salinan*'s bridge, listening intently through an

Valor 219

open commlink as Susanna relayed the Marines' progress. And much like everyone else, he offered a silent thanks to God as the combat concluded without the mining vessel blowing apart.

"Sir, Colonel Demood is asking that we proceed with hull patching and come alongside to receive prisoners," the communications officer said.

Khattri offered a grin. "The Marines are getting a little too used to ordering us around."

"Maybe you should demonstrate to the colonel sometime that your kirpan isn't just for show."

"Well, I am a student of several martial arts techniques."

Wilson snickered. "I hear Demood prefers pugil sticks."

Khattri made a face. "Swinging around giant swabs isn't my thing."

"Touché." Wilson barely avoided cracking up. "Okay, let's get on with it. Navigation, all ahead one-third, and bring us within docking range of Master One."

Twenty minutes later, the *Salinan* glided alongside the mining vessel and eased over a few meters at a time toward docking tube range. The navigator also expertly placed them so that the long robotic arms used for positioning and spot-welding sheets of alloy for hull patches could reach two out of three holes.

The salvage team had already jettisoned the rescue enclosures while applying a temporary polymer-based sealant to the interior. That left the *Salinan* free to weld two large panels of alloy over the gaps in the ship's structure. They repeated the procedure on the third breach before extending a rescue tube from the *Salinan* to an exterior airlock.

"Comms, get me Colonel Demood on a point-to-point link."

"Aye, aye, sir."

Calvin's voice crackled through the speaker in Wilson's chair a few minutes later. "Your boys did real good, Major. Good show. Hell, I'm surprised we're still alive."

"Yeah, that was touch-and-go for a few, wasn't it?"

"The best kind of op, Major."

"Well, what more can the Marine ferry service do for you today?"

"That little ship of yours can tow stuff, right?" Calvin replied with a chuckle.

Wilson's face heated. He hated having the *Salinan* called *little* or *tiny*. "Oh, it can."

"Then let's do that. Drag us back to Zeivlot orbit, because I don't trust anything on this thing not to explode if we look at it wrong."

"We could use an umbilical to provide power, if you'd like, and have an engineering team crawl over the reactor."

"Perfect. Once we get the detainees off, have your people come aboard, and I'll leave them to their thing. It's important we dump as many of their memory cores as possible." The speaker crackled several times with bursts of static.

"Roger that, sir." Wilson pursed his lips. "Anything else?"

"That'll do it. Well, except that I will be making sure a case of the good stuff makes its way to Senior Chief Stokes. That was a crazy stunt he came up with, and it worked perfectly."

Wilson grinned. "I'm *quite* sure the senior chief will appreciate it, sir. *Salinan* out."

The commlink cut off with a click.

"Enough excitement for one day, I think," Khattri said.

"Yeah. Won't argue with that one." Wilson let his head fall back to the chair. *I remember the days when all I had to do was haul disabled ships from point A to point B. Wouldn't mind going back to them either*. But as soon as he processed the thought, he knew he wasn't being honest with himself. He enjoyed being in the thick of the action. *We're making a difference, which is much more rewarding than moving a disabled ship back to space dock.*

24

DAVID HAD DECIDED before Iskv-Selagan arrived that it would only be them and a single master-at-arms in the conference room. *All the better for me to take the measure of the man as much as I can.* Thinking of the adage "Better safe than sorry," he'd withdrawn a compact sidearm and strapped it to his ankle. *Just in case I'm wrong.*

As David waited, he studied some of the shadow boxes on the walls. Each was a tribute to a battle the *Lion* had fought, from the Second Battle of Canaan to the capture of Unity Station to the shipyard campaign in the Orion arm and finally to the climactic Third Battle of Canaan. Each was remembered as a triumph by the CDF.

Moreover, they're recognized as my *victories.* David celebrated each one, even those that had brought him great personal pain. He thought back to Sheila and her death. More than anything, he'd hoped there would be a break from war after the defeat of the League. *Since we arrived in this galaxy, however, it's been one conflict after another. But who am I to feel sorry for myself? The species who live here have to endure this hellscape. Perhaps we can make it better.*

Valor

David's repose was ended by the hatch swinging open. In walked Iskv-Selagan, who wore an alloy exoskeleton over his clothing. "I greet you, General," he said as he clasped his hands to his arms in a crisscross style and bowed.

"Welcome aboard the *Lion of Judah* once more." David stood and extended his arm. The two shook hands before he gestured to the table. "I thought we might get more done with only us in attendance."

Iskv-Selagan pointed at the master-at-arms who had entered with him. "And this individual is to protect you in case I dishonor my word?"

"Yes."

"Prudent. I would take the same precaution." Iskv-Selagan slowly lowered himself into one of the chairs.

"I'll start by expressing my regret for the loss of life among your people." David bit his lip. "While we took what steps were necessary to defend ourselves, humans—and Jews in particular—believe all life is sacred."

"We, too, place a high value on sentient life. Did any of your people perish?"

"The last casualty count I saw said we had six confirmed dead and a few dozen wounded."

"Far less than us." Iskv-Selagan said somberly.

"I hope our joint rescue teams are able to pull many of your citizens from the disabled vessels."

"Even if they are, I despair over where we will house or feed them. Each ship is well calibrated after eons in the void, General. We must maintain a balance at all costs, or the whole will be lost."

"Why not build more ships?"

"Because the Admari no longer have that capability. You do not understand, General Cohen. While I have only seen a small portion of your vessel, I know it is new. Humans do not yet understand the price the void extracts for living in it. You don't know the pain of your elders and infirm being forced to end their existence before their time so that the whole may continue."

David blinked slowly. "You mean to tell me you execute your old and sick?"

"I can see in your eyes you believe us to be monsters. Yet it is not that simple, because there are so few resources that if we tried to sustain those who cannot contribute, all would perish."

"Yes, Iskv-Selagan. What you said goes against every fiber of my being, ethics, and religion."

"It is easy to make such pronouncements when your stomach is full, there is power to spare, and every system works as intended."

Would we revert to extreme measures, killing our wounded and the elderly just to survive? Is that worth the price? David's initial reaction was it would be better to die than give in to such horrible sins. *But what would we do if faced with the harsh reality?* No answer mattered except the one provided if the *Lion* ever reached that point.

"I'll concede you have a point, Iskv-Selagan. Yet we are responsible for anything your species does with the technology given to it. Frankly, *I* am responsible."

Iskv-Selagan placed his small, thin hands on the table. "How? It is our choice what we do with the weapon once we have it."

"That doesn't absolve us. If you, say, invade a populated world and kill its inhabitants, that falls on *me*."

"I have difficulty understanding why you would agree to discuss giving us the weapon if you cannot trust us."

David shrugged. "Because the outcome of annihilating your species is abhorrent." He sucked in a breath. "We must

Valor

find a way for you to give reasonable assurances that you won't abuse the technology."

"What possible method could be used for this?"

"In exchange for specifications to neutron beams, we want your FTL tracking technology. Assuming it's not a QET planted during the last visit." David smiled thinly.

"A QET?"

"Quantum entanglement tracker."

Iskv-Selagan blinked. "Our sensors pinpoint the exit point of an artificial wormhole, and any subspace wake."

David leaned back. *Well, that would surely be an improvement to our capabilities.* "If you give us that, we can find you if you abuse the neutron beams. Hear me Iskv-Selagan, when I say Terran Coalition technology will *not* be used to commit aggression against innocents."

"Surviving in the void is harsh, General. There are acts my people have undertaken for which we are not proud, but we never leave another stranded nor take so much from them that they cannot survive."

"You pirate others, then?"

"Pirate?"

"Steal from them."

"On occasion, we have taken from those with much." Iskv-Selagan shifted. "It is necessary. The instant-transfer device makes this easy."

"There are planets and solar systems with FTL capabilities. We have encountered one. You could trade with them."

"Our kind is not welcomed, General. We are seen as pests, or we were when previously attempting contact with others. It has been many generations since that was attempted."

"Then let's try to change that after some confidence-building steps."

Iskv-Selagan stared, his expression inscrutable. "You are a strange species, General Cohen. We did attack you."

"Yes, and we defended ourselves. But I'm not willing to wipe the Admari from the galaxy. I'm not God, and I don't get to play God."

"God?"

"Kind of a catch-all term humans use for the higher being we believe created the universe and whom we worship."

"Ah. Religious belief."

"Yes."

"We abandoned such trivialities eons ago," Iskv-Selagan replied. "Our belief is solely in ourselves and our own abilities. Even if such a being did exist, it would not be worthy of respect or worship."

David frowned. "It is difficult for me to wrap my mind around that concept."

"If God, as you put it, existed, then this supreme being allowed my people to be nearly eradicated. Why would we even acknowledge such a deity after what has been done to us? When we lived on the surface of other worlds, there were those who did believe. Perhaps I would've then. But not now. Your people do not understand the horrific conditions in which we live."

I bet I could make some educated guesses. David knew just how low humans could go from his decades of military service. *Take away our creature comforts and put us in highly stressful situations in which others are trying to kill us... and some portion of even the best humanity has to offer will turn into feral animals.*

"I'm not here to judge you, Iskv-Selagan. But hear me when I say there is a better way, and at some point in the future, we can get your people properly fed and find ways to

Valor 227

either build new vessels or repair the ones you have. For now, let's put an end to killing one another."

"The neutron-beam plans and a working prototype in exchange for our wormhole-tracking sensor technology?"

David inclined his head. "Those are my terms."

"I wish, perhaps, we had taken a different tack with you and the other humans the first time."

"While I will never apologize for defending my ship and crew, Iskv-Selagan, I, too, wish we could've done this first. Will your people agree to this?"

"Yes. It is a fair bargain. What of yours?"

"In my capacity as the commanding officer of this fleet, I speak for all humans in Sextans B."

Iskv-Selagan blinked. "I see. No others have a say?"

"The military isn't a democracy. Our government back home is elected by our population, and the Coalition Defense Force takes its orders directly from our civilian leader. But out here, no, the only thing that works is maintaining the chain of command."

"Then I see no impediments to our agreement, General."

"Very well. Shall we get to it?" David stood.

Iskv-Selagan gingerly pushed himself up. "I will return to my ship and take the vote." As he turned toward the hatch, Iskv-Selagan paused. "General, a question. You indicated your people believe in a deity. Do you?"

David nodded and touched the Israeli flag on the left shoulder of his uniform. "Yes. I'm a practicing Orthodox Jew."

"But you mentioned that the *Lion of Judah* was tossed here from millions of light-years away. If this is true, how can you still believe in an entity that appears indifferent to the suffering of your crew?"

"Well, Iskv-Selagan, I dispute that HaShem shows indifference by allowing things such as our trip from the Milky Way galaxy to occur. But beyond that, none of this is mine." David gestured around the room. "It's God's. I and everyone in the universe are mere stewards of what He's given us. There is a story from the Tanakh of a man named Job. He worshiped God with all his heart, and he had everything. A large family, riches, lands. And one day, God allowed the adversary to take it all away. His children were killed, his lands destroyed, his wealth stolen."

"If a being would allow such calamity to fall on a person who followed its teachings, why should anyone worship it?"

"Because as Job put it, I came out of my mother's womb with nothing. Everything I've been entrusted with comes from HaShem. The Lord has given, and He has taken away. No matter what he decides, blessed be the name of the Lord."

Iskv-Selagan stared at him for several seconds. "I do not understand, General Cohen. But I do not need to. On behalf of my people, I wish you peace, and may you avoid the pestilence."

"Godspeed." He extended his hand and shook with the alien, being careful not to squeeze too hard.

Iskv-Selagan inclined his head before leaving through the hatch.

David spent a few minutes alone after the Admari leader left. When they'd first arrived in Sextans B, he'd felt significant doubt about why God would do such a thing to them. Over time, David had made peace with it as much as possible. But having the ever-present question tossed into his face brought those lingering thoughts to the surface. *I studied the Book of Job for years, and I always noted that HaShem didn't directly address Job's questions. Maybe that's the point, though. In the end, our minds are so much smaller. Still, I want to understand. It would make this easier. Especially the small matter of Hebrew writing on the obelisk on Zeivlot. That, I still don't understand.*

———

LESS THAN AN HOUR LATER, the Admari had officially notified David of their acceptance of his offer. As he sat at the head of the deck-one conference room table with Aibek, Hanson, Merriweather, Ruth, Amir, Dr. Tural, Major Almeida, Master Chief Tinetariro, and Hayworth, the air was thick with tension, like many of their meetings lately.

Most of them probably disagreed with his decisions, but the uniformed officers would never publicly let that slip. *The job is so much harder without civilian leadership to fall back on. I keep questioning how far I can push my crew, which isn't quite how I thought about things back in the Milky Way.* He'd toyed with having an advisory council, but since Hayworth was the only human civilian aboard, there weren't enough to make it work.

"How will the exchange occur?" Aibek hissed.

"They're sending a shuttle over with a tech team to pick up a neutron beam. I told them we'd 3-D print a small-enough version to function on their ships," David replied.

"And the sensor module will come with them?" Hanson asked.

"Yes."

"Plenty of opportunity for them to screw us." Hayworth crossed his arms. "This entire thing stinks."

"Is that your scientific opinion, Doctor?" Ruth asked with a smirk.

"Don't mock me, young lady. I've simply got the... What

do you military types call it? Oh yes, the *balls* to say what everyone else is thinking."

"If somebody wants to give me a better option, I'm all ears. For instance, a way to jam the Admari sensors."

Hayworth let out a sigh. "Which is the only reason I can find tacit moral justification for this course of action, General." He shook his head. "I apologize. I lack religion, as you all know. But noninterference is sacred to me. The fact that we keep shredding it, even in the name of doing good... It bothers me to my core. And I believe those we supposedly help will pay the price in the end."

"What are we going to do with the Admari prisoners?" Tinetariro interjected. "We've got almost sixty of them in the brig, which we're not really designed for long term."

"I plan to return them as soon as we're sure the sensor tech works."

Merriweather cleared her throat. "And we're going to trust this device isn't a Trojan horse?"

"Trust but verify, Major," David replied with a thin smile. "Test it in a firewalled computer first, and we'll probably install the thing on the oldest Ajax-class destroyer in our fleet then replicate the technology here."

"I will oversee that effort," Hayworth rumbled. "No offense, but I have more experience than any enlisted engineer."

"None taken, and we'd be grateful for the help, Doctor."

Hayworth snorted.

At the end of the table, Almeida leaned forward to make eye contact with David. "As far as we can tell, the teleportation technology is ship based. Nothing in the Admari exoskeletons accounts for the ability."

"That tracks with my examinations of them," Dr. Tural added. "They show reduced skeletal structure and general ill health. Lack of food and long-term oxygen deprivation. These people are barely surviving. Without the exoskeletons, at least some of them couldn't walk on the *Lion of Judah*."

David raised an eyebrow. "Extended periods without artificial gravity?"

"Certainly seems to be indicated."

"I can't imagine trying to live on starships as a void-dwelling species. Space is where we work, not where we *live*."

"Tell the Admari that," Almeida replied. "If they're in the sharing mood, the ability to appear out of thin air on an enemy warship could come in handy."

Hayworth grunted, "Do you know why that sort of technology doesn't exist in the Terran Coalition, Major?"

"I kick doors in, Doctor." Almeida grinned. "And leave the white-coat stuff to the eggheads."

"Unless this species has access to some new understanding of quantum mechanics, it's matter replication, not transfer."

David tilted his head. He had a passing understanding of the concepts Hayworth had mentioned. The CDF had tight regulations on technology deemed dangerous to humanity, such as true artificial intelligence or self-replicating machines. "Meaning that it would make a copy and destroy the original?"

"Precisely. Even as a dyed-in-the-wool atheist, I find such a thing disturbing."

"It would still be useful to move material. Imagine teleporting a fusion warhead inside a League ship," Ruth said.

"We'll pass on that." David set his jaw.

"But—"

"Captain, remember Pandora and her box. We're not

going there. That's partially a religious judgment but also a belief that some technology isn't worth the moral cost. If we were to obtain the teleportation tech and use it as a weapons-delivery system or to move cargo, you can bet every credit that everyone in this room has—"

"It would eventually be used by spies then elite soldiers and finally all of us," Hayworth finished. "And now you understand why I don't create weapons, General."

David nodded. "On this, we agree, Doctor. Such a device is an abomination." He shuddered. *Do beings who go through with it still have a soul? I don't want to find out.*

An uncomfortable silence followed as each seemed to process the implications.

"Moving on," David said finally. "Once we're done with the exchange here, I want to get back to our primary objective: getting past the nanites. The precursor civilization is the key to getting home. I refuse to give up on doing so." *Yet at every step of the way, it seems like there's a detour.* He detested the feeling.

"General, the only safe way to proceed is using stealth fighters to perform recon," Amir said. "We both know this."

"And I suppose you still plan to fly the mission yourself?"

Amir nodded. "Yes, sir."

David felt a horrible pang of regret, knowing that he was sending one of his oldest friends into a situation where, if the swarm discovered them, he and any other pilot with him would perish. *Yet this is what we do. Every day with the League. So why is it so much worse now to send them into harm's way?* "Do you have a flight plan?"

"Two of our SFS-4 Ghost stealth fighters. Parabolic course through the system, with an eye to being within range of Lagrange points in case of an emergency jump."

Valor

"Except the Lawrence drive generator on a Ghost is too weak to safely jump anywhere but the edge of the system," Ruth interjected.

"No, but it would still be a chance." Amir pursed his lips. "I prefer slight odds over none. That is less tempting of Allah."

Ruth shook her head. "I don't want to lose another friend out here. You might be a pilot, but you're good people," she said with a smile.

Amir's eyes twinkled. "I'll take the compliment, Captain. Do not worry—I have no intention of dying. We must see what's on the planet. This is the best way. The only way. I leave the rest in the hands of God."

David knew his old friend was right, as he usually was in the proper use of the *Lion*'s fighter wing. *Doesn't mean I have to like it.* "Mission plan ready to go?"

"Yes, sir."

"We'll jump into deep space, close enough for it to be a one-hop trip for the Ghosts. Say, tomorrow morning?"

Amir nodded. "We'll be ready, *inshallah*."

"Good. Then I've got nothing else except... Dr. Tural, do you have an update on our casualties?"

The doctor licked his lips. "Most of the engineering personnel are already back on duty. The Admari seemed to prefer nonlethal energy weapons. A number are still in critical condition, and we have six confirmed fatalities."

David sucked in a breath. *Six more young men and women won't be going home. On my watch.* He resolved to write letters to their families, though HaShem only knew when they would be delivered.

"And among the crew compliment of our escorts?"

"None."

"I'll tour sick bay later today, once our after-action reports are completed. Thank you for your efforts, Doctor."

"I am but a humble servant. It is a blessing that Allah uses my hands to heal."

David nodded before glancing around the conference room. "Any saved rounds, people?"

Silence was the only reply.

"Then let's get back at it. Dismissed."

25

IN SOME WAYS, Amir felt as if he was preparing for death. He'd visited the mosque aboard the *Lion of Judah*, prayed before Allah, and tried to cleanse his soul as best he could. As he sat strapped into the SFS-4 Ghost fighter, there was a strange emotional cross. Part of him relished the chance to test his skills against the most dangerous opponent he'd ever faced. On the flip side, perhaps Amir had gone insane. He wasn't sure.

Based on a design that dated back to the outbreak of the League of Sol–Terran Coalition war, the Ghost had an odd shape compared to most space superiority fighters. Its body was long but narrow. It had no hardpoints for external munitions, only a small number of anti-fighter missiles housed in internal weapons bays, and a long-range neutron cannon was mounted under the nose.

While the stealth craft had strong shields for its size, the hull was paper thin. But it had a singular advantage in being the only Terran Coalition fighter-sized vessel capable of Lawrence drive jumps. A unique, highly classified exterior coating coupled with sharp edges and a black paint job rendered the Ghost nearly invisible to League sensors.

But will it hold up against the nanites?

Amir went through his preflight check and tried to remember how to fly the craft. It was a far cry from the SF-106 Phantoms he was used to. The cockpit was roomier than anything he'd been in besides a cargo shuttle.

"How's it going over there, sir? Remember what the buttons do yet?" Captain Clare O'Sullivan, commander of the Black Bat recon squadron, chuckled. She hailed from Eire and had been assigned to the *Lion* a few weeks before their ill-fated wormhole transit to the Sextans B galaxy.

Amir laughed. "O'Sullivan, I was born from my mother's womb able to fly."

"High speed, low drag, sir?"

"That's what the Americans say, anyway."

"Funny. I thought I'd finally made it when I got posted here."

"Then we were tossed into the great unknown." Amir clicked through the last check. His Ghost was ready to paw the vacuum.

O'Sullivan snorted. "We're still in one piece, at least until we hit these nanites. The briefing on those things is positively terrifying."

"I... How does my friend Demood put it? Got myself right with God before this mission."

"Me, too, sir. But that's before every mission in a Ghost. We're not made to blow things up like your Phantoms or the big, ugly, fat fu—apologies, sir. I'm aware of your rules on cursing."

"Nothing to apologize for, Captain. Are you ready to fly?" Amir avoided profanity like the plague, something he had in common with David.

"Yes, sir. Green across the board."

"Then I will obtain final clearance." Amir toggled his commlink to the command channel. "This is Black Bat One requesting permission for launch."

The voice of the air boss echoed. "Approved, Black Bat One. Good hunting, and Godspeed."

"Understood and acknowledged. Godspeed to you as well. Amir out." He gripped the throttle with one hand and the flight stick with the other. "O'Sullivan, we have a go. Full power now."

The Ghost accelerated rapidly, zipping down the launch tube and into the vacuum of open space. One of the *Lion*'s escorts, the CSV *John Manners*, loomed in front of Amir's cockpit. He rotated his craft to the left and jammed the throttle to maximum. "Status, O'Sullivan?"

"Clean launch, sir. Ready to jump on your command."

Amir pulled up the preloaded FTL coordinates on his navcomp. "Engage Lawrence drive."

With the use of unique energy capacitors integrated into the Ghost's systems, a small wormhole opened in front of each fighter. Once the maws were fully formed, both craft roared through.

The inside of the wormhole was a multicolored kaleidoscope that only lasted a few seconds but so disoriented Amir that he had to repeatedly open and close his eyes upon emergence. His head spun.

"Black Bat Two to Black Bat One. You okay over there, sir?"

"The transit was rough." He continued to feel as if the cockpit were falling.

"Close your eyes for five seconds, sir. I forgot to tell you to keep them closed while traversing the wormhole. Something about it messes with most pilots' minds."

Amir did as she suggested, and when he was done, the feeling retreated, though a wave of nausea was still working its way through him. "Thank you, Captain." Sensors had snapped on, and Amir confirmed they were in the proper place. "No sign of the nanites or hostile vessels observed earlier."

"Same here, sir. Clean scope."

"Perhaps the enemy has retreated to the planet the distress signal is coming from."

"Do you want to stick with the parabolic course, sir?"

Amir nodded, even though she couldn't see him. "Yes. I'll overlay it." He toggled the navcomp to share his projected path and adjusted speed to sixty percent output. Reduced thrust would reduce their sensor signature.

"ETA is a little over twenty hours at this speed, sir."

Thank Allah these craft have an integrated waste relief system. For food, they had a few ration packs and water. In truth, fatigue would be the biggest enemy, other than the nanite swarm. "Maintain course and speed for now, Captain. I may try for more, depending on how far we get in without making contact."

"Yes, sir. Nothing more to do except sit back and enjoy the in-flight movie."

Amir snickered. He'd heard O'Sullivan was a bit of a smart aleck but enjoyed the banter. "Make sure it's a good one. Preferably something we haven't seen before."

"Dunno about you, sir, but I've watched almost everything worth viewing in our entertainment library twice. Not having GALNET access sucks."

"It's the small things in life," Amir replied.

"That, it is, sir."

He went quiet, thinking about the situation they were in. His family was never far from his mind, even in the face of death. Staying silent and stealthy went against every fiber of Amir's being. He announced himself on the battlefield by putting anti-fighter missiles into every League vessel he could and dogfighting intensely to the point that he lost situational awareness of the larger battle. He'd had to work on that as a leader, to maintain overall control of the battle-space with nearly two hundred combat spacecraft under his command.

Amir thought about engaging in a conversation about O'Sullivan's life aboard the ship and who she'd left behind, but the peacefulness of the void was comforting. A distant nebula painted the heavens, its blue and orange coloring a background against which stars were born. Everywhere he looked, bright orbs filled the sky, each one holding the possibility of a new race or another example of Allah's handiwork.

For the next ten hours, the Ghosts headed farther and farther in system. The glare from the blue giant was so intense that Amir practically turned his cockpit canopy opaque to keep from burning his eyes. The third planet was farther out from the star than the most distant worlds in a main-sequence system, but that put it in a zone where solar radiation wouldn't destroy the atmosphere or poison the ground. *Though it is exceedingly rare to find life in such a place.* The closer they got, the more apprehension built in Amir's soul. *We should've seen the nanites by now. They challenged the Lion of Judah far sooner.*

"Black Bat Two to Black Bat One."

Amir checked to ensure the transmission was a tight beam, not a general commlink, as his heart skipped a beat. He also double-checked his outgoing protocol before replying, "Go ahead, O'Sullivan."

"We're close enough to kick off a detailed scan."

"And attract the attention of anything in this system."

O'Sullivan's chuckles echoed through his headset. "Whenever we light it off, sir, the effect will be the same. I don't know about you, but if we're going to get wiped off the face of the universe, I'd rather get it over with before my legs cramp further."

Amir couldn't help laughing. The release of humor was nice, though it didn't change their situation. "I suppose you have a point, Captain." *She is right. This will either get us the information we need or seal our fates.*

"So... ready?"

"Why not? You may begin the scan when ready."

Allah, protect us in whichever way you choose.

Minutes passed, and sensor data flowed back to O'Sullivan's craft before disseminating to Amir through the tactical link. The results weren't what he expected. It appeared a society of some sort had existed on the third world at some point, but even while the surface was scoured of all life, what was left showed little sign of advanced technology. *Though I suppose it could've been lost to the eons of time.*

"You seeing this, sir?"

"Indeed, I am, O'Sullivan."

"No sign of the nanites, either."

Amir reconfigured his sensors to search specifically for the source of the distress signal. As far as he could tell, it was on the northern continent of the third planet, next to a large body of water. *No life signs, no metallic objects, no structures.* "Do you show anything different on your sensors? I feel as if we were led into a trap."

"Given the lack of anything on this world, specifically around where that signal emanates, I have to concur, sir."

"It is time to turn around."

A pregnant pause followed. "Yes, sir."

Valor

Amir banked his fighter around and executed a one-hundred-eighty-degree turn. "Return to my wing position, and we'll head back to the system's edge."

The flight back felt even longer as they waited for death to fall on them at any moment. Yet it never came. For that, Amir was thankful and cherished another day in the universe in which they might yet find a way home.

———

THE SWARM TOOK final measurements of the distance between it and the last piece of the creators' puzzle. Situated on a garden world, in a distant solar system, the object would allow them to finally regain complete efficiency. Their course altered as space and time bent around the field, allowing the mass to maintain FTL speeds.

Needing raw materials to complete the journey, the swarm had located a suitable world that was within a few light-years, reachable within a couple of weeks, and contained everything needed for the interstellar journey. The Jinvaas scan results had proven invaluable in increasing their warp capabilities.

All that remained was the execution of the plan. The hive mind was never wrong, and it judged there was no possibility of defeat.

26

WITH A MILLION THOUGHTS running through David's head, dinner in his officers' mess was a small solace. While the space could be used by any senior-grade officer, by tradition, only the commanding officer and department heads entered without permission. At that time of night, he was the only person there, aside from a mess steward and the unseen chef who toiled away in the kitchen.

The view of the void through the large windows was beautiful. Numerous stars were visible, as were nebula. Some were brighter than others, but all of them were a reminder to David of the creative power of HaShem.

"May I join you?"

David glanced behind him to see Bo'hai standing there, still in her white lab coat. "Uh, sure. I was having a late dinner."

She slid into a chair across from him. "You still appear troubled."

"It's been a rough twenty-four hours."

The mess steward scurried over. "Sir, I didn't realize you would be joining us tonight."

David waved a hand. "I wasn't sure, either, but don't make a fuss. I'll have whatever's leftover from the evening meal."

Bo'hai offered a smile. "And I, the same."

"Of course."

As the steward departed, Bo'hai stared into David's eyes. "What's bothering you?"

David chuckled. "Isn't it obvious? The ship is assaulted by nanites then by a race that's been searching for a weapon to defeat those same nanites... and in the end, I give them some of our premier weapons technology and pray they don't do awful things with it."

"And that troubles you?"

"Of course it does. I don't like playing God. I exist within a set of rules and regulations. First within my faith then within those of the CDF." David gestured. "Except in Sextans B, there are few rules—because I am the final arbiter of right and wrong for this fleet."

"Are you not making the best decisions you can?"

David licked his lips. "Based on available information, well, I think I am. But there's a truth about humans that I suspect extends to most if not all sentient races. We judge ourselves based on the intent of our actions. We judge others on the *outcome* of their actions. There are so many ways that all of this could blow up in our collective faces that I can't count them."

Bo'hai put her hand on his. "The Maker works through you. Of this, I am certain."

"I'll take your word for it." *Because right now, I feel far from HaShem.*

"Could you have made a different decision with the Admari?"

David shook his head. "I could've killed them all. That wasn't an option."

"Why?"

He locked eyes with her. "Because it would've been *wrong*. I just... knew we couldn't do it. *I* couldn't do it."

"But you're not at peace with the decision."

"There wasn't a 'good' choice. Only shades of worse." David chuckled. "Those sorts of calls are the worst because, above all else, I prefer black-and-white outcomes where there is a clear right and moral way to proceed."

"Hmm. So do all of us." She smiled. "But that is not often the way of life."

"It was when I was fighting the League... at least, most of the time."

Bo'hai steepled her fingers. "You are being forced to grow as a person, then? And do uncomfortable things?"

A unique way of looking at it. "I suppose you could say that."

"Then perhaps, somewhere underneath the hardship, there is a truth the Maker wants you to learn."

"If HaShem is trying to give me an object lesson, He needs to do it differently without endangering my crew," David replied dryly.

"I doubt we get any choice in the matter."

The steward reappeared, carrying a tray with two plates of piping-hot food and water glasses. "Is there anything else I can get for you?"

David shook his head. "I'm good. Thank you, Private."

"I have everything I need," Bo'hai replied with a dazzling smile.

As the steward strode off, David bowed his head and offered a prayer in Hebrew to bless the food. Then he opened his eyes to take in the meal. It consisted of some type of meat charred and coated in seasonings, mashed potatoes, and some Zeivlot root vegetables. *I'd give my right arm for a steak dinner.* He shoveled a forkful of potatoes into his mouth and reminded himself they were lucky to be eating anything other than C-rats.

"I see you've developed a taste for some of our food," Bo'hai said as she took a bite.

"Somebody figured out a spice rub that masked some of the meat's unpleasant... to us, anyway... flavors." David chuckled. "Be assured we're grateful to have gotten fresh provisions from your government."

"I've been trying your different forms of combat rations. The, ah... meals ready to eat?"

David's eyes widened. "They're awful. And primarily for combat situations when no other food is available."

"Oh, I know. But I like exploring the different facets of humanity. Besides, some of them taste good. That pork rib meal, for instance."

"I wouldn't know." David smiled. "Pork is not on my list of approved foods."

"It isn't considered kosher?"

David shook his head. "No. Admittedly, there isn't a kosher kitchen on the *Lion*, nor *mashgiach*, so nothing I eat on board is kosher, unless it's specially prepared and sealed meals. Those run out a few weeks into deployment, usually. But even though I may break the dietary laws to avoid starving, I still keep as many as possible. And there's no such thing as kosher pork, period."

"You believe that the Maker honors your commitment to His law, I assume?"

"Yes." David chewed his food and swallowed. "It's a test of our faith."

"It seems as if both of us are enduring various tests."

Bo'hai shuddered. "These nanites, as Dr. Hayworth refers to them, seem like the embodiment of evil. I hope he is able to use the new sensor module to track them."

"That research is his primary focus now," David replied. "How goes your work?"

"Long, with little progress. Trying to determine how a dead language works is... challenging. But I welcome it. If nothing else, the work makes time go by faster." She set her glass down. "What of you?"

"One day at a time. Once the doctor can integrate the FTL sensor module, I'll probably order us back to Zeivlot for resupply, then we'll take another run at the precursor capital system. Perhaps the zupan will allow for a larger expedition. Five hundred researchers working the problem will make more progress than fifty. It's also possible we could further investigate the obelisk on Zeivlot if things there have calmed down." David shrugged. "Eventually, a discovery will be made. Or enough time will pass that it will make sense to redefine our mission."

Bo'hai blinked. "You would give up on getting home?"

"That's unlikely, but at some point, if it becomes clear there is no easy path to such an outcome, since I'm the commanding officer of this fleet, it will be incumbent upon me to ensure the safety and well-being of my officers and crewmen. Maybe that looks like sticking to the Zeivlot and Zavlot system and helping your people overcome their differences. Or perhaps it would be founding our own colony somewhere and ensuring our species survives in Sextans B." The implications of either were overwhelming, but saying them aloud helped David process where he was mentally.

"Regardless of your decision, I wish to stay with the *Lion of Judah*."

David tilted his head. "This might come across as indelicate, and I apologize if so, but are you sure you'd want to remain among a crew of humans? Surely you have plans to get married and maybe have children. I understood those things were important to you from our previous discussions."

"They are." Bo'hai set her fork down. "But perhaps they will unexpectedly happen for me. After all, our two species are quite similar, at least visually."

David almost choked on the piece of charred meat he was chewing. He'd harbored feelings for her that went beyond simple friendship for some time, but it was impossible to act on them. "Excuse me. That almost went down the wrong pipe." He took a sip of water and got his wits about him.

"Would you consider visiting one of our religious services? Some of us like to meet once a week, and Pastor Estrada graciously lets us use her chapel."

"I'd be honored. Are there any specific rules I need to abide by? Covering my head, special garments, et cetera?

She shook her head. "No. Only come as you are. We lack a minister, so some of us gather to pray, read from the great book, and discuss our faith."

"Then let me know when." He took another bite, chewed, and swallowed. "Tomorrow will be another day. We will press on, no matter what."

"Yes." Bo'hai smiled.

The meal continued, and for a moment, David allowed himself to forget about everything else and focus on Bo'hai's company. *It's a shame I can't act any further on my feelings. But that is part of being in command. Perhaps someday.*

27

CSV *Salinan*
Zeivlot Orbit
23 August 2464

WILSON GLANCED around the small conference room where he and the senior staff would meet. The room was nowhere near as impressive as one found on a capital ship, and the holoprojector was a fifteen-year-old model that couldn't do half the things the newer ones could. But it was his. Khattri was the only other one present for a hastily called conference of all ship commanders that Calvin had sent out a couple of hours before.

"Demood give any idea what's going on?" Khattri asked as he fiddled with a tablet.

"Nah." Wilson smirked. "Come on. We're just the peons amid royalty out here."

"Until the *Magen* or the *Yulia Paievska* needs an emergency tow."

Wilson laughed. "There is that. Okay, it's time. Pull it up."

The holoprojector sprang to life with images of Calvin, Major Gabriella Acuna, commanding the *Magen*, and Major Moshe Scholsberg, commanding the *Yulia Paievska* in their various conference rooms either aboard their ships or planetside. It appeared as if Calvin and his team were somewhere on Zeivlot, with the number of uniformed Zeivlot military officers in the room behind him.

"Got a lot to relay and not a lot of time to do so," Calvin said and cleared his throat. "First off, I want to thank Major Wilson and his team, especially Senior Chief Stokes, for their exemplary performance. Because of them, we've got valuable intelligence and some idea of what's coming. Which brings us to this briefing. Corporal Nussbaum, if you would."

A young woman Wilson recognized from a few interactions leaned forward. *Susanna Nussbaum. Somebody said she was Amish, which makes her service unusual. I bet there's an interesting story there.*

"The analysis team, working with Zeivlot forensics specialists, took apart the mining vessel we captured. Most of the systems on the ship had been wiped, including its navigation computer."

"So there's no indication of where the ship had been?" Scholsberg asked.

Susanna shook her head. "I didn't say that, Major. Only that the data cores had been wiped. Tracing the vessel's path when it was on scope for the sensor stations around the belt gave us a good idea of the area it worked in."

Wilson grinned, impressed. *Good for you, corporal. Don't let rank push you around if you know what you're doing.*

"There was virtually no ore on the ship, either. All we

found in our search was trace residue of radiologics, conventional explosives, and ore-drilling equipment. Our assessment is they were preparing another attack."

"But there's been no evidence of unnatural orbit changes in any asteroids so far. We've helped both planets set up early warning systems," Acuna interjected. "I don't doubt they were up to something, but the question remains... What? Did you gain any HUMINT from the captured hostiles?"

Calvin took that one. "I questioned every detainee, as did several other interrogators from Zeivlot and Zavlot. We walked right up to the line, and they didn't give us anything except rantings about how the Maker was going to kill every human for defiling their world, blah blah blah."

Susanna seemed to pull herself slightly straighter. "I have a theory. We found drilling equipment and explosives because whoever was behind the first attack correctly realized that sending a single asteroid wouldn't be enough. I believe they've installed ion engines or fission rockets on multiple asteroids, possibly massive, civilization-ending-size, and at a time of their choosing, they'll send everything they've got at Zeivlot or Zavlot. Which one, I don't know for sure. But if I was guessing, I'd say Zeivlot because it's where the obelisk is."

"Those observations fit the available facts," Wilson said. "Corporal, do you have any indications when these terrorists might launch their assault?"

"No, sir. Only that I wouldn't expect them to dawdle. They've got to know by now we captured one mining ship and destroyed the other. If I were them, I'd assume my operation was compromised."

"We should get the Zeivlot and Zavlot military involved.

Valor 251

They both have limited spaceborne assets that could be used for picket duty," Scholsberg said.

Wilson groaned inwardly. They'd repeatedly seen that both planets had a real problem with insider threats. *We need to do this with CDF personnel only.*

"Absolutely not," Calvin replied. "I'll apprise the leaders of both planets, but it's too great a risk to link in partner forces. We'd have no idea someone was passing information until it was too late. Beyond that, they have such limited offensive capabilities that I doubt indigenous spacecraft on either side could do much of anything here."

"Then we'll need to execute continuous patrols, making sure none of our commands are within a gravity well that would prevent a microjump," Acuna said. She glanced around the different screens. "I realize the *Salinan* isn't a traditional combat vessel, but we'll need everything in the cupboard, Major."

"We've got neutron beams, missile tubes, and a crew well-trained in their use, Major Acuna," Wilson smiled thinly. "The Battle-E is painted on my vessel for a reason."

"Hey, you've got some real John Wayne guys over there, Major," Calvin interjected. "I'm sure the rest of your crew is cut from the same cloth. Whatever happens, I've got a feeling we'll all be up to our necks in it before too long. There is one other thing Corporal Nussbaum didn't mention. She's traced the currency used to buy the two mining ships we tracked down through half a dozen shell companies, cut-outs, and other money-laundering tricks, which surprisingly work for aliens as well as they do back in the Terran Coalition."

Chuckles swept the vidlink.

"I will be asking Zupan Vog't for permission to kick down the door of the individual identified. In the meanwhile, you squids can sort out patrol routes and maintain complete readiness. We can't know when the enemy will attack, but we can be as prepared as humanly possible. Any questions?"

Silence settled in before Calvin nodded. "Okay, then. Go forth, do great things, Godspeed, and all that. Demood out."

The holoprojector blinked off, and the lights automatically returned to full brightness.

Wilson leaned back. "So, what do you make of that, XO?"

"These guys are pretty determined to wipe one another out."

Wilson snorted. "A few of them are, anyway. Damn. Well, I suppose there're worse things to do in the CDF than shoot down asteroids."

Khattri raised an eyebrow. "You're not worried the terrorists have something more up their sleeve, sir? So far, they've been a canny and unpredictable opponent."

"Of course I am," Wilson snapped. His expression softened. "I'm sorry. That was unkind. Yes, I'm concerned. But as the commanding officer, I don't get to show worry to you or anyone else on this crew. Remember? I'm the old man. My job is to see us through. Can't do that if there's a whiff of indecision about me, now, can I?"

"You don't have to do it all alone, sir."

Wilson pursed his lips. "Thanks. Well, let's get up to the bridge. Lots of moving parts to oversee."

"Yes, sir." Khattri stood.

Wilson followed him out. He had a feeling, almost a premonition, that the worst was yet to come. *Lord, give me wisdom to face whatever threat is coming.* Their training, technology, and perhaps, just perhaps, grace from the Almighty would have to be enough.

CSV *Magen*
Zeivlot Asteroid Belt
24 August 2464

SUSANNA GLANCED up from her workstation deep within the SCIF on the *Magen*. She and a few other intelligence analysts had returned to the vessel to provide a real-time common operating picture and ISR support to the fleet for the duration of the crisis. Someone had taken the time to hang the motto of CDF Intelligence on an empty wall. The banner read: In God We Trust. All Others, We Monitor. Like many others, she found the motto amusing, though her upbringing in the Amish faith left her wary of invoking God in a military enterprise. That would probably never change.

Her workstation was more than a single monitor. Instead, she had three separate screens, each showing different sensor displays, and on one was raw output logs. Every so often, Susanna averted her eyes and blinked a few times. *I feel another headache coming on.* Working for shifts of ten hours in a dimly lit room had that effect on her.

"Corporal, you seeing that thrust plume?" Private Matsu Harada, an analyst even more junior than her, asked.

Susanna opened her eyes. "What sector?"

"Fourteen by six."

It took a moment and a few more blinks to find what Harada was talking about. *That's strange.* The listening posts the Zeivlot and Zavlot governments and the CDF had set up to detect missile launches in hopes of preventing another tragedy gave insight into most of the inner solar system and the large asteroid belt. *Space rocks don't move on their own. They especially don't move in straight lines.*

"Can you confirm what we're seeing on the *Magen's* sensors?" Susanna asked.

Harada nodded. "Yes, Corporal. Bridge control confirms."

On Susanna's screen, other rocks started moving out of their orbits. Alerts triggered, filling her workspace. Most of the contacts seemed clustered together, but half a dozen others were headed on different trajectories. *Where are they going?*

"Private, start an analysis algorithm immediately. We need to trace where all these asteroids are headed. Make sure it accounts for the system's gravity as a variable."

"What's going on, Corp?"

Susanna shook her head. "As insane as this sounds, I think this is proof the terrorists strapped engines to these space rocks." She glanced up. "I can think of no other reason why that would happen. Quickly. I need to figure out where they're going so that we can alert command."

Focusing on the brightly lit display, Susanna realized that some of the rocks were headed into orbits that would bring them closer to the listening posts. Her mouth went dry as she reached for an input device to bring up the bridge intercom.

Without warning, a bright light flashed, and a blast of hard gamma radiation went off only a few hundred kilometers from the farthest sensor system. Embedded on a large miniplanetoid-size asteroid, the device had no shields or armor. It was only there to offer a warning.

Immediately, sensor data dropped from the affected node. *My God, they're going to blind us.* The scope of the attack became clearer as more blasts appeared in the void before the harsh gamma radiation snuffed out the delicate electronic that was their target.

Susanna decided to bypass the *Magen*'s command staff and instead sent a gold-priority message to Colonel Demood. He would know what to do. He had to, because she was out of her depth. *Lord, please help me.* The objective of whoever had staged the attack was to once again scour all life from one or both worlds that made up the system. *Help me to stop this evil, Lord. Please use your servant.* Resolutely forcing herself to suppress the emotions raging inside, Susanna did the only thing she could: gather information to help the destroyers and the *Salinan* do their jobs.

28

Government Center
Zeivlot
24 August 2464

LESS THAN A DAY... or a rotation, as the Zeivlots called it... later, Calvin and Menahem marched through the doors to Vog't's office. Both wore dress uniforms with all their medals, ribbons, and insignia. Calvin thought the display of brass might help give weight to their argument. *After all, we're both professional warriors who have fought battles in two galaxies. Nothing like showing that to the civilians from time to time.*

Getting through the first round of administrative "professionals" had taken Calvin finally going around the chain of command and contacting Vog't personally. That might've explained some of the nasty looks directed his and Menahem's way as they sat down with her and a few high-ranking Zeivlot officers.

Valor

"Thank you for having us, Zupan."

Vog't tilted her head. "We are always glad to receive our allies in the Terran Coalition."

Man. Ever the politician, this one. "Thank you, ma'am. I have news about the previous attack on the space elevator."

One of the Zeivlot flag officers cleared his throat. "Colonel, we've reviewed your warnings about additional threats—"

"And?" Calvin interjected.

"It's difficult to believe that even one asteroid was targeted at Zavlot. It's far harder to believe others are up there. Our analysts believe you're chasing a ghost."

Calvin sucked in a breath. *Count to three.* "We captured a mining vessel involved in this plot, War Leader. I lost a good Marine trying to take another one whose crew *blew the thing up* rather than be taken alive. Does that sound like the behavior of a ghost to you? Or perhaps you know something about spirits I don't." A smug smirk spread across his lips.

"I didn't have this information."

"No, because I don't know who we can trust in your military."

The man's face turned bloodred. "How dare you—"

"Stow it. I spent most of the last few months cleaning up after your military intelligence—so porous that the enemy seemed to always know when we were coming—and eliminating most of the terrorists on Zeivlot."

The flag officer's face looked like someone had stuck a knife in his chest.

Vog't smoothly interrupted. "We are grateful for your efforts these past months, Colonel Demood. Yet what you sent over in the prebrief was... Well, you must understand it's a shock. And somewhat far-fetched."

"General Cohen likes to say that when you have eliminated the impossible, whatever remains, however improbable, must be the truth. Yes, it's a bit over the top to fling asteroids at planets and space stations, but somebody's doing it. And I think I know where the money is coming from."

Before anyone could speak or Calvin could continue, an emergency-override commlink pinged his handcomm. He paid it no heed.

"Do you have information on this suspected individual, Colonel?" Vog't asked.

Calvin nodded and handed her a portable data cartridge. "Yes. Right here."

Again, the emergency override sounded on his handcomm. With significant annoyance, Calvin glanced at it. *What's Nussbaum want?* He brought the device up to his lips. "I'm in with the zupan, Corporal. This had better be good."

"Sir, it's happening. Multiple early-warning systems are offline as a result of direct asteroid strikes. My best guess is that Zeivlot is the target."

Alarm spread across the faces of everyone in the room.

"Best guess, Corporal?" Calvin asked. "I need better than that."

"With the early-warning sensors gone, sir, it's virtually impossible to determine. I'm basing that projection on the trajectories and velocities observed as the platforms were destroyed."

"Understood. How much time do we have here?"

"Hours, worst case. Days, best. It depends on how fast they accelerate."

Calvin gritted his teeth. "Understood. Feed me the targeting information, and I'll get our assets deployed."

"Yes, sir."

The commlink cut out, and Calvin returned the device

to his pocket. "I'm sure you'll want to double-check this on your own systems."

Vog't had paled. "We will do whatever is needed, Colonel."

Calvin turned to the war leader. "I don't suppose any of your spacecraft are anywhere near the asteroid belt and capable of linking up with our forces?"

He shook his head. "They can't keep up with your ships."

Kinda knew that already. "Okay. I will put one destroyer at each planet and task the *Salinan* with supporting the *Magen*, which will be stationed at Zeivlot. Depending on how much time we have, perhaps additional ships can be vectored in."

"Madame Zupan, we need to get you to a secure location immediately," the war leader said. "You're welcome to join us, Colonel. We can coordinate a response from there."

"I'd like to take a crack at—"

"After the current crisis is over, Colonel," Vog't replied. "For now, we have one goal. Brief me further en route."

"Yes, ma'am." *This is gonna be fun. Not. I really need some bad guys to shoot.*

———

Fourteen hours later, Wilson checked the sensor plot one more time. *It's not going to magically change if I turn my head away.* Dim blue light bathed the *Salinan*'s bridge. He'd decided to go to condition one when they received word of the early-warning sensors going offline. *Bursts of gamma radiation mean one thing to me... fission warheads going off at close range.* "Anything, TAO?"

"No, sir."

"Sir, the CSV *Magen* has entered our AO. She's

requesting we initiate a tactical network link," the communications officer announced.

"Do it," Wilson replied.

The two Ajax-class destroyers left behind to guard the Zeivlot and Zavlot solar system were the Block I variant dating back roughly five years. Wilson wished they had Block IIs instead, as those vessels had an upgraded point-defense package and a vertical-launch system that could fling many more missiles into the void. *But if wishes were horses, beggars would ride.*

Moments later, the common operating picture from the *Magen* superimposed on Wilson's tactical plot. She had superior scanners to the *Salinan* and expanded their range a good bit. Still, there were *a lot* of gaps.

Wilson set a series of waypoints on the plot, drawing off an area they could hope to crisscross in thirty minutes. "Navigation, build a grid search pattern around what I just sent you."

"Aye, aye, sir."

"Engage at max sublight."

Khattri raised an eyebrow. "Looking for a needle in a haystack?"

"Yeah. That's the only thing I can think of. Let's hope we'll get lucky."

"Ground-based sensors on Zeivlot will eventually pick up incoming asteroids if they're out there," Fazel interjected.

"The sixty-four-thousand-credit question is: When? As long as we can get to them soon enough, rocks won't last long in front of our neutron beams."

"From your lips to God's ears, XO." Wilson continued to stare at the plot. Similarly to towing a warship or watching a salvage operation, time seemed to slow to a crawl, as if the universe itself ceased functioning.

"Conn, TAO. Got a series of sensor echoes at extreme range. Can't make it out, but they appear to be headed toward Zeivlot."

"Highlight them on the tactical plot." Wilson's gaze never left the screen as several gray dots appeared. *If I turn to chase them down, I can forget about the grid search.* "Thoughts, XO?"

"Right vector," Khattri murmured. "But could also be a few mining ships coming in to help."

Such a thing was implausible but not impossible. Wilson searched his gut. More often than not, its instinct was more reliable than computer screens, or so he believed. "Navigation, come to heading two-eight-seven, mark positive forty-six."

"Rolling the dice, sir?"

"Just this once." Wilson willed the sensor resolution to increase. With each minute, the range closed, and their ability to resume a methodical search decreased. "TAO, anything?"

Fazel shook his head. "Not there yet, sir."

Wilson licked his lips as his pulse quickened. The trick in a potential combat situation was to closely monitor his heart rate and breathing. *I want my senses heightened but not pushed too far.*

"Conn, TAO. Multiple asteroid contacts *confirmed*, sir. They're headed straight toward Zeivlot."

"Designate them as hostile, Lieutenant." Wilson sat up straighter.

"Aye, aye, sir. Populating the board with Master One through... Sixteen. There could be more, but those are confirmed."

That's a hell of a lot of space rocks. Wilson zoomed in on the detail sensor view. *Several of those things are three to five kilometers wide. My God, that's a civilization-altering or -ending strike.* Anger erupted inside him. *What the hell is wrong with these people? We saved them once already from disaster. Who in their right mind tries to end all life?* "Navigation, intercept course on Master Seven."

The closest inbound asteroid, it made an acceptable first target.

"Aye, aye, sir."

The little ship pushed forward, and the stars changed as she swung around.

"Communications, TAO, deconflict with the *Magen.* I don't want to be shooting the same thing."

Both officers echoed their responses, and the *Salinan* charged on.

29

"Conn, TAO. Entering maximum effective range for our neutron beams, sir," Fazel called over his shoulder.

Wilson drew in a breath and studied the tactical plot. He'd been watching the thing like a hawk, searching for any change in the number of asteroids. Something was off, though. "Lieutenant, am I seeing things, or are our hostiles accelerating?"

"As strange as it sounds, I think so, sir."

"They probably have gravity drives or mass drivers attached." Wilson balled a fist.

Khattri cleared his throat. "Whoever did this knows their business."

Wilson turned. "Agreed." He gave it a few more seconds to ensure there would be no issue with hitting the incoming. "TAO, firing point procedures, forward neutron beam, Master Seven."

"Firing solution set, sir."

"Match bearings, shoot, forward neutron beam."

The *Salinan* didn't have much in the way of anti-ship

weaponry, but to defeat a giant rock zipping through space, it didn't need to. The emitter on the vessel's bow glowed, and a spear of blue energy shot out from it at the speed of light. It connected with the targeted asteroid, melting through meters of rock and alloy. A brief, overwhelming flash of white light filled the bridge.

Wilson involuntarily closed his eyes and averted his gaze. "What was *that*?"

Fazel turned his head. "Fission explosion, sir. Master Seven has split into dozens of smaller rocks."

"Shit," Wilson muttered. "How big?"

"Large enough to track, sir."

"This certainly complicates things," Khattri said. "We could get in close and use our point defense to help clear out the largest ones."

"Yeah. Just remember, iron shards moving at the kind of velocities we're seeing here will shred armor and hull."

The scope of the terrorists' plans came into focus. Wilson licked his lips and wondered if his face was pale. He felt as if he'd walked by his grave. "Like a giant shotgun in space." *What are the odds that all these rocks have a nuke buried in them?*

As the incoming spread out farther, Wilson plotted his next step. *Best to find out.* "TAO, firing point procedures, forward neutron beam, Master Three."

"Firing solutions set, sir."

"Match bearings, shoot, forward neutron beam."

Again, the *Salinan*'s weapons suite lashed out into the void. Much like before, the blue energy melted its way through the asteroid's exterior. Fazel had subtly modified the emitter's width, causing the beam to envelop the rock thoroughly. As it reached the center, another bright-white flash lit up the inky blackness of the void.

Valor 265

"It would appear we have a major problem," Khattri said quietly. "There is no way we and the *Magen* can shoot down all these little iron-and-rock pieces."

Wilson gritted his teeth. "I know. Open to any suggestions here, XO."

Before Khattri could open his mouth, Fazel interjected. "Not to add fuel to the fire, sir, but I ran some calculations. Even with fission warheads blowing them apart, some of these things will be large enough to cause extreme damage to the surface. If a fifty-meter-wide meteor hits Zeivlot, we could see areas the size of several city blocks flattened."

Not an option. "Can we take some of the stragglers out with our missiles?"

"Too spread out. We can't throw sixty warheads at once at the problem like the *Lion of Judah* could."

While Wilson already knew that, he did want to validate it. "ETA on *Magen*?"

"Ten minutes, give or take."

And about forty until the incoming hits the orbital station, followed directly by Zeivlot.

A sudden inspiration hit Wilson. "TAO, retract our ventral bay doors, and prepare the tractor beams."

Khattri turned sharply. "Sir?"

"I've got a next-level-crazy idea. TAO, set them for a wide dispersal pattern, and overload the power output as much as possible. Put every scrap of energy we've got in." *Well, this will either work or rip my ship apart.*

"Aye, aye, sir," Fazel replied.

"Navigation, put us five thousand meters above the asteroid formation, and match bearing and speed with them."

"Aye, aye, sir."

Wilson pulled his uniform shirt down. "Communications, send to the commanding officer, CSV *Magen*. *Salinan* will deal with hostile contacts approaching Zeivlot. Take up position next to the space elevator, and extend shields to cover it from iron shards."

Okay. Now I've just got to pull this off.

———

In the Zeivlot continuity-of-government bunker, there was barely controlled pandemonium. Calvin had never been inside it before, but Vog't and the others acted like they had. Those there seemed to know where things were, which was a small but significant detail. *I wonder if this is where they rode out the near destruction of their planet all those months ago.*

He would've much preferred to be out doing something. *Anything. Like kicking some doors down and shooting the people responsible for this fiasco.* The sheer absurdity of the situation was mind-blowing to Calvin. He couldn't get his brain around the idea that inhabitants of a planet would try their best to destroy it. *Who does that?*

Vog't's insistent voice brought Calvin out of his thoughts. "Colonel, did you hear me?"

"Ah, sorry, Zupan. What did you say?"

"I asked if you would move the CSV *Yulia Paievska* to Zeivlot orbit. It seems as if the *Magen* and the *Salinan* are overmatched."

Calvin shook his head. "Major Acuna indicated when I contacted her a few minutes ago that it wouldn't help but *would* leave Zavlot undefended. The problem is these asteroids... They're dense enough with solid-iron cores. I don't quite get the particulars, but it's not as simple as blowing them apart."

Valor 267

"My people said the same." Vog't pursed her lips. "I don't know what else to do."

"Ground interceptors?"

"Well, we had a great many fusion warheads." Vog't chuckled bitterly. "But those were entirely expended on trying to kill everyone on Zavlot."

"Maybe that seems like a poor decision now."

Vog't blinked. "Was that, ah... What do you humans call it? An insult, Colonel?"

Calvin snorted. "Look, you want the truth? I'm sick of putting my people in harm's way to stop crazed terrorists who want to kill everyone around them, including themselves. I don't freaking get it. I like being alive. I enjoy getting up in the morning, having a good breakfast, talking with my fellow Marines, experiencing the universe, and going to new places. Hell, I even like meeting new people sometimes. This fixation on death, it doesn't compute for me."

"Our cultures are different—"

"They're not that different. We're motivated by similar pursuits and desires. General Cohen had a bunch of fancy words for saying that, but the truth is humans, Zeivlots, and Zavlots are a *lot* alike. It would be nice if these assholes would quit ruining my days off. I mean, I can't even get a beer without somebody trying to blow your planet up."

Vog't smirked. "You have a way with words, Colonel."

"Just a Marine, ma'am. We're all like this."

"I pray to the Maker that your compatriots will be successful." She shook her head. "At times such as these, I feel a deep despondency over the actions of some of my fellow Zeivlots."

"Then do something about it, ma'am."

"If we survive, perhaps I will try something different."

"Sounds good to me." Calvin's gaze went back to the giant screen showing the incoming asteroids. *Dunno what Wilson and his people are up to, but I hope it's insane enough to work.*

30

WILSON WATCHED the tactical plot like a hawk. The *Salinan* steadily closed on the incoming rock formation, and he thanked God they were so tightly clustered together. *Otherwise, what I've got in mind would have no chance in hell of working.* The deep-space rescue vessel wasn't a combat warship, but he'd still drilled his crew with pride, like a ship of the line. It had been enough to get them the coveted battle efficiency ribbon, or Battle E, at the previous year's Valiant Shield exercises. Wilson hoped it would be enough to see them through the crisis, as it had the initial intervention at Zeivlot.

"Conn, Navigation. Aligned on your target course, sir."

"TAO, where are my tractor beams?" Wilson rubbed his hands together.

"Ready to go, sir," Fazel replied.

"Shunt every ounce of power into them, and override the safeties to extend their width."

"Sir, we could burn—"

Wilson cleared his throat. "I'm well aware of what could happen, Lieutenant. Override the safeties."

"Aye, aye, sir."

"Activate all tractor emitters. It's critical we snare all the asteroids around us, TAO. We're only getting one shot at this."

Fazel nodded. "Aye, aye, sir."

On the tactical plot, the rocks around the *Salinan* turned purple one by one, indicating a successful tractor lock.

"Nav, adjust heading ten degrees to starboard. Maintain current thrust."

Wilson blew out a breath. While the vessel moved as he instructed, almost immediately, the emitters showed signs of stress. The little ship seemed to lurch as it tried to drag the rocks, and red warning lights flashed on his screen. He keyed the intercom for engineering. "Wilson to Benoit."

"Go ahead, sir."

"Push the reactor to one hundred ten percent power, and route all additional juice to the tractor system."

"Sir, those emitters are stressing into the red now. With more power, they'll blow out or shear half the ship's superstructure off."

Wilson bit his lip. "Captain, execute my orders. Bridge out." He clicked the intercom off.

"You okay, sir?" Khattri asked.

"Not in the mood for second-guessing at the moment," Wilson replied. His entire focus was on the asteroids.

A few moments later, more power flowed to the tractors, and the *Salinan* glided through the void more smoothly.

"Sir, we're about to lose the third ventral emitter," Fazel said. "I have to shut it down to avoid failure."

"Negative, Lieutenant. Maintain power levels, and spread the load out among the others."

Fazel looked ready to argue before nodding. "Aye, aye, sir."

Valor 271

"We might not be able to repair the ship, sir," Khattri whispered. "Worst case, we could get a major hull breach."

"Yes, and? It doesn't matter if *any* of those rocks get through," Wilson replied tightly. He was acting on instinct. There was nothing in the towing-and-salvage manual for how to deflect civilization-killing asteroids with a tractor beam. *Call it a wing and prayer.*

"Conn, TAO. Third ventral emitter has fused and melted, sir. One, two, and four showing increased strain."

"Steady as she goes." Wilson did his best to project Zen. *This beats our crazy maneuvering when the Leaguers almost found the PASSCORE sensors.*

While the *Salinan* was tiny next to the *Lion of Judah*, a fleet carrier, or even an old Thane-class escort carrier, she was purpose-built to move things in deep space. As such, the cluster of asteroids strained against the powerful tractors, but their course gradually adjusted onto a heading that would make them miss Zeivlot and fly off into the void.

Thirty more seconds, and we're home free.

"Microfractures across our forward port quarter," Khattri interjected. "Sections six through ten, decks two through five."

"Master Chief, sound collision alarm. Clear all external areas in the indicated zone," Wilson barked.

Moments later, a klaxon blared through the ship, though it quieted after a couple of blasts on the bridge. In the affected portions of the vessel, crewmen would rush to secure their stations and set up localized force fields. As a former boson's mate, Wilson well remembered the drill.

"Conn, TAO. Emitter One has failed. Two and Four are redlined, sir. Strongly recommend we—"

A harsh, guttural sound of ripping alloy came from deep within the *Salinan*, and for a moment, Wilson thought they'd bought the farm. When it ceased, he blew out a breath, surprised they were still in one piece.

"All ventral emitters have failed, sir."

Khattri paled. "Hull breach, deck two through four. From my screen, it's a miracle we didn't lose the ship."

Lord, please let it be enough. Wilson stared at the updated course projection for all tracked asteroids. Most of them showed green, overshooting Zeivlot's atmosphere or skipping across it in a few cases. But not all. Four would impact the surface.

"TAO, get me sizes on the remaining threats."

Fazel turned. "Three are small enough that if we shoot them down, they'll burn up during reentry, for the most part. The fourth is a planet killer, sir."

Wilson quickly did some math. "TAO, firing point procedures, neutron beams, and Starbolt missile tubes one and two. Target the non–planet-killer asteroids."

"Firing solutions set, sir."

"Make tubes one and two ready in all respects. Open outer doors."

"Doors open. Tubes ready."

"Match bearings, shoot, neutron beams, and both tubes."

A flurry of blue particle-energy spears erupted from the bow and the starboard quarter of the *Salinan* while two Starbolts shot out of the forward missile launches. Their engines ignited, and the warheads accelerated into the void.

On Wilson's monitor, he watched as the two blue dots indicating their outgoing missiles sped away from the ship and eventually merged with the targeted asteroids, blowing them into small chunks. Meanwhile, the third target broke apart, and what was left exploded in a thermonuclear explosion.

Valor 273

Fazel turned around. "Three down, one to go, sir."

"Effectiveness of our weapons suite against that rock, Lieutenant?"

"Not good, sir." Fazel shook his head. "Large fragments will get through. Enough to destroy cities or worse."

Wilson double-checked the plot. *Nor is there enough time to get the* Magen *here.* "Navigation, intercept course on the final asteroid. I want our dorsal profile presented. Maximum speed."

"Aye, aye, sir."

"TAO, ready the emergency tractor beams on the dorsal quadrant."

"Uh, sir..."

Wilson set his jaw. "I know, Lieutenant. They're for pulling in escape pods. That doesn't matter. Max out the width, and divert every scrap of power into those emitters."

Fazel nodded. "Aye, aye, sir."

The *Salinan* steadily closed the distance with the final, planet-killing-size rock, which was nearly five kilometers in diameter, and the deep-space rescue vessel looked like a pebble next to it.

"Conn, TAO. We're in range, sir."

Wilson stood. "Listen carefully. The moment I give the order to engage the tractors, Nav, I want you to put full thrust on a course thirty degrees to starboard of our current position. Neutral declination. Everyone clear?"

At Fazel and the navigator's nods, Wilson cleared his throat. "Activate tractor beams."

Wilson nearly fell as the *Salinan* latched on to the asteroid, kicked off its engines, and started the turn. Instead, he kept his feet under him and stood over Fazel's shoulder, staring at the raw scan data. They were pulling the rock but not fast enough.

"Sir, everything's burning out. I told you they're not made for this."

"Steady, Lieutenant. Get every second you can."

"Yes, sir." Fazel reallocated power on the fly, trying to get everything he could out of the three auxiliary tractor beams.

One by one, they failed. The last kept going a few seconds longer than it had any right to, which Wilson ascribed to good old-fashioned CDF overengineering. Regardless, he was thankful. *Lord, please let that be enough. We're out of tricks, and the Zeivlots need a miracle.*

The asteroid's new course was calculated on the tactical view, and the plot was updated. It took a moment for Wilson to realize it, but the rock would skip off the atmosphere and head into the void. He took a deep breath and let it out slowly. *Thank you, Lord.* He returned to his chair. "That... was some outstanding work, ladies and gentlemen. We just saved a planet."

Hoots and hollers broke out, including from Wilson and Khattri.

The celebration went on for thirty seconds before Wilson held up a hand. "Okay, people, we've still got work to do."

"We're going to need yard time," Khattri commented as the tumult died down. He flipped a screen around to show multiple areas of the hull blinking red. "Also lucky to be in one piece."

Wilson grinned. "Can't let our fast space-warfare brothers and sisters have all the fun."

"Feels nice to be the big damn hero for once." Khattri snorted.

"Amen." Wilson chuckled. "Communications, let the *Magen* know our situation, and request they chase down and destroy the remaining asteroids." He'd been proud of

Valor

his crew on many occasions. *But this takes the cake. I'm gonna have to get these guys shore leave at some point.*

———

CALVIN WASN'T much of a praying man, as everyone around him probably knew. But as enough asteroids headed toward the planet to kill every living thing on it and probably crack the crust open, from what the zupan's advisors were saying, he found the time to speak to God. Then he waited to die.

His thoughts were with his wife, and he was filled with deep sadness that he would depart the mortal plane having never met their child.

Wild cheering caused Calvin to open his eyes. It took a minute for the translator in his ear to pick up what the Zeivlots were screaming along with large amounts of clicks that seemed to indicate joy.

"They missed! They all missed!"

Zeivlots hugged one another and were even dancing in the command center. Calvin took it all in, shocked he was still alive.

Vog't touched his arm. "Your people saved us once more. The salvage ship dragged the rocks off course, while a destroyer saved the space elevator. Truly, humans are touched by the Maker."

Calvin shrugged. "I'm just an old Marine, Zupan. About the only thing I'm touched by is the Corps." After making peace with death, he found it difficult to believe he was still alive.

"You know better."

He regarded her for a moment. *Yeah, leave it to an alien from a planet four and a half million light-years from home to put things in perspective. The Coalition, particularly the* Lion of Judah, *wins more than our fair share of battles.*

"I believe you wanted my permission to go after the financier behind these recent attacks?"

Calvin's eyes glinted. "Yes, ma'am."

"Granted."

"I'm going to enjoy kicking this next door in." He stood. "No time like the present, ma'am."

"Godspeed, Colonel."

"You, too, ma'am." Calvin inclined his head before heading toward the exit. *Now, this is where I can do my job and feel good about it. The bastard who nearly wiped out six billion people will rue the day he encounters me.*

31

Deep Space—Sextans B
CSV *Lion of Judah*
31 August 2464

DR. HAYWORTH and Hanson had spent a long, arduous week of testing the Admari technology on the CSV *John Manners* and, once they were sure it wasn't a threat, installing it in the *Lion*'s sensor system. After that, they began a search for the nanite swarm. The process was equally slow and challenging. Hour after hour, the scanner-control teams, made up of half a dozen enlisted ratings, worked methodically through the void around SB-WE163-8.

Throughout the process, David carried on as best he could. If they could find the nanite swarm, then it would be relatively simple to avoid it while the *Lion* kept searching for enough data on the precursor race to unlock its secrets and get home. Returning to Zeivlot within the next couple of weeks was also at the top of his mind. David wondered daily what Calvin and the rest of his personnel were dealing with. *I hope the situation has remained calm and peaceful.* Something in the back of his head said that was unlikely.

"You appear as if you are in another galaxy," Aibek hissed under his breath.

The comment jarred David out of his rumination. "Eh, yeah. Thinking about Colonel Demood and our people back on Zeivlot."

"I am sure the good colonel is hating life."

David raised an eyebrow. "Why?"

"Because he is a true warrior and would rather be out here, fighting unknown threats."

"Perhaps." David chuckled. "Somehow, I think we'd all rather be *home*." He still felt guilty for asking Calvin to join the last diplomatic run the *Lion* went on. His wife was pregnant. *But I asked him for one last trip around the Coalition to fly the flag. I thought we'd all earned a victory lap.* David shoved the introspection out of his mind. It would have to wait until later.

"Conn, TAO. Possible FTL contact. Range, six light-years," Ruth called out.

"Another wild goose chase, Captain?" David forced a grin. "The last eight have been."

"Won't know till we check it out, sir. But this one's registering as considerably more massive than the others. And it's headed toward a solar system. Main-sequence star, roughly the same size and output as Canaan."

The way Ruth described it got David's attention. "Navigation, plot a Lawrence drive jump to the edge of that system."

"Aye, aye, sir," Hammond replied.

"What if she found the nanites?" Aibek asked quietly.

"We'll confirm our readings and jump out."

Valor   279

"Prudent."

For the next ten minutes, orders and replies went back and forth as the *Lion of Judah* prepared for the FTL jump. After an uneventful transit, she exited the artificial wormhole at the edge of the targeted solar system. Their sensors took a few seconds to clear after the charged particles dissipated from the ship's hull.

"Conn, TAO. No contacts within a quarter million kilometers."

"FTL wake?"

"Headed toward one of the planets, but I'm not sure which yet."

Unlike the blue-giant system, a main-sequence star had a far smaller diameter for the orbits of its celestial bodies. As a result, the *Lion*'s sensors could see most of them, and without the harsh radiation blasting out of the corona, their resolution was significantly higher.

"Fourth planet, and it's inhabited." Ruth turned. "Sir, this wake reminds me of the Vogtek drive system. It's not the same, but there's a real similarity in waveforms."

David turned toward Tinetariro. "Master Chief, get a master-at-arms to Dr. Hayworth's lab. I want him up here immediately." *I should've done that earlier. Blasted mental fatigue.* "TAO, execute as deep a scan as possible with the scientific sensor suite."

"Moving further in without risk is possible," Aibek hissed. "We are able to jump out of this gravity well with impunity."

"It would still take a few hours to traverse the system at full combat speed. I don't want to double jump and risk severe damage to the fleet if we had to execute a third, emergency jump."

Aibek raised an eye scale. "Yet we lose nothing by starting in."

Am I being overly cautious? As usual, his XO—and friend —had solid advice. "You're right. Navigation, plot a course to the far side of the fifth planet. All ahead full." A large gas giant, it would make for a convenient object to hide behind.

"Sir," Ruth interjected. "I'm pretty sure we're looking at a late-twentieth-century-human-technology level, perhaps the early twenty-first century, for the indigenous species. There are satellites in orbit but no manned spacecraft showing up."

David stroked his chin. *Which means they probably won't be able to see us unless someone gets incredibly lucky.* "Below the Zeivlots, then, in terms of space access?"

"Absolutely."

What would the nanites want with this system, though? It has no technology that could be useful to them. Perhaps we're reading another ghost. David kept his concerns to himself as the *Lion* plodded farther toward the gas giant. In the meantime, Hayworth arrived and took up his nominal station toward the back of the bridge after pointedly confirming they were not going to contact the new species or reveal the fleet's presence. Little new information was gleaned aside from transmissions from the alien world's entertainment networks. They possessed crude video transmission equipment and apparently spent a great deal of time making such recordings.

Roughly an hour later, things started happening —quickly.

"Conn, TAO. Aspect change. New contact emerging from an Alcubierre warp field, sir. It's..."

"Report, Captain."

Valor 281

"I... Sir... You'd better look for yourself. On the tactical holoprojector."

David spun around, thinking he'd rather hear it from Ruth. All such thoughts left his mind as he took in the scene on the projector. A spherical object the size of a large moon or a small planet had appeared only a few hundred thousand kilometers from the fourth planet in the system. "Composition?"

"The same alloy that seems to be employed by the nanites as their primary building block," Hayworth replied. His voice held a tone David had never heard from him before.

He sounds scared.

David went through what he could've done differently. They didn't have enough time to translate the language of the indigenous species, even if they'd been working on it for the last two hours. He turned to Taylor. "Any chance of warning them?"

"I don't think so, sir."

"By the Prophet," Aibek hissed.

David turned back toward the holotank to see a mass of red dots moving away from the sphere. There were so many that the sensor system was having trouble differentiating between all the different contacts. "Same things we engaged?"

Ruth sounded as if something was caught in her throat. "Yes... sir. Yes. Confirmed. Same configuration."

"My God." David stared in shock, his OODA—observe, orient, decide, act—loop compromised. The cloud of dots accelerated, heading for the inhabited world. Dozens of possible courses of action raced through David's brain, but they only boiled down to two broad choices. Try to fight the nanites or jump out. *I'd chance it if there were twenty, forty, or even a hundred of those ships.*

"Communications," David managed to get out, as his mouth had become parched. "Try every known language and frequency. Tell them what's coming."

"Aye, aye, sir."

Though it was a small thing, it let David hang on to the thought that he'd done some part of his duty.

"Sir, we have to help," Ruth interjected. "Maybe we could save some of them. Let their civilization survive."

David had sorted that idea into the long-shot category moments before. "Based on the nanite construct's present speed, how long until they're in orbit?"

Ruth bent over her console for a few moments before turning her head. "Fifteen minutes or less."

"That is not enough time. They would overwhelm and destroy us before anyone could be extracted from the surface, even with a double jump."

Aibek just said what we're all thinking and dreading. "We'll stand by to help any survivors."

"There will be no survivors. I now think I understand the level of devastation observed on all these worlds. The hive mind wants something, and it will scour whatever that something is from this planet until nothing else exists," Hayworth said. "And we should leave before the swarm realizes we're here. It can obliterate us with ease."

David shook his head. "Not yet. Have you made any progress on the weapon we discussed?"

Hayworth stood. "General, you're not hearing me. Now, I may be just a civilian, but I am also an old man with no desire to die in a hopeless battle where we would give our lives for nothing. The optimum solution is to jump out as quickly as possible."

Valor   283

"Doctor," David replied as he, too, stood, "listen to me very carefully. There may come a time when I decide the proper thing to do is give my life and this command for a lost cause. That time is not today because, as you put it, there is nothing we can do to change the facts on the ground. But what we can do and will do is bear witness to how this race perishes from the universe. That is the *least* we can do. If you can't wrap your mind around that, get off my bridge."

Anger rose to the surface, though David knew it was misplaced. Hayworth was right. *That doesn't change that I feel we're somehow not doing our duty.*

Silence spread, and in its wake, an oppressive atmosphere filled the area.

Ruth turned and spoke, breaking the moment. "Sir, aspect change here. A lot of new contacts coming from the surface of that planet. Assess them as missile launches."

"Pipe it into the holotank," David replied.

"Aye, aye, sir."

Thousands of blue dots populated the holoprojector. They raced away from the planet, headed straight for the nanite constructs. To David's amazement, no attempt was made to turn away or even shoot down the incoming warheads. He prayed softly in Hebrew that the weapons would be effective and hoped the inhabitants of the planet had some advanced technology that wasn't readily visible.

As missiles connected with the onrushing nanite vessels, the masses of icons representing them disappeared. David thought his eyes were playing tricks on him, because *none* of the red icons blinked out. "TAO, are those missiles having *any* effect?"

"They're fission and fusion bombs, sir. I'm pretty sure they were intended to hit planetary targets and were retargeted on the fly." Ruth licked her lips. "The nanite vessels were barely affected. Maybe one or two went down."

David sank back into the CO's chair. The nanites continued their relentless assault, spreading across the blue-green sphere's surface. Minutes passed, and the world turned gray before their eyes.

"Virtually all outgoing communications have ceased," Taylor said, choking back emotion. "There's a few still. I don't have to speak their language to know they're begging for help."

"There were billions of beings down there," Ruth said in shock.

David felt empty and lifeless. Every fiber of him wanted to do *something*. But there was nothing they could do, no last-second miracle to pull off. He set his jaw. *There is* one *thing I can do.* "God, filled with mercy, dwelling in the heavens' heights, bring proper rest beneath the wings of your angels, amid the ranks of the holy and the pure," he began, reciting a Jewish prayer for the dead. Typically, it would be spoken in Hebrew, but so the others would understand, he chose English instead.

"Illuminating like the brilliance of the skies the souls of the beloved and blameless who went to their eternal place of rest. May You, who are the source of mercy, shelter them beneath Your wings eternally and bind their souls among the living, that they may rest in peace. And let us say: amen," Ruth and a few other enlisted ratings finished.

"Amen" echoed throughout the bridge.

"Navigation, plot a Lawrence drive jump as far away from here as possible." David forced the words out of his mouth as if they caused physical pain.

"Aye, aye, sir," Hammond replied, sniffling.

"May the Prophet guide vengeance on this scourge, and may he use us someday as his instrument," Aibek hissed.

David had never seen the expression on his XO's face, but it looked far scarier than any he'd ever seen on it before. *So that's what rage looks like on him.*

"Conn, TAO. The nanites have noticed us, sir. One hundred–plus contacts headed our way."

Time to go. "Navigation, status of the jump?"

"Coordinates plotted, sir. Ready to engage."

"Communications, order all escorts to follow us through. I don't want to take a chance on anyone getting left behind. Navigation, activate Lawrence drive."

The lights dimmed as the massive FTL generator drew as much power as it could consume from the antimatter reactor. The deck plates rattled, and a small vortex opened in front of the *Lion*. As it grew ever larger, he wondered what would happen to the souls of the beings who'd just been brutally erased from the universe and thought of the age-old question, "Why do bad things happen to otherwise-decent people?"

"Wormhole is stable, sir."

"Take us in," David replied.

The *Lion of Judah* accelerated and slid through its artificial tunnel between space and time. The nanites didn't pursue, and all David had to do was come to terms with the deaths of billions of people and his inability to do *anything* about it. As the morning watch continued, the bridge resembled a tomb. He couldn't remember it ever being so somber. *Something horrible would be wrong with us if what we witnessed didn't shake everyone to their core.*

Davⅰᴅ ʀᴇᴛʀᴇᴀᴛᴇᴅ to his day cabin after completing the morning watch. Emotionally, he was a wreck. Over and over, the images of the planet turning gray as the nanites devoured its surface and people played in his mind. It hadn't helped that the science team spent the hours after the jump refining the sensor images and information about the solar system. *More than four billion. That's how many beings died.* It bothered him that they would never be able to put down a more accurate number, as if it meant those lives wouldn't be remembered. *How do you sit shiva for a world?*

Flipping through the Psalms on his tablet, David stopped on one of his favorites. *The Lord is a refuge for the oppressed and strength in times of trouble. And those who know Your name will put their trust in You alone, for the Lord does not forsake those who seek Him.*

The entry buzzer interrupted his thoughts before the hatch swung open.

Hayworth stood there, one hand on the alloy frame. "May I?"

"Of course, Doctor." David gestured to a chair in front of his desk.

He closed the hatch behind him, crossed the few meters quickly, and sat while affixing David with a hawklike stare. "I was out of line earlier. Before anything else, I must apologize for that."

"You were right." David steepled his fingers.

"Perhaps. But I'd be lying if I said I wasn't deeply affected by what we all saw."

"Fear has a different effect on every person, Doctor. After twenty years in the CDF, I can control mine pretty well. Mostly, I wield it as a tool to keep me at the top of my tactical game."

Hayworth inclined his head. "That is something I know little... nothing, in truth, about."

"What's on your mind?"

"That transparent, am I?"

David forced a smile. "Doctor, we've known each other for a long time now. I suspect you know my expressions and tone as well as I know yours."

"Ah, yes. Quite." Hayworth glanced away. "You shouldn't punish yourself for not being able to save them."

Perhaps he does understand. "If only it were that simple, Doctor. I have so many questions after seeing that happen in real time. When you walked in, I was contemplating what happened to the souls of that species. All of them wiped out in one horrible moment."

"You're a student of Marcus Aurelius, yes?"

David pursed his lips. "I've read his book. It's required at the Coalition War College."

"But I've heard you use its wisdom."

"I didn't realize you were a stoic, Doctor."

"Well, I'm not, but he had some decent points." Hayworth gave a thin smile. "Nor are you a stoic."

"Not entirely, no. But one must have some level of stoicism to survive twenty years of combat. At any rate, go on."

"If there are gods, and they are just, then they will not care how devout you have been but will welcome you based on the virtues you have lived by. If there are unjust gods, then you should not want to worship them. If there are no gods, then you will be gone but will have lived a noble life that will live on in the memories of your loved ones."

"Not how I see it, but I'm not debating the existence of God today."

Hayworth shrugged. "Nor was I suggesting we do. Only

that those aliens, whose species we don't even know, will live on in our minds. Because even if only for a moment, we saw them fight to live against impossible odds. I don't have to be a military man to know valor when I see it. And if there is some higher being in the universe, I would expect it feels the same way."

But it's not that simple. HaShem expects our obedience to His Law, yes. But He also wants faith. I wonder, though... How does He treat those who didn't know Him? Or does He simply ensure every world does, in some manner or form? "An intriguing thought, Doctor."

"I can't seem to get you to debate me anymore." Hayworth harrumphed. "Exchanging ideas with someone who can give me a run for my money is far more interesting than demolishing the arguments of the less learned."

David chuckled. "I think what you mean is that you enjoy debating the merits of the argument rather than faith."

"There's no argument against faith that works."

"Precisely, Doctor." David nodded. "It is impossible to convince me that my faith is wrong. But the same is true of you."

"I've begrudgingly admitted that in the past and still do." Hayworth's expression softened. "If such a being existed, created the universe, and went around dictating our paths in life... it would not punish you for what happened a few hours ago, General. There is nothing you could have done, short of sacrificing all of us in a lost cause."

"Some would say that a lost cause is the *only* type worth fighting for."

"At one point, the Terran Coalition defeating the League of Sol was the very definition of an impossible cause. But we had time, and we weren't fighting something so far beyond our understanding that it made it appear like insects. You did everything you could."

"I know. Intellectually, I *know* we couldn't have done anything differently."

"But it doesn't help your emotions?" Hayworth replied.

"Not at all."

"Hmm. Sign of a good man." Hayworth closed his eyes. "What I'm about to tell you will do little to assuage your guilt, in that case."

What now? It can't get any worse. David blew out a breath. "Oh?"

Hayworth took David's tablet off its cradle and typed a few things before flipping it around. "We were able to program the sensors to track the Alcubierre warp wake generated by the nanites."

David stared at the map of Sextans B on the screen. It took a few moments to process the track of the swarm and its projected line. His mouth went dry. "How sure of this are you?"

"Of the current trajectory, completely. Whether they stay on course... I cannot say."

"That's what they got from our computer core." David put his hand in his hands. "My God... I've sentenced two species to die. They must be heading to Zeivlot for the artifact."

"Yes, that's my conclusion as well. I believe these nanites seek out precursor technology for their own ends. You must understand they would've gotten there eventually."

"Small comfort, Doctor," David replied bitterly. "*Damn* small comfort."

Hayworth raised an eyebrow. "You don't cuss."

"I'm directly responsible for this, Doctor." David let his hands drop and leaned back. "You warned me. You said that one of these days, I was going to cause something awful to happen. Well... congratulations. It happened sooner rather than later."

"It doesn't matter. The question for you is: What now?"

David met Hayworth's gaze. *Feeling sorry for myself has no place in this office or on the* Lion of Judah. "How long do we have?"

"Two years, give or take."

Relief washed over David. *At least there's enough time to try to find a way to fight them.* "Why so long?"

"The FTL system the nanites use is vastly less efficient than the Lawrence drive. It's similar to what the Jinvaas use. I postulate that the energy requirements for opening a wormhole large enough to allow an object the size of a moon to transit are beyond the scope of their technology. Regardless of why... it does give us some time."

David nodded. "Time is an important ally, Doctor. Are there any other pertinent facts?"

Hayworth shook his head. "Not at this point. But we're continuing our review of the data, and I'm pursuing several lines of research."

"Good. We'll hold a staff meeting later today."

"I figured you would." Hayworth offered a crooked grin. "After all, the military can't do anything without a meeting and a memorandum in triplicate."

While David figured the older man's comments were meant to make him feel better or perhaps lighten things up, he wasn't in the mood. "If you'd excuse me, Doctor... I've got a lot to consider."

Hayworth stood and shuffled toward the door. "I'll see you later, General."

As the hatch clanged shut, David licked his lips. *First things first.* He touched a button for the bridge intercom.

"Yes, General?" Aibek asked, his deep voice crackling through the speaker.

"Have Lieutenant Hammond plot a course back to Zeivlot, with full cooldowns between jumps, but we'll want to move as quickly as possible aside from that."

"Yes, sir." If the XO had any questions, it didn't show in his tone.

"And prepare a staff meeting for seventeen hundred hours. Make sure to include Dr. Hayworth."

"Yes, sir."

"Thanks, XO."

David clicked the device off and let out a sigh. *A week or so to get back. Then the hard part starts.* He had three hours and change until the senior officers assembled. Before David put his mind to developing a plan, he bowed his head. *HaShem, please, grant me wisdom. I'm at my limits, and any mistakes will cause countless innocents to die. I've never asked You to help me win a battle, but this time, I will. These... nanites are a force of pure evil. Please, help me and my crew. Amen.*

With the prayer complete, David opened his eyes. *Time to get to work.*

32

IN THE DAYS after yet another near-death experience for the citizens of Zeivlot, much had happened. Calvin noted with satisfaction as he and Major Wilson strode into Zupan Vog't's office that they had saved the lives of millions of people once again. Protests were ongoing in the streets of most major cities throughout the planet and on Zavlot. They demanded an end to religious and political extremism and, so far, had been peaceful. Calvin hoped it would translate into more than just talk.

"Colonel Demood, Major Wilson, thank you both for coming." Vog't stood and walked around her desk, extending her hand in the human fashion.

Calvin first came to attention before relaxing and shaking her hand. "Zupan."

Behind him, Wilson also went ramrod straight.

Vog't moved down and shook his hand as well. "Gentlemen, please, join me." She gestured to the chairs in front of the ornate desk before returning to her seat. They were alone, aside from two Zeivlot protection officers who accompanied the zupan at all times.

Valor 293

"Thank you for having us, ma'am," Calvin replied. He sat with his hands in his lap.

"It has been a tumultuous few days." The translation devices still had a lag, but after so long, everyone had acclimated to the effect. "And I am again in the Terran Coalition's debt."

Calvin shook his head. "I'm only carrying out my orders, ma'am. Well, mostly." He grinned wryly.

Vog't turned to Wilson. "Major, your quick thinking saved millions if not billions of lives. There is nothing I can do to repay you."

"All part of the service, ma'am." Wilson smiled as well. "Defending those who cannot defend themselves is part of the Coalition Defense Force's job description. I'm just glad the *Salinan* was in the right place at the right time."

"You will receive our highest honors along with all soldiers involved."

"I wouldn't mind some R and R," Wilson deadpanned.

Calvin chuckled before turning serious. "I'd like to know if you got any actionable intelligence out of Nur Ve'si. His people gave up without much of a fight."

"People who hide in the shadows and enjoy a life of luxury... are far more susceptible to coercion, Colonel. Let us say that there will be many arrests, though for the sake of our planet's stability, we will not announce all of them, and there will be modified terms for some financiers."

Calvin raised an eyebrow. "So they walk."

"No." Vog't pursed her lips. "Some will be allowed to remain free while we monitor every aspect of their lives—quietly, of course—and roll up anyone and everyone connected to them."

What does the general call it? Realpolitik. I hate this crap. He forced his expression to remain as neutral as possible. "I see."

"You disagree."

"It's not for me to agree or disagree, ma'am. The military's job is to carry out policy, not define it."

"Yet I suspect you'd line up every last one of those people and shoot them if it were up to you."

Calvin pursed his lips. "Sounds about right, ma'am."

"Sometimes, I wish I could have such clarity of thought and act on it, Colonel. Should you ever find yourself in a position such as mine, however, you will realize compromises must be made."

"Which is why I'll stick to what I'm good at. Kicking down doors and putting down bad guys." Calvin flashed a thin smile. "Keep me away from politics."

Vog't nodded. "Oh yes, Colonel. Still, this is a good day. I think we may have finally seen the end of organized terrorism on both worlds."

Yeah, kinda doubt that. Calvin had been around the block more than once and had a cynical view of those who used violence to achieve their aims. It always seemed that somebody else showed up when one group was knocked down. *That seems to be the order of things.* He thought back to the lessons in school about how humans once determined how they interacted with one another based on skin color and religion. *Some of us still do.* However, Calvin had never met a citizen of the Coalition who engaged in such beliefs and hoped he never did.

"We live in hope," Calvin said finally. "And until then, my Marines and I will help you keep a lid on it, Zupan."

Vog't's lips curled into a smile. "Well said, Colonel. Take a few days off, courtesy of our government."

"Thank you, ma'am."

Valor 295

"Well, gentlemen, if you will excuse me, I must get back to the matters of state."

Calvin sprang to his feet and came to attention. "Of course, ma'am. Thank you for your time."

Wilson quickly followed. The two of them exited the office and made their way out of the building with little said. A private conversation could not be had, and Calvin was allergic to bureaucrats.

Once outside, they walked back to a newly built shuttle pad where Menahem and Susanna waited in the passenger area of a Marine transport. Both of them came to attention.

"Oh, at ease," Calvin said as he walked up the ramp. "We're off the clock as of right now." He dropped into one of the padded seats and strapped in.

"Speak for yourself, but I've got to return to the *Salinan*." Wilson climbed into a harness and secured it.

"Hey, the zupan said we had some time off."

Wilson snorted. "We've got a station to fix."

"Let me introduce you to my minions here." Calvin smirked as he gestured. "Master Gunnery Sergeant Ruben Menahem and Corporal Susanna Nussbaum."

Wilson eyed them in their sand-colored camouflage battle dress uniforms. "Ah, nice to meet you both in the flesh. Especially you, Corporal. You did one hell of a job in a rough situation."

Susanna blushed. "Thank you, sir."

"So, where are we off to, Colonel?" Menahem asked. "I was promised fun and beer. I don't see either."

Calvin chuckled. "How about hover dune buggies and as much beer as you can put down? At least, what passes for beer around here. They call it some kind of ale." He made a face. "After a while, it stops tasting like piss."

"Where'd you get dune buggies?"

"Zupan's office asked what I wanted for a vacation. I told 'em we wanted fifty dune buggies, a resort somewhere on a beach devoid of anyone except Marines, and enough alcohol to float a boat."

"And they agreed?"

"I mean, we just saved the planet from getting hit by a bunch of asteroids."

"Technically, Colonel, that was my guys," Wilson interjected with a grin.

"Shore leave's approved for everyone."

"Uh-huh." Wilson winked. "I know better than to mix squids with Marines. We'll end up with half our people in jail."

He's right about that. Calvin didn't respond and, instead, pulled a small patch out of his pocket and tossed it at Susanna. "Had that made for you, Corporal."

She stared at the small piece of cloth emblazoned with a blue background and a relief of a horse-drawn buggy to the left. "You know there's more to us than the horse-and-buggy thing, right, sir?"

"Yeah, I know. Gotta admit I'm not too up on the Amish, though. Anyway, I thought it was time you had something to put on your uniform that was unique to you."

Susanna stared at him before smiling. "One of the things I like most about my service is how we are all the same."

"Eh? How do you figure?"

"In my culture and religion, we seek sameness. Every barn we raise is built the same way. Our clothes are plain and similar. Even our buggies are built to the same specifications as they were five hundred years ago, and none differ." Susanna touched Menahem's uniform. "In the CDF, we all wear the same uniform and use the same tools, and everything is designed to be interchangeable. It is just like things were back on Freiderwelt."

Wilson grinned. "You forget the tech. That's a big difference."

"Major, what counts is what's in here." Susanna put a hand to her chest. "*That* is the same for all of us."

A tear came to Calvin's eyes. "Corporal's got a point. Dark green. Light green. We're all Marines... and you squid pukes."

They all laughed.

"All right, enough sappy stuff. All aboard for some fun. Oh, and, Corporal? I know you don't drink, so I took the liberty of bringing water bottles for you."

Susanna smiled. "Thank you, sir."

"Damn, she can't even tell when I'm razzing her."

"Oh, I can, Colonel, but I choose to turn the other cheek and ignore it."

Laughter pealed from Menahem and Wilson.

Menahem said, "She got you good there, sir."

Calvin affixed a stare on Susanna. "Yeah, keep trying, young whippersnapper. I'm only impressed by squids who can kick my ass with a pugil stick." His expression softened. "But... And don't repeat this, because they'll think I'm getting soft. You did *real* good."

Susanna beamed as if she'd just been told she had won the lottery. "Yes, sir. Thank you, sir."

As the shuttle ramp closed and the engines cycled to lift off, Calvin leaned back. *Yeah, we all did well.* He looked forward to a few days off, punctuated only by regret that he wasn't back home with his wife, Jessica. *Well, until I get there, I'll do the best I can.*

––––––––––

298   DANIEL GIBBS

ONLY A FEW HOURS had passed since David met with Dr. Hayworth and began planning the *Lion*'s next steps. He was still fleshing out possible options. The single most significant objective in front of them was to get back to Zeivlot and Zavlot. Once they were there, both governments would be informed of the civilization-ending threat to their societies. *It sounds so antiseptic. Civilization ending. That's a nice, tidy phrase for billions of people being erased from the universe in fifteen minutes.*

No matter how much David tried, he couldn't wipe the images of the nanites devouring a world out of his mind. Whenever he closed his eyes, it happened all over again. *Sleep will be difficult.* A glance at the clock on his tablet reminded him that the staff meeting was about to begin.

David sprang to his feet, exited the day cabin, and took the few steps to the deck-one conference room. As he entered, everyone stood and came to attention.

"As you were."

The *Lion of Judah*'s entire senior staff, in addition to Dr. Hayworth, sat down. The Zeivlot and Zavlot scientists as well as the lone Otyran were explicitly excluded, as David wished to brief Bo'hai privately. She had become their unofficial leader, and he felt it better to explain the situation to her in detail. *Why am I concerned about what she'll think?* David filed the thought away and cleared his throat.

"First, I'd like to thank you all for your efforts in this dire hour." David sat at the head of the table as he spoke. "This situation isn't getting better, as I'm sure you all know by now. Before we continue, I want to apologize for how things ended today. I wish I could've somehow found a way to change the outcome."

"There was nothing you could've done, sir," Ruth

Valor 299

replied. She had dark circles under her eyes, and her nose was bright red and puffy. "Or any of us, for that matter."

"No, there wasn't. That doesn't make the tragedy any less. Going forward, the *Lion of Judah* has only one mission: eliminate the nanites, by any means necessary."

"What about getting home?" Hanson asked.

"It's a secondary concern." David spread his hands out on the table. "I know that's a lot to ask all of you and the crew. But... we can't turn aside."

Merriweather shook her head. "General, I know this isn't a democracy, but you're asking thirteen thousand soldiers to stop searching for a way home and instead focus on defeating a galactic-extinction-level threat. In a galaxy, I might add, that for the most part doesn't seem to have FTL-capable species, much less peer military powers."

"We have a moral obligation to try, Major." David set his jaw. "Suppose we find a way to recreate the wormhole that got us here tomorrow. Would you be okay with flying through it, knowing this threat would continue to slaughter billions?"

While she initially appeared ready to argue the point, Merriweather eventually bit her lip. "No, sir."

"As someone who argues for noninterference, I must echo General Cohen's sentiment."

David snapped his head around, shocked at Hayworth's comment.

"Don't look so surprised." Hayworth shrugged. "Here is a truth to keep in perspective. If the hive mind driving this entity can decode the artifact's secrets on Zeivlot, odds are it would be able to upgrade itself enough to fly to the Milky Way quickly. Which means our homes are at risk too. Beyond that, since the nanites learned about the location of the obelisk from our computers, we bear some level of responsibility."

"Correction—I bear responsibility."

"I've assisted you of my own free will throughout our time in Sextans B, General. And I wager the vast majority of your officers and crew throughout the fleet agree with and wholeheartedly endorse your actions. It's who we are as humans. We *want* to help others."

"Doctor, I know you have a stringent policy against weapons research, but—"

"Yes."

After a few moments of silence, during which David stared into Hayworth's eyes, he nodded. "Thank you, Doctor."

"Out-of-control self-replicating machines that destroy entire civilizations are worth bending my 'no weapons' rule for. Allow me to caveat that by saying I will work solely on a means to destroy the nanites. However we're able to accomplish this, it will not involve some new superweapon. I'd rather focus on disrupting the bonds between the nanites."

"I'd be happy to help wherever I can, Doctor," Ruth interjected.

"Me too," Hanson said.

"Make it three." Merriweather flashed a small smile.

Hayworth pursed his lips. "I'd be glad of any assistance."

"What will we tell the Zeivlot and Zavlot governments?" Aibek hissed.

"The truth. All of it," David replied.

"Have you considered they might not take kindly to the nanites obtaining their address from us, as it were?" Amir asked.

His light humor didn't land.

Too soon. "I expect them to be furious. But... it doesn't

matter. By the time we get there, I'll have several options for them to choose from. We'll see what they want to do."

"What if they tell us to screw off, sir?" Ruth raised her eyebrows. "I mean, it's not outside the realm of possibility."

"Then we'll collect our people and regroup. Speaking of which, I'm very much looking forward to seeing Colonel Demood and his merry band of misfits."

"Who knows what trouble they have gotten into or glorious battles the colonel has fought," Aibek said with a grin.

HaShem help us if we walk into another dicey political situation. "I'm hoping everything is stable. It'll make what I have to tell them easier."

"Hope is not a strategy, sir," Ruth replied.

"Yes, I do like to say that, Captain." David blew out a breath. "All right. We will begin nonstop efforts of finding a way of defeating the nanites as the fleet heads back to Zeivlot. Tall order. Beyond that, our plans must wait for both governments to weigh in. You all know I hate overly long meetings, so any saved rounds?"

Dr. Tural leaned forward. "In times such as these, calling upon the wisdom and help of Allah seems prudent. In all my years as a healer, I have never seen such a terror as this. We should be careful not to rely solely on our faculties and be sure to ask God's favor in our task."

Memories from several pivotal moments in the war against the League flooded into David's mind. He also remembered the message given to him rather directly that he should stop relying on himself and instead turn to HaShem's grace. *And when I did, a League auxiliary plowed into the side of the enemy flagship when all hope seemed lost.* His first stop when the session ended would be the shul.

"Perhaps we should pray," Ruth added.

Her words sent a mental bolt of lightning through David. He avoided introducing direct prayers into military settings or putting his subordinates in a position that they would have to join him. It was one thing to privately ask God for help but another to assume all others were inclined to do it in the same manner as he was. *And the small matter of Dr. Hayworth being an atheist. I have no desire to insult him.*

Before he could speak, Hayworth beat him to it. "Don't avoid doing so on my account. While I do not believe in a higher power, I realize the comfort most take from that belief. And on the off chance there is something larger than us out there with the ability to control the universe... we could use its help on this matter."

David inclined his head. "Thank you, Doctor."

They all joined hands, and he began to pray aloud in English.

33

AFTER HOURS SPENT IN ENGINEERING, going over schematics for the neutron and particle beams, Ruth pushed the hatch open to the quarters she shared with Taylor. She'd worked with Hanson to try to narrow down improvements to the energy focuser and power couplings in the hopes of improving their weaponry to the point that it would be effective against the nanites for more than a few shots.

She had no reason to think it would be done in a day, but after a full watch rotation, another six hours had left her completely drained. It didn't help that they'd seemingly made no progress. Hanson, ever the optimist, kept telling her every failure was just another chance to succeed. *After hours of that, I don't ever want to hear it again.*

"Hey, honey!" Taylor called out and set down the tablet device he was holding. "Late night, eh?"

"Yeah." Ruth plopped herself on the small couch next to him. "Whatcha up to?"

"Trying to help with translating the precursor database. Honestly, I'm not sure what I'm contributing, but General Cohen asked me to look for patterns or ciphers. You?"

"Weapons research."

Taylor put his hand on hers. "Bad night?"

"Robert, we saw billions of sentient beings get devoured by a swarm of tiny, intelligent self-replicating machines. It's been a bad day, and it'll probably be a bad week, month, and next couple of years."

"Yeah. I know." He put his arms around her. "Believe me. I know. The communication nets were jammed with voices. I couldn't understand a word said, but... I didn't need to. Those people were begging for help and just to see their loved ones again before the end."

Ruth turned and got closer. Tears came to her eyes. "I'm sorry. I didn't even think. I am so selfish sometimes." *He heard all that. All I had to do was watch the screen.*

"Not selfish to be worried, hurt... scared." Taylor kissed the top of her head, even when she recoiled slightly from his touch.

Whenever I try to pull away, he tries harder. Even though affection didn't come naturally, Ruth forced herself to count to five and not try to get away. "I don't know what we can possibly do in the face of such power. The main entity was the size of a moon, and that was after it sent maybe half its mass to destroy the planet. Sure, the *Lion of Judah* is powerful..."

"My dad used to say it's not the size of the dog in the fight but the size of the fight in the dog."

Ruth rolled her eyes. "Stop talking like you're a one-hundred-year-old man dispensing wisdom to his great-grandkids."

Taylor chuckled loudly. "Hey, it's true. We've been in some tight spots before, and General Cohen's always managed to save the day. You have to keep the faith. Somehow, all of us will find a way to win."

Valor   305

"I think we might need a miracle this time." Ruth sniffed and adjusted herself to fit under his chin. "Did you hear what the general was doing tonight?"

"No, been heads down on that database. I can barely see straight."

Ruth shivered. "I heard some of the enlisted fire controlmen talking. He went down to the shul and asked everyone else to leave. They said he stayed in there for hours, and passersby could hear him begging God for help. Last I heard, he was back in his day cabin, working on a strategy for defending Zeivlot and Zavlot."

Taylor squeezed her shoulders. "Nothing wrong with asking for some divine help about now or planning for the worst."

"But—"

"It's okay. We've got time, and it won't be solved tonight."

Ruth let herself try to absorb what he'd said. "How are you able to compartmentalize all this?"

"Men are boxes, remember?"

"And women are pasta. Yeah, I think I read that book too." Ruth forced a smile, but her heart wasn't in it. "At least I'll get to see Susanna."

"Do you think she'll want to be one of your bridesmaids?"

Ruth whirled around so fast that it broke their embrace. "*What?*"

Taylor's eyes widened. "I mean, she's a female friend."

"Robert, there is no way we can, in the middle of all this, drop everything and get married. It wouldn't be okay."

"Why not?"

The simple way he asked made her do a double take. "We might not be alive in a year."

"So? I can't think of anything I'd rather do, especially

given the state of things, than marry you. And if the end comes, then so be it. At least we'd be together."

Ruth's lip quivered, and a moment later, she was full-on crying while clinging to him. "I'm sorry," she said between sobs. "That just hit me."

"It's okay." Taylor embraced her tightly. "I meant it."

"I know."

Taylor ran his fingers through her hair. "We'll get through this."

More than anything, Ruth wanted to believe him. But after she'd seen the vast destructive power of the nanite hoard, doubt was difficult to set aside with positive thinking alone. "Maybe." She clung to him for a while before finally pushing back and wiping her eyes.

"You okay?"

"No, but I'll get there. Have you eaten?"

Taylor shook his head.

"Then let's go sneak something in before we go to bed. Tomorrow's going to be another long day."

"Deal." He stood and straightened his shirt. "I heard the officers' mess on the engineering deck somehow ended up with a few steaks. Might still have a few."

Ruth grinned. "Probably Hanson working his logistical magic. I'm game."

Taylor stuck his arm out as if to formally escort her. "Then if you would, my lady?"

"Why... are you so gosh darn cute?" Ruth interlocked her arm with his. "Lead on."

Laughing, they entered the passageway and headed toward the gravlift. Ruth forced herself to focus on the here and now. *I guess I should get around to asking Elizabeth to be a bridesmaid.* She and Susanna were the only two female friends she had. *Not that I have many male friends either. It'll be okay*, she told herself over and over. *The* Lion of Judah *always comes through*. But the doubt was still there. And it lingered despite every attempt to will it away.

———

DAVID WAS NOT one to feel apprehensive. In virtually everything, he made a decision, executed it, and let the chips fall where they might. But planet-sized swarms of nanites weren't quite an everyday occurrence. Standing outside Bo'hai's quarters, he felt more disturbed than he'd ever felt. It even eclipsed his near breakdown after Shelia's death.

He'd spent the last few hours praying, thinking, and trying to reason out what to do next. While there were numerous possibilities, they only had a few days until they reached Zeivlot. *And the chickens come home to roost, as my mother would say.* David knew HaShem heard his prayers, but he longed to receive a direct answer.

This discussion isn't going to do itself. He pressed the call button.

"Who is it?" Bo'hai asked through the wall-mounted speaker.

"It's Gen... ah, David."

The hatch swished open automatically. Bo'hai was seated in the living area of her quarters. She stood. "Please, come in. I wasn't expecting company this late."

David flashed a small smile and stepped inside. The holoprojector was on and frozen with an image he couldn't quite make out. "Catching some entertainment?"

"*War Patrol.*"

"Seriously?" David laughed.

She raised an eyebrow. "You don't care for it?"

"May I?" He gestured at an empty chair.

"Of course."

David sat and shook his head. "I don't like the show. It gets far too many things wrong about military life and how things work on a starship. There's got to be dramatic license. I get that. But come on. Get who salutes whom right."

Bo'hai chuckled. "I can see how that would matter to you. If someone made a story about my occupation, I would also want those little details to be correct."

"How're things in the scientific unit?"

"Good. Your Major Hanson tells us we have to drink from a fire hose. I had to look up that idiom to understand it, but the mental image is quite apt. I've learned more in the last few months than my entire life."

"Knowledge is good for the soul."

"I sense you did not come to make small talk," Bo'hai said softly.

David shook his head. "No." He took a deep breath. "There's been a series of... developments today."

"Would that have something to do with the general sense of fear I saw descend on the faces of every soldier on this ship?"

"Yes."

Over the next few minutes, David explained the scope of the nanite threat, what they'd witnessed, and that the *Lion* was returning to the Zeivlot system to sort out what to do next. As he talked, her face went ashen, and several times, she placed her head in her hands, visibly shaking.

"I know this is a lot."

Bo'hai blinked a few times. "You have a knack for understatement." She licked her lips. "Why are you telling me this privately?"

"Because you're the ranking scientist, and I know

everyone else looks up to you. You are, in effect, their leader."

"I don't think of myself as such."

David shrugged. "Sometimes, leadership is foisted upon us rather than sought."

"Was it that way for you?"

"Hmm. At one point, I had no interest in continuing to serve in the Coalition Defense Force. In fact, I made it loudly known as soon as my draft enlistment was up that I was leaving and going to rabbinical school. But... things change." David pursed his lips. "I became an officer, and once that happened, command was a way of life. Though I must tell you—being in charge of this ship was something I never considered. I figured the destroyer I was given, the CSV *Yitzhak Rabin*, would be the pinnacle of my career."

"Clearly, the Maker had other plans."

"Yes." He continued, "I need you to help Dr. Hayworth inform the rest of the science team tomorrow."

Bo'hai tilted her head. "And after that?"

"Our mission has changed. Getting home is secondary. Our primary objective is to stop those nanites by any means necessary. You and your fellow researchers will help us understand the enemy and, I hope, develop weapons to fight them."

"You would stand against this evil with eight ships?"

"I once went to fight twenty-five hundred League ships with less than two hundred of my own. I've got some ideas. I need to flesh them out then get your political leaders to buy in. Whatever happens, if we must sacrifice ourselves to save innocents, I won't hesitate to."

"It won't come to that. The Maker will intercede on our behalf."

"I believe with all my heart that HaShem helps us. In

many different ways." David thought back to how he'd felt when seeing a League auxiliary vessel lose control of its thrusters and fly into the side of the enemy flagship at the Third Battle of Canaan, tilting the battle in favor of the CDF. "But given what we're up against here, we'll need a no-crap miracle."

"Then I shall pray for one."

He stood. "Thank you for taking the time to speak with me."

"Any time, David." Bo'hai sprang to her feet and stepped toward him to put her hand on his. "Remember that it is darkest before first light."

"Thank you." *I can't believe how well she took this.* David squeezed her hand and turned to leave.

But Bo'hai didn't let go. Instead, she clasped his other hand. "If anyone can stop this scourge, it is you, David. The ancient texts foretold you and your people's arrival and that you would keep us from destroying ourselves. I know that even this enemy can be overcome."

David forced a weak smile. "As my friend Colonel Amir likes to say, if God wills it. Now, if you'll excuse me... I have more work to complete before trying for some rack time."

"Of course."

After withdrawing his hand, David made his way to the hatch. "Good night."

"Good night," Bo'hai replied.

Walking through the passageway, back toward the gravlift that would take him to his quarters, David saw dozens of soldiers, more than he would expect to see at that time of night. Most of their faces held expressions of worry and downright fear. As he passed each one, David smiled and forced as much confidence as he had to show. Once he was in the gravlift, when the doors slid shut, doubt returned.

What are we going to do? David gritted his teeth as the lift took off. *I've got to think this out logically, one step at a time. And pray for wisdom constantly, because I need it now more than anything.* It wasn't much of a plan, but it *was* a start. *He who watches the wind will not sow, and he who stares at the clouds will not reap.* The proverb from Ecclesiastes jumped into his mind as the doors swooshed open.

My bed's made, at least. That gives me the promise of a better day.

The Lost Warship: Book 4 – Justice:
The discovery of an advanced civilization with the means to assist General Cohen and his crew in their fight against the nannies brings unexpected perils as all is not what it seems.
As David intervenes in yet another alien society, will the price finally too much to bear?
Now available on Amazon!
Tap HERE to read NOW!

THE END

ALSO AVAILABLE FROM DANIEL GIBBS

Battlegroup Z

Book 1 - Weapons Free

Book 2 - Hostile Spike

Book 3 - Sol Strike

Book 4 - Bandits Engaged

Book 5 - Iron Hand

Book 6 - Final Flight

Echoes of War

Book 1 - Fight the Good Fight

Book 2 - Strong and Courageous

Book 3 - So Fight I

Book 4 - Gates of Hell

Book 5 - Keep the Faith

Book 6 - Run the Gauntlet

Book 7 - Finish the Fight

The Lost Warship

Book 1 - Adrift

Book 2 - Mercy

Book 3 - Valor

Book 4 - Justice

Book 5 - Resolve (Coming in 2023)

Book 6 - Faith (Coming in 2023)

Breach of Faith

(With Gary T. Stevens)

Book 1 - Breach of Peace

Book 2 - Breach of Faith

Book 3 - Breach of Duty

Book 4 - Breach of Trust

Book 5 - Spacer's Luck

Book 6 - Fortune's Favor

Book 7 - The Iron Dice

Deception Fleet

(With Steve Rzasa)

Book 1 - Victory's Wake

Book 2 - Cold Conflict

Book 3 - Hazards Near

Book 4 - Liberty's Price

Book 5 - Ecliptic Flight

Book 6 - Collision Vector

Courage, Commitment, Faith: Tales from the Coalition Defense Force

(Anthology Series)

Volume One

ACKNOWLEDGMENTS

An incredible thirty-two novels are now complete - wow. There are times when I am at a loss for words. This is one of them. To think that one book, six years ago, would turn into this... is beyond my imagination.

Thank you to all those who have helped me along the way: you know who you are, and I couldn't do all this without you.

To my special Kickstarter backers -
Brian Clairmont
Avi Beidani
Lonnie Bristol
Alexander Roth
Christopher Hayes
Lewis Brande
Oridon

Thank you all - and we'll do it again soon!

Godspeed,

Daniel Gibbs

Printed in Great Britain
by Amazon